DREAMLAND

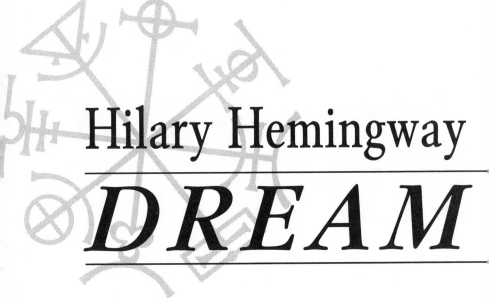

Hilary Hemingway

DREAM

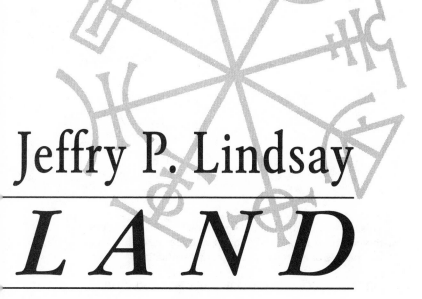

Jeffry P. Lindsay

LAND

A NOVEL OF THE UFO COVER-UP

A Tom Doherty Associates Book / New York

DREAMLAND: A NOVEL OF THE UFO COVER-UP

A Forge Book
Published by Tom Doherty Associates, Inc.
175 Fifth Avenue
New York, N.Y. 10010

ISBN 0–312–85631–8

First edition: February 1995

Printed in the United States of America

0 9 8 7 6 5 4 3 2 1

For Doris and Hannah

ACKNOWLEDGMENTS

Sincere thanks to those who generously gave assistance and guidance during the writing of this novel: Susan Crawford, Doris Hemingway, Natalia Aponte, Dr. August Freundlich, Tommie Freundlich, Lorian Hemingway, Bill Held, Bill Feuer, Marianne K. Sweeny, Det. Jim Chambliss, F.D.L.E., Det. Allison Chambliss, Metro-Dade Homicide, Lieut. Greg Terp, Metro-Dade Police Bomb Squad, Det. Ralph Garcia, F.D.L.E., Dr. George Mulder, Dept. of Psychology, Cal. Tech., San Luis Obispo, Tahoma Hemingway Mulder, Advice on Engineering and Physics, J.E.H. Dept. of Defense, and for the hard research of Dr. David Jacobs and Budd Hopkins.

Upon one tree there are many
fruits, and in one kingdom many
people. How unreasonable it would
be to suppose that besides the
heaven and earth which we can see,
there are no other heavens and no
other earths?
—Teng Mu
     Thirteenth-century philosopher

A stormy wind came out of the
north, a great cloud, with
brightness round about it, and fire
flashing forth continually, and in
the midst thereof the colour of
amber came a fiery sphere. Also out
of the midst thereof *came* the
likeness of four living creatures.
And this *was* their appearance; they
had the likeness of a man.
—Ezekiel 1:4,5

ONE

The Bible tells us Joshua fit
the battle of Jericho and the
walls came a-tumbling down.
—Colonel John Wesley
Head of MJ-12

H e moved through deep space without a sound. Around
him, a ship; his viewpoint from the edge of the main room.
Not the corner, since this ship seemed to be round and had no
corners. Ahead of him, through a—window? Yes—he saw the
velvet blackness of space. And he understood that he saw from
the perspective of another.

Behind him he sensed calm, unhurried movement from the
crew. His view rotated and he knew the ship was turning, although he felt no sensation of movement.

Now a planet swam into his field of vision and he picked
out the familiar continents, oceans and islands: Earth. It grew
steadily larger as the ship rushed downward at unimaginable
speed.

A sudden alarm in the ship behind him: not a siren, not a

bell; just the sure sense that something had gone very wrong. And then—

Colonel John Wesley forced his eyes open. The dreams were not new, but they were bad and often brought on by flying.

Even strapped securely into the UH-60 Black Hawk helicopter that hurried over the Maryland marsh, he found that the dreams could shake him.

He did not look like a man easily shaken: powerfully built, with white brush-cut hair and cold eyes, a veteran Cold Warrior.

He did not speak about the dreams, not ever. His thoughts were "classified." To others, they might seem symptoms of paranoid psychological dysfunction. Whatever they might be, he made certain that nothing ever showed on his face, especially when someone watched him, as someone did now.

Arthur Randall sat across from him, an overweight, red-haired National Security Agency operative.

"Colonel?" Randall began in his Louisiana twang, "just where the hell did you boys hide this base?" Randall smiled to show that he was not afraid, but Wesley could see the fear in his eyes. *Fat bastard,* Wesley thought.

The Colonel looked out at the vast marsh below. They would arrive at the complex in a few minutes. The pilot had already begun his bank to the west.

"It's supposed to be down there somewhere, isn't it?" Randall went on.

"We spent four billion to conceal it," Wesley told him. "I doubt you'll find it."

"Four billion? Jesus H. Christ." Randall pushed his head against the chopper's transparent canopy. But he saw nothing. Nothing the late-November frost hadn't already turned swampy brown. The only breaks in the sea of dead grass were small patches of gray rock and, here and there, a few larger islands.

Wesley's cold blue eyes turned back to his guest.

"Mr. Randall, you are the first outsider we've had to MJ-12. I'm not accustomed to giving tours."

"I understand." Randall nodded, his double chin jiggling.

"I think I should warn you—hold on."

"What's that?" Randall leaned closer, not sure he had heard right. Suddenly his shoulders smacked hard against the seat restraints. The black chopper dove. Down it went, down toward one of the islands in the most inaccessible portion of the marsh.

"Wesley—!" Randall sputtered, panicked.

Wesley just stared.

The pilot held course. Only seconds remained before impact.

"Oh shiiit!" Randall's voice screamed above the whine of the motor. Sweat streaked his face and terror filled his wide eyes. The Colonel turned to watch him and smiled.

At the last moment, when the helicopter was clearly about to crash, the island's surface wobbled in electronic waves—

—and the hologram of rocks, shrubs and marsh disappeared, revealing instead a large man-made cavern.

The chopper nosed up and settled down on a spotlessly clean landing pad inside.

"Oh, my God," Randall gulped. "What the hell—"

Wesley smiled thinly and pointed up. Randall looked out the window and saw the electronic waves flicker back across the cavern's ceiling. The green and brown lasers had a criss-cross pattern. The hologram of an island's surface had been restored.

The base was again invisible. To the eye it was a patch of swamp. To a spy satellite it would look like a quite ordinary geo-thermal hot spot.

"How the hell did you do that?"

"Another tech spin-off from SDI."

Wesley did not explain that the hologram was only one part of the security at MJ-12's "Country Club." If someone or something penetrated the grid without clearance, it would be ash before it hit the floor. An N-9 Trident reactor kept the security grid criss-crossed with UH voltage. The structure had a higher protection rating than the Strategic Air Command bunkers.

The chopper's rotors wound to a stop and a double line of very tough-looking young soldiers ran out to the landing bay. They wore dark fatigues and, like their Colonel, a black beret with a triangular patch of crossed lighting bolts on a field of gold and blue.

The troopers formed two facing lines and snapped to attention as the chopper's door swung open. The Colonel stepped out, followed by Arthur Randall.

"Ah, Colonel, your Black Berets." Randall said, recognizing them from his Intelligence dossier. He wiped the sweat from his forehead with a sleeve.

It was a thrill for Randall finally to be at the home base of the Majestic-12 Working Group. He couldn't wait to meet the engineers, intelligence officers and scientists who conducted the research and development of the "visitors" technology. In his seventeen years in Washington Intelligence he had heard only whispers about any of it. And now he was really here. Here, to find a way to stop Wesley.

The Black Berets saluted their Colonel as he passed through their ranks. Wesley felt a strong pride in these men. He had hand-picked each as a raw recruit. He had watched over them through training and made them the finest elite corps in the world. But then, they had to be, considering who and what they guarded.

"You got some real tough-looking boys, Colonel. Change their oil every ten thousand miles?" Randall loosed a short nervous laugh. Wesley paused a half beat, then continued his stride.

"Yep, hell of a fine operation. You know, NSA doesn't want to lose this base or Dreamland. Your work with, uh, them has been very valuable, nobody is saying otherwise. But I— Holy shit—" Randall broke off as they stepped around the chopper and the sheer size of the complex hit him.

It spread before them, a football field wide and seven stories deep, with seamlessly smooth walls—similar, Randall thought, to the Stealth's blend of liquid polymer, boron-carbide armored and stainless steel. *We can't give this up.* He stepped up his pace to catch up with the Colonel.

"That shit you pulled in Washington scaring the President? That's got everybody hopping mad. I mean, Jesus' tits, Colonel, this has been a black project for over forty years—look at where it's come. This is *not* the kind of decision you force from a President who's out in eight weeks. It needs to be reviewed, studied."

Wesley stopped and faced Randall. "We don't have time to dick around with politics, mister. We'll be damn lucky to stop them at all. I've been given eight weeks— eight weeks to build JOSHUA and *use* it. I don't care what the National Security Council, Department of Defense, or Central Intelligence says. I answer only to the President and for now I've got his support."

Randall's face frosted over. "Then hear this, Colonel. If you fail to engineer JOSHUA on schedule, I'll guarantee my report to the incoming administration will put a stop to this hostile approach—and to your career. Got it?"

Randall had just barely finished his threat when the back side of Wesley's forearm hit him hard just below his double chin. He fell to his knees, his stubby fingers grasping at his crushed windpipe.

"Yes, Mr. Randall," Wesley said. "I got it."

Randall clutched his throat, unable to breathe.

But Wesley did not let him die of suffocation.

At the far end of the hangar, Major Michael Andros waited. He ran his fingers across the top of his blond hair. Tall and lean, he was classically handsome but unaware of it. His work had been far too important to permit him the distractions of a social life.

He had not heard what the heavy man had said to Wesley, but he knew the Colonel's temper. And he had seen Wesley's sharp jerking twist of the red head, followed by the thud of the lifeless body hitting the floor.

Andros held back his revulsion. His comfort came in knowing that the Colonel's days were numbered—if Andros could stay alive and if his plan worked.

"Sir!" Andros said coming to attention as Wesley approached him. "Welcome to the Country Club, Colonel."

Wesley returned his salute with a snap. "Thank you, Mike. Let's roll." They turned toward a chromium steel double door built into the cavern.

"How was Washington, sir?"

"I got what I needed and got rid of what I didn't. Is everybody here?"

"Yes, sir." Andros stepped up to the security pad in front of the door. It scanned them for fingerprints, body temperature and retinal patterns. The heavy doors slid back.

"Dr. Keller arrived about twenty minutes ago. The others came in last night. They're all waiting in the main conference room."

"Good." They stepped into a turbo lift that quickly descended two hundred meters into the earth before opening into a wide hallway.

There were no doors in the metallic and highly polished hallway. The two men strode side by side silently. Finally Andros turned to the Colonel.

"Sir, you're still thinking of this as a showdown—"

"Save it, Mike. I've had a bellyful in Washington, and I won't hear it here—not from you, not from anybody. We're going ahead with it."

They turned the corner. The new corridor, still polished, was lined with doors. A sign on the first door said:

GENETICS

"Sir, I know some form of detente is still possible. The benefits would be staggering—for both sides."

Colonel Wesley stopped.

"Benefits? We've had those bastards for over forty years, Mike, given them over forty years of the very best security and protection in the world—and what benefits have we gotten out of 'em?"

"Colonel, you know as well as I what they've given us. From amniocentesis all the way to Stealth technology—"

"That's not the point and you know it," snapped Wesley. "That stuff is *peanuts* compared to what they're sitting on. God damn it, Major." He pointed a finger at the genetics laboratory. "You think I don't know you're up to something in there? And don't give me any crap about genetic sampling—they didn't come here to play with babies—those aren't even real babies!"

"Actually, sir—"

"And even if everything else was exactly the way they want us to believe it is—did you really think we'd let them *go?*"

Wesley stared hard at the Major and then spun away into the walnut-paneled conference room.

There were twelve chairs around the black marble table. Nine of the chairs were filled by middle-aged occupants leafing through their notes or chatting quietly as they waited for the Colonel. A tenth man stood at the far side of the room, drawing a cup of coffee from an urn into a black porcelain mug.

All ten looked up as Wesley and Andros entered. Wesley took the seat at the head of the table.

"Let's get started, shall we?"

Major Andros slid in at the table's far end.

"You all know what we're up against. The decision to go ahead has not been easy. We need now to decide what is the fastest and best way to build JOSHUA. Dr. Keller, your report?"

Wesley looked four seats down to a bearded man who took a battered meerschaum pipe from the pocket of his Harris tweed and stuffed the bowl with Borkum Riff tobacco.

"Well, Colonel, we've spent a great deal of time with the new data over in Tech Section. Ran it through VR mock-ups, numerical analysis, the works." Keller paused, smoke trickling from the corner of his mouth.

"The thing is, there seems to be one key piece missing. Best guess is, they have intentionally withheld their technology on this project."

"Of course they have. Wouldn't you, if you knew it would be used against you?" Andros interrupted.

"Major, how would they know we are planning to use it against them?" a Navy Vice-Admiral jumped in.

"Look, we have had an understanding that has been in force for forty years and we've all done well by it. If there's data missing now from one of their designs, then that's a *message*. They must *know* this kind of technology could be used against them."

"And that is the best damned reason I've heard yet for building JOSHUA!" stormed Wesley. "We've tried kinetic-energy cannon, Starstreak high-velocity missiles, chemical-energy warheads. Nothing even worries them as long as they're behind that damn retaining wall. Only our directed-energy weapons—our subsonics, microwaves and particle beams—have even made them blink!"

"Perhaps," said one of the academic-looking women, "your reading on JOSHUA is all wrong. They could intend us to fill in this missing piece ourselves."

"Or," said Keller, "they have some rather extraordinary means to get it built without our knowledge."

The Vice-Admiral slammed his hands on the tabletop to get everyone's attention. "What if JOSHUA ended up being some sort of weapon for them? Under the guise of teaching and helping us, we build a device that enables them to gain control. We already know about their experiments in biochemistry to create a hybrid life-form. This might be all they need to stick around and recolonize."

"Exactly," Wesley said. "I've thought about that. Every piece of technology they've given us has in some way benefited *them*. And unless we build JOSHUA I don't see that we have any defense. There's just too much at stake now."

"Sir," Andros said, "don't you think there's a lot at stake for them, too? It's been over forty years. They just want to go home—"

"And regroup to flatten us!" the Vice-Admiral fired back.

"No." Andros shook his head. "If we could just trust that they—"

"Trust?" snorted Colonel Wesley. "Mister, I've spent my life staring down the barrel of a gun and if I've learned one thing, it's this: Trust comes only when you have just as much ability to wipe out the other guy as he has to wipe you out. That's what JOSHUA gives us. It's our insurance, and without it they have us over a barrel!"

"And so we build JOSHUA, and what do they build that's bigger, better, even *more* threatening? Where does it all stop, Colonel?"

"It stops when we're on top, Major! Now God damn it, Mike, pick a side here! With your own kind! Those bastards are barricaded behind their retaining wall and we don't know *what* they're up to, or even what they're capable of! The only thing we know is they don't like DEW weapons and JOSHUA is just that!"

Wesley looked around the table. No one else seemed to side with the Major. "All right then, we go ahead as planned." No one disagreed.

"With the committee's permission, I would like to farm JOSHUA out to Aerocorp in New Mexico. Priority track one."

There were nods, shrugs, around the table, except for Major Andros. Wesley noted his look of alarm. *I thought so. So it's New Mexico after all. New Mexico and the babies . . . Genetic sampling my ass, Major.*

"Good," said Wesley, "I'll head out there to set it up." His eyes locked on to Andros. *This time, Major—I'm going to hunt you down and skin you, like the animal you are.*

Andros met Wesley's stare with his own. But he didn't dare hold it too long. He looked away, hiding his triumph.

The plan was working.

TWO

Trust comes only when you have
just as much ability to wipe
out the other guy as he has to
wipe you out. That's what
JOSHUA gives us.
                    —Colonel John Wesley
                    Head of MJ-12

T he city of Los Alamos, New Mexico, has a high proportion of scientists. A lot of them do defense work.
Like most defense work, it offers good pay and benefits
to some of the nation's better minds.

Stanley Katz certainly qualified. So did his wife,
Anne, as far as IQ went. But her specialty was not de-
fense-related. Stan seemed happy enough as a civilian
engineer at Aerocorp, a large defense contractor. Anne,
an astronomer, worked out of the defense loop. Still, she
liked it here. She had found an excellent and satisfying
career in a small observatory in the hills outside town.

Tall and dark-haired, Annie was good-looking without being glamorous. For most of her thirty-four years
she had been too busy with books and telescopes to learn

makeup—but then, she didn't really need it, either, with her large, wide-spaced violet eyes.

At the moment those eyes showed a small trace of worry. Her experience with OB-GYN doctors had not been positive so far, and Stanley, who had promised to be there for moral support, was late.

Dr. Dolan stepped into the OB examining room. She slapped the file folder of Annie Katz's medical history into a slot in the wall rack with a small, professional smile and began to examine her patient.

Annie wore a hospital robe, open in back. Dr. Dolan raised the robe and ran a tape measure down Annie's stomach.

"It's not even showing yet," Annie said. "It's making me crazy."

Dr. Dolan nodded. "It won't be long now, Annie. In the fourth month you'll start a real growth spurt. Soon you'll be sick of all the Goodyear blimp jokes."

"I—don't think I'll ever get sick of it, Doctor. Just as long as . . . I mean, is there still a chance that . . ."

"There's always a chance you'll lose it again, Anne," she said gently. "But I think we're past the worst of it. Second trimester is always just a little safer. But for God's sake, no heavy lifting, no touch football. Use some common sense."

"I will," Anne promised, smiling.

"See that you do." Dr. Dolan sounded a trifle grumpy as she turned to the fetal-growth chart on the wall. The doctor had allowed herself to like this distracted first-time mother, victim of three miscarriages and hoping against hope not to lose a fourth.

Dolan pointed to the fourth picture on the chart, which showed a twelve-week-old fetus.

"There's what Junior looks like about now."

"My God," Annie said, "it looks like some kind of space monster."

Before Annie could study it any longer, the door crashed open and Stan Katz rushed in.

Rail-thin, fiercely gawky, but with a wicked smile, Stan Katz seemed unable to arrive on time—except at work, of course.

"Hi, honey, I'm really sorry—" he started.

"Stanley. Close the door, I'm practically naked."

"Oh, sorry—" Stan swung the door shut and smiled at Dr. Dolan. "Hey, Doc. Did I miss anything horrible?"

"We saved it for you, Stan," Dolan said as she smeared Vaseline on Annie's stomach. "You're just in time to see your wife anointed with the ceremonial bear grease."

Dr. Dolan placed the ultrasound fetal monitor into the "bear grease." A tube ran from the wand to a clean, stainless-steel box that held a video monitor and a sensitive speaker.

Dr. Dolan fiddled with the dials on the monitor for a moment, and then the room filled with a noise that sounded like a destroyer going overhead in a World War II submarine movie. Stan jumped back, surprised.

"That's your baby's heartbeat," she said, and then frowned. Annie's heart skipped.

"Is something wrong, Doctor?"

Dr. Dolan cocked her head to one side and listened to the heartbeat. "Wrong? Nnnoo. . . . Sounds healthy. . . ." The doctor listened hard for a moment and then looked up to such a raw-nerved expression of terror in Annie's violet eyes that she straightened and smiled. "Nothing wrong at all, Annie."

Stan and Annie shared an emotional moment. The baby was alive and sounded good. *We're really going to have this one,* Annie told herself.

"This is going to take some getting used to. . . . We've tried so hard, those other times—"

Stan squeezed his wife's hand and kissed her forehead.

"This time, it's going to be okay."

"Let's hope so," said Dr. Dolan. "But you are definitely not out of the woods yet. Just don't do anything dumb."

"I won't do anything dumb," Annie assured Dolan.

"Don't say that, then go back to peeking through that damn telescope eighteen hours at a stretch—"

"You don't peek through a radio telescope, Doctor, you—"

"I don't care if you put it up your nose, Annie. The point is, don't overdo it. This baby won't stand for it."

"I'll keep after her, Doctor," Stan said.

"Do that." Dolan turned back to the ultrasound

equipment. She punched up the grainy black-and-white picture. "There's your baby."

Annie and Stan stared at the picture for a few moments.

"It's got your looks, Stan," the doctor joked.

"You think so?" It bore almost no resemblance to anything human, with its bulging head, large eyes and stubby, clawlike hands.

Annie smiled. "We'll hope it gets my personality."

THREE

The temperature was colder in the midwestern part of the country. In fact, Frank Cassidy was freezing.

But he shrugged it off and pulled hard on the cold metal tape measure. He had work to do, and there was nobody else to do it. The puzzled, gray-haired farmer standing beside him couldn't help. Only Frank himself knew what to do.

He knelt and brought the tape right up to the edge of the circle. Forty-six feet six inches exactly. Again. He wrote down the familiar numbers on his legal pad.

In the 300 cases of crop circles he had investigated, he judged 110 to be the real McCoy. This was about to become number 111.

He considered several factors: size, a lack of footprints around the crop circles, design patterns—though these had become increasingly more complex—and, perhaps most important, examination of the crops themselves.

In hoax circles, the crop stalks had been broken into a twisting pattern. In real ones, the stems were bent from the root and unbroken.

Frank looked down at this one and knew it was real.

"It's freezing out here. You done yet?" an old woman yelled from the beat-up Chevy just off the road.

"Just a minute, Dot," the farmer called back. He turned to Frank. "Can you hurry it up some? We've been out here over an hour. Don't think I won't hear about it. The wife says I was crazy to call you."

"Well, I'm glad you did," Frank said, standing.

He looked out at the field. The surface showed a light dusting of snow over the stubble of the fall's crop, except for the circle and its joining paths. They seemed punched into the surface as if a giant cookie cutter had fallen from the sky.

"You've got a genuine mystery all right. Kinda beautiful, if it weren't for this." He glanced down at the black-and-white carcass of a Holstein cow. Rigor mortis had set in. The cow had been dead at least twelve hours, but the farmer had sworn that the crop circle had appeared only in the last four.

Frank bent down next to the heifer. The usual: blood completely drained, not enough left in the whole carcass to fill a thimble. It had a ripple incision on the underside, reproductive organs removed. The incision had cauterized the wound as it cut, the mark of a modern surgical laser.

Except this kind of laser wasn't developed until the mid-1980s. And cattle mutilations started turning up in the late 1950s. So far, more than fifteen thousand had been reported by ranchers across the United States.

"Damn weirdo cults," the farmer said, blowing on his fingers. "I called Tom Jr. Told him one of his cows was dead over here."

"You mean this isn't yours?"

"No, that's Tom's tag in the ear. I don't have livestock, just oats and corn. Damned glad of it, too."

"Where does Tom live?"

"About twenty-five miles south. Just off route eighteen."

Frank pulled off the animal's green tag and wrote down the rancher's name, sure it was a dead end. But he would follow up anyway.

Before he could leave, Frank needed a sketch of the pattern. If this had been designed, he hoped to find the designer.

At the far side of the circle he saw the connecting T-shaped path cut into the frozen ground. On the opposite side another path began. He followed it. Twenty feet out, he found two short paths that crossed it. No footprints led from the road, except his own and the farmer's. Whoever or whatever had made this had left no clues.

Frank came back and showed the farmer the drawing. "Don't take off for my lack of artistry."

The farmer squinted. "I kinda like it."

"One of the prettiest I've seen," Frank agreed.

"Looks like some kind of ancient symbol."

"Does it mean anything?" The farmer dug his hands deeper into his coat. The wind seemed to be picking up.

"Don't have a clue."

"What kind of investigator are you?"

"Smart enough to know *not* to blame the weather."

"It's one of those devil-worship cults," the farmer said.

Frank shook his head. "I don't think so. If humans were involved, we'd have footprints."

Frank pulled a zip-lock and garden spade from his jacket. "Can I take a soil sample?"

"Help yourself. I got four hundred acres more."

At noon Stan and Annie left the obstetrician's office. Annie leaned forward to give him a kiss.

"Just relax and get back to work, Stan. Carol's going to pick me up in a few minutes."

Stan groaned. "The witch doctor of Gotham. . . . You should go home and rest."

"She's a psychiatrist, Stan, a respectable medical profession."

"Yes, bwana. And her have evil eye, too."

"Psychiatry is not voodoo. Carol does Jungian gestalt."

"Okay, so it's Swiss voodoo—oh, damn!" Stan noticed that his parking meter had expired and he had a ticket.

He reached to snatch the ticket from the windshield, and a car horn blasted next to him. Stan jumped.

At the wheel of a green VW Super Beetle was Carol Blum. "Yo Stanley," Carol drawled in her thick New York accent. "You in trouble with the law again?"

"You couldn't put in a quarter for me? You sat here and watched 'em write out a thirty-dollar ticket?"

"But they pay you so much to build bombs, I know a little thirty-dollar ticket means nothing to you."

"They don't pay me *that* much," Stan snarled.

"Then get an honest job. If the money isn't great, stop doing something you hate and only do because the money is great. Go back to teaching."

"Sure." Stan was really warming up to it. "And you go back to reading rabbit entrails, back to honest mumbo jumbo. Think of the overhead you'll save."

"Think how much I'd have to spend on broomsticks."

Annie stepped in and gave Stan a kiss on the cheek. "I'll see you tonight, honey," she said, and slid into the passenger seat of Carol's Bug.

"So I take it the visit to the doctor went well?" Carol asked. "I saw you and the yutz you married making kissy-face."

"I wish you wouldn't needle Stan like that. . . ."

"Me? Needle him?" As she pulled into traffic, Carol

grinned. "He's a good guy. And I am so happy for the two of you, honest to God, I could bust."

A Ford with local plates dared to slow for a turn. Carol leaned on her horn. "Move it, asshole!" she bellowed. "These people should all be herding sheep somewhere."

Annie clutched the dashboard and told herself that after all these years she should be used to Carol's driving style.

Carol's house was on a street that, in her words, "looks like off a Norman Rockwell." Her contract with the Air Force had brought her here, to review pilots for flight-worthiness, and although she loved her work, Los Alamos was too quiet for the spirit of Manhattan that raged in her like a three-day sale at Bloomingdale's.

When Carol opened the door into her strangely dark house, Annie sensed something wrong. "Carol, is something funny going on?"

"In Los Alamos? Nothing funny here since they stopped making knock-knock jokes. Close the door for God's sake, you're letting all the excitement out."

Suddenly a bright light flared. "Surprise!" came the yell. Blinking to clear her sight of a blue dot from a flash-bulb, Annie saw a dozen friends and baby-shower decorations.

Carol led Annie to a chair.

About half of Annie's friends had children and half didn't. From their gifts it was easy to tell which was which. Jayne, who ran the public defender's office, had none. She gave Annie a stuffed tiger that growled when you squeezed it. It was beautiful, expensive, and velvety soft, but as two of the mothers giggled, "That thing would scare a kid to death."

Kathleen, a florist with three kids, gave "the ultimate in practical gifts." Inside the package was a blue nylon bag filled with things Annie had never seen before—a blue rubber squeeze bulb, a tube of Desitin and another of lanolin, and a bundle of hand-towel-sized white cloths Kathleen referred to as "blarp rags."

An elaborate bow-splattered box, wrapped with such maniacal abandon that it could only have come from Carol, contained a car seat. "Hang on to it, Annie. They won't let you check out of the hospital without one."

"There's one more," Carol said, handing Annie a battered plain brown package. Annie fingered the rumpled paper. The writing seemed somehow familiar. She raised a questioning look toward Carol.

"From your mother," said Carol. Annie's face fell and she dropped the package to the floor.

Carol reached for the package. "It's been a lot of years. She's your mother. You can't shut her out forever."

"I can. I have."

"Please, just see what she has to say. At least look at the card. . . ." But Annie would not look up. "I'll open it then."

Carol began to read aloud:

Dear Daughter,
    A new life is a time to heal old wounds and I
hope and pray we can heal this one.

"That's not so bad," Carol smiled.

I know so much has happened between us and I
am sorry, truly I am. I have asked God to forgive
you for marrying that Jew . . .

Carol's voice trailed off into dumb shock. Although
she knew Annie had not spoken with her parents for
many years and she had heard them referred to as blind
bigoted fundamentalists, Carol had thought she exag-
gerated, and had believed she did a good thing by writing to Annie's mother about the shower.

Carol snatched up the package from the floor. "Anyway, let's see what she sent," she trilled with forced gai-
ety. She removed the wrinkled brown paper and held the
box out to Annie, silently praying the gift would not be a
further insult.

Annie was somewhere in the fog of her long-ago un-
happy childhood as she looked at the floor, telling herself, *Breathe, just breathe . . . in, out . . . just breathe . . .*

She had worked for twenty years to make her world
better than the dim place of bitter damnation her parents
had brought her into. But childhood is always three steps
closer to us than we know.

And now, from a very great distance, she heard
Carol's voice saying, "Open the box, Annie."

She took a deep breath and opened the box with mechanical nonchalance. But tears came to her eyes as she
saw the battered teddy bear inside. "It's Gruffy Bear,"
she said in a small, faraway voice. "When I was little,
Gruffy Bear was my only friend."

Annie clutched Gruffy Bear, tears rolling down her cheeks, and turned to Carol. "If you tell me to let it all out . . ."

"I won't. But don't keep it all in, either. There's just so much about your childhood . . . I didn't know. . . ."

"There's a lot I'd rather forget. A lot . . . I'm not even sure of—anymore."

FOUR

Project JOSHUA has been deliberately crippled—perhaps while
both sides maneuver for position.
—Dr. Keller
MJ-12 Tech Section

Tom Jr. stood six-three in his stocking feet, and now he wore cowboy boots with two-inch heels. He stood even with the cow's head, covered with blood. He pulled the last stitch through and tied it off. The two-year-old Holstein looked like Frankenstein's cow, with the gouging rip along her neck and her forehead sewn closed.

The barn door slammed shut and Tom Jr. looked up, annoyed. The cattle stirred and a loud hum came from the milking machine gone dry. Frank Cassidy had arrived.

"Anyone here?"

"Be with you in a minute." Tom's voice sounded tired. A strong smell of antiseptic blended with the stench of cow manure.

"What can I do for you?" Tom said as he walked over, wiping his hands on a towel.

"Ah." Frank pointed at Tom's blood-soaked overalls. "Are you all right?"

"Sure," Tom laughed. "Isn't mine. Something spooked 'em last night. Had one get tangled in the barbed wire."

"Oh." Frank smiled. At least that tied in with the time of death on the other cow. "I'm Frank Cassidy. I'd like to ask a few questions about the cattle mutilation down at the Dunning farm."

Tom nodded. "I haven't seen it, but if it's like the rest . . ." He shrugged.

"You mean you've lost more?"

"This will be the sixth, I guess, in maybe—ten years? It's gotten so the Sheriff won't even look into it."

"Did you see anything unusual—I mean, before or after one of these?"

"Who did you say you work for?" Tom Jr. looked a little annoyed.

"I work for myself, strictly a research investigator. I've put twenty years into this sort of thing."

"I see. Well—when I told folks what I saw, nobody believed me. I'm not used to that sort of thing. All the jokes . . . I'm not crazy, but what I saw, or thought I saw, well, I can't really blame 'em. It was just easier to stop talking about it."

"Everything you say will be kept confidential." The big man still hesitated. "Please believe me."

"Why?"

"Because I'm betting that whatever happened to you is a lot like what's happened to others. That's what I research. Things like this."

"Huh. What've you found out so far?"

Frank smiled at him. "Not a lot. Just enough to be sure it's going to continue unless we can all get together."

Tom Jr. leaned against the barn door and mulled it over. "Okay, I guess. . . . Ah, it happened maybe seven years ago. I was upstairs getting ready for bed, when something just lit up the sky. Bright—whew, I thought there'd been an explosion. But there was no sound.

"Out my window I saw this slow-moving fiery orange ball. It came over the hills, like it was following the road." Tom Jr. smiled a little, then shook his head.

"Suddenly it just turned, headed straight for my barn. I was trying to make sense out of it, figured it must be a plane on fire, about to crash. So I grabbed my first-aid kit and ran.

"But when I got outside there was no crash. This—thing—was just hovering. It went from being all orange to turning silvery gray, and then a blue light shot out and hit my barn. I turned to get my twelve-gauge. But I couldn't move. I mean, I had absolutely no control. My legs were like solid.

"That's when it happened—" Tom paused, then finished, "That *damn* blue light hit me."

He closed his eyes; his face tightened.

"It's okay," Frank said.

"No, it's not okay. They had no right. They just . . . had no right. To . . ." He trailed off, frowned, shook his head. "It doesn't make sense." Tom Jr. wiped his face. It was an odd sight, a giant of a man so scared. But Frank had seen it before. He might not know everything about what caused it, but he knew a lot about how to deal with it.

He put a hand on the big man's shoulder. "Tom, take my card." Tom looked at him, puzzled. Frank met his gaze. "What happened to you has happened to a lot of other people." The big man looked at Frank, a haunted look in his eyes. "A whole lot. *You are not alone.* If you want to talk to some others, we meet on the third Wednesday of this month."

Annie heard Carol's refrigerator open and close. When Carol came back, she carried a package wrapped in white butcher paper as well as her shoulder bag.

"Not more surprises . . .?"

"This one you'll really like. And old what's-his-face, too." She moved to a small electronic panel on the wall near her front door. "Umm, what's my birthday?"

"An alarm system? Some people in Los Alamos don't even lock their doors."

"I want their names and addresses—okay, out the door. We've got twenty seconds."

On the porch, Annie asked again, "Why? You must be the only person in town with a burglar alarm."

Carol made a face. "I didn't want it, but I keep prescription drugs for my head-shrinking business so the base insisted. Hey—I got a deal—a free panic button in every room. So if some maniac junkie breaks in, I hit the button and the cops are here in two minutes."

"Two minutes! Are you serious?"

Carol shrugged. "That's what they say. But this being Los Alamos they would probably get here the next day."

"In New York, they wouldn't come at all unless there was a Dunkin Donuts on the corner."

"In New York there is a Dunkin Donuts on *every* corner."

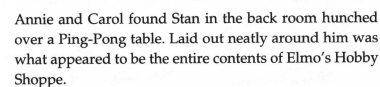

Annie and Carol found Stan in the back room hunched over a Ping-Pong table. Laid out neatly around him was what appeared to be the entire contents of Elmo's Hobby Shoppe.

Stan had a giant pile of tunnels, trestles, barns and farmhouses, and a mound of clay for sculpting a landscape.

He looked up, surprised and embarrassed. "I had this meeting with the advisory board. They made me head engineer for a new project, but it's on hold until the guy from the Pentagon gets in. I had the rest of the day off. So . . . I, ah . . . I never had a train when I was a kid." He shrugged. "I figured our kid should." He turned to Carol, "How's the head-shrinking trade?"

"No shortage of business here. But guess what I have for you?"

"Secret hostility?"

"That's not secret, schmuck." She took out the white

paper package and ripped it open. "All the way from Brooklyn—genuine New York pastrami!" With a flourish she shoved a three-pound chunk of pastrami toward Annie, who instantly turned green and ran down the hall.

"And you thought you only did that to me," Stan said.

Annie's queasiness didn't last long, and soon they were eating a bland dinner. The so-called morning sickness had been hitting Annie late in the day, around dinner-time—which, as Stan pointed out, had been severely cutting into what he could expect to find on the table for dinner.

"Especially onions. Show her even a *picture* of an onion," he told Carol, "and she runs from the room. I like onions, too. But, hey," he said, lifting a large bowl of mashed potatoes for Carol's inspection. "This is it. Until the baby comes, we're living on potato flakes."

"The doctor says the morning sickness will be over soon," Annie said. "Besides, this baby is worth a few months of potato flakes, Stanley."

Stanley quickly got up and gave her a big, gentle hug, and a passionate kiss on the cheek. "This baby," he told her, "is worth all the pastrami in Brooklyn, Chicago and Miami. Forget the damn onions."

Just an hour after a spectacular desert sunset that ran through the entire spectrum of reds and cooled into purples, the whine and whuff of a Black Hawk helicopter's engines grew clear as it came in to land at an unmarked military base in Groom Lake, Nevada.

Two large aircraft hangars stood side by side. A military sign on one read:

AREA 51:54
NO ADMITTANCE

A squad of Black Berets led by an incredibly thin man with captain's bars on his shoulders moved to meet the helicopter.

Stepping out of the chopper, Colonel Wesley returned the Captain's salute. "Captain Crouch."

"Colonel, welcome to Dreamland, sir."

"Always a pleasure, Captain." Wesley half turned. "And you remember Major Andros, I'm sure."

It was clear from Crouch's face that remembering and liking were not the same thing, but he snapped Andros a salute. The Major hesitated a moment longer than necessary before returning the salute, which left Crouch frozen in his salute.

Wesley led the way toward the hangar. Crouch fell into step beside him and Andros trailed behind, looking at the stars and marveling at the clarity of the air that made them seem so bright. Wesley and Crouch conferred in low tones.

"Any change?"

Crouch gave a slight shake of his head and unconsciously pitched his voice so Andros couldn't hear him. "No, sir, they're staying behind that retaining wall. Except when they slip out for their experiments." He glanced back at Andros. "Nothing we can do to keep tabs on that, sir—but Major Andros might be able to tell us more."

Wesley turned and saw Andros craning his neck up at the stars. The Colonel shook his head. "Sometimes I don't think the Major knows what planet he's on. What is the timing on the intervals?"

"Increasing, sir," said Crouch as they headed into the larger of the two hangars. "And I believe the Colonel is right in assuming this new activity indicates an increased risk of containment failure."

Wesley shook his head. "They're not going anywhere. I'm going to get JOSHUA operational and in eight weeks I'll have their wall down."

"Yes, sir."

"You are keeping the low-frequency subsonics on, Captain?" Wesley asked as they approached the retaining wall.

"Yes, sir. It's the only thing that seems to penetrate that goo." Crouch glanced at the series of small black parabolic dishes focused at the clear gel-like wall. "Stirs them up pretty good from what we've been able to track."

Wesley took a step closer to the strange wall. It seemed to rise from the ground and completely encase a huge, gray dome. It was made of a thick, translucent jelly-like substance, a substance that had proven effective in absorbing and stopping all known tactical weapons.

When it first appeared, Wesley had ordered a squad of Black Berets to a frontal assault. Three of them were armed with Strike Force fire cannons. For a brief moment, it had appeared that the flamethrowers had been successful in burning an opening into the wall. But as three soldiers advanced, the wall resealed and trapped them like flies caught in thick honey.

They recovered two of the bodies. Technically, the soldiers were not alive or dead, but in some kind of cellular suspension, an active sleep in which their bodies failed to age. The top minds of MJ-12 were still working to analyze it.

From where Wesley stood now, he could see the third Beret still buried deep within the translucent wall, his eyes and mouth wide in what might be considered a scream of terror. Wesley preferred to believe it was a shout of victory. The soldier had actually touched the dome before being encased.

Damn good man, Wesley thought again.

Finding a way to breach the retaining wall had become a top priority. With it up, Wesley knew he could not stop them, hold them, or even accurately monitor them. But JOSHUA would end that.

Wesley turned to Crouch. "Keep the subsonics on— maybe turn it up a notch. I want that missing data and it doesn't stop until they give it to us." He half turned his head to Major Andros. "You can tell them that, Mike," Wesley said.

"Sir?" he said, pretending he hadn't heard every word. But Wesley and Crouch moved past the retaining wall toward Wesley's office door at the end of the hangar.

Andros was left alone with the night sky and the sound of crickets and that was fine with him.

Such brilliant stars, he thought. *Pleiades. Orion . . .* he ran over the list in his mind.

There it is: Vega . . .

.

FIVE

Annie's observatory sat on the peak of a high desert mountain, far from light and radio-wave pollution, and shielded from Los Alamos by the rock walls of the peak itself. Outside the small building a large parabolic dish pointed skyward.

Inside the observatory Annie sat at the console of a computer. A computer-generated image of the stars in the Vega system played across the screen. Annie typed in a string of instructions and the image began to rotate along one axis.

Her problem had begun several weeks earlier, when she had run a routine chart-deviation check. She had punched up the small but well-known Vega system and discovered an anomalous gas cloud. The fact that it shouldn't have been there was one thing, but the way this cloud acted was another. Class-E nebula clouds did not emit distorted-frequency waves similar to those emitted by a small planet or moon.

Annie stared at the star chart's image on the screen, but she could not get her mind to focus on it. *There's something about this gas cloud. I know something about it, but I can't remember what. I can't even remember how I know it.*

She concentrated, waiting for her subconscious to tell her what to do, hoping that either something would come to her or the irrational thought would go away and let her work.

"Well!" said a soft voice at her elbow, and she almost went through the roof.

"My God, Max. You scared hell out of me."

"Sorry." Max smiled easily and sat on the edge of Annie's worktable.

Blond and stocky, Max was one of the most easygoing people Annie had ever known, and since they had begun to work together they'd never had a cross word.

Max sipped from his coffee cup, which was decorated with a large picture of an owl and his name in big blue letters.

"So have you decided on a name yet?" he asked.

"Well, I thought MV-3974 would be nice—the catalogue recommends it."

"It's very nice, Annie. But I meant a name for the *baby.*"

Annie gave up her clumsy subterfuge, glad she could talk openly. "Oh, Max, I don't know what to do.

Stanley won't listen. He wants the baby to have a family name."

"What's wrong with that?"

"His *family* is wrong with that: it's Clarence, Ludwig or Adolph if it's a boy, and Gertrude, Mavis or Birgut if it's a girl."

"Oohhh," he said. "Oh, boy." He sipped his coffee. "Ludwig is nice."

Annie showed him teeth. "If you say that to Stanley, I'll poison your coffee. Besides, he likes Adolph. He says it's a very misunderstood name."

Annie sighed and told the computer to turn the antenna.

Max watched her work, absorbed and curious.

"Where are you going?" he asked as she settled the dish in a new area and started to fine-tune it. She punched up the audio, and the room filled with the sounds of deep space, a white-noise roar of random hisses and crackles.

"Um, I'm not sure. I just— The other day, it occurred to me . . . and I thought I'd try it over here . . . maybe listen to this thing on a different . . ." She spoke in a way that put off discussion. The truth was, a piece of a dream had just come back to her. But now it seemed more like a memory.

Although she remembered few details, one that stuck had to do with finding a Vegan anomaly using a slightly different approach.

It had to do with the principle that a frequency wave might be better observed as it traveled away from, rather than toward, an object. If it held true, she could find this signal in a skip off another planet as it headed away.

This principle could not be used in normal star charting. Because every heavenly body emits a radio-frequency signal, it would be nearly impossible to separate a particular planet's signal and what was just added in a bounce or skip. But because the observatory's computer already knew the Vega system, it could theoretically eliminate the charted signal and hear only what was left.

Annie had been hoping to try it without Max looking over her shoulder.

"Right about here," she said as she locked on to Vega directly. "I thought it might—" Abruptly the sound changed from the massive static sound to something completely different, unlike anything either of them had ever heard before.

It was music.

The new sound was so clearly musical that it was impossible to think of it as noise. It filled the room with a symphonic twirl of sound, as though somebody had taken the bleeps and chirps of telemetry and composed an eight-bar fugue with it. The music rose to a soaring, ethereal climax, died away, and repeated from the beginning again.

Annie stared dumbly at nothing, too numb with shock to touch the controls. The first thought that came to her was almost as surprising as the sound itself. *I know that music,* she thought. *I've heard it before.*

Max muttered over and over, "It's not possible. It's just not possible. It's not—"

"Roll the tape, Max," Annie snapped. "For God's sake, *roll* it!"

Max lunged for the rack-mounted Ampex and patched it quickly into Annie's output.

"What the hell is it?" he asked Annie.

"Um—" Annie frowned with concentration. "It's probably just, uh, you know . . ."

"Right . . ." Max said, and they both stared as the music faded, and then began again.

Annie sighed with relief as the music repeated. "We're going to get it. We'll get the whole thing now."

Annie found herself carried away by the music—not so much by the beauty of the simple fugue, but by something connected with her first thought; *I know what this is,* she thought again. *Maybe not this exact thing, but something very close, very much like it,* and she tried to think how that could be possible and couldn't come up with anything except a huge blank wall blocking off the memory somewhere far in her past, so far back that it made no sense and it seemed futile even to worry about it. *But I know what this is,* she thought again.

Annie glanced at Max. He seemed disturbed rather than excited. But she had no time to wonder about that and turned back to the computer.

"Hey, maybe it's a solar flare?" Max said.

"For God's sake, Max, we're not in any alignment that could possibly pick up the sun. And it's not a short-wave skip, and it's not any known satellite, all right?"

She took a deep breath, and shook her head to clear away the seductive beauty of the music—seductive to her alone, for she could see that Max was growing more nervous with each repetition of the fugue. "Call NORAD," she told him, more to follow correct procedure than out of any real conviction that NORAD had an answer.

"Right," he said, "of course, absolutely. It has to be one of their dark birds. Has to be."

"I don't think so," she muttered, "I don't think so."

Max moved to the corner of the room and reached for the telephone receiver. This should have been one of the happiest moments in his life. After all, he had devoted his life to the study of astronomy from childhood through college.

But it was not a happy moment for Max. The problem lay in the four years during which he had *not* studied the stars. He never talked about that period. If he had, it would have surprised Annie more than the sound now pouring out of the speaker.

During that four-year period, Max had been a special agent for United States Intelligence under the direct orders of Colonel John Wesley.

His placement at the observatory had not been an accident. He looked on it as a reward for time spent in high-tech intelligence in East Berlin, monitoring the Soviet

Bloc for sudden and unusual technological break-throughs.

Now a breakthrough had arrived. His job was to report it. He talked softly and intensely. "Colonel, we have a confirmed lock on . . . an intense low-frequency radio emission from the Vega region. The pattern is not random, repeat, *not* . . . Yes, sir . . . Acknowledged."

Max hung up the phone and glanced toward Annie. She hadn't heard him. Her entire focus was on the signal, which was starting to fade. He watched her work up a sweat trying to keep the signal.

"Come on," she hissed, "stay with me, damn you." But the signal stopped—and then resumed, faster, more urgently, but the same sequence. Furiously, Annie fine-tuned and plotted the position. *Where are you? What are you?* she thought as it started to take shape, then suddenly faded. *Don't go.*

But it was gone. Annie wilted for a moment, then lunged at her controls and fought to get the music back. But it was no good. It really was gone.

"NORAD says it's not theirs."

"No kidding."

"They said, maybe it's Chinese. . . ."

"Chinese. *Chinese?* Did that sound Chinese to *you*, Max?"

"Well, no, but . . . It has to be *something*."

"Well, I have to agree with you there, partner. It does have to be *something*."

"Are you going to call the SETI people?"

Annie shrugged. "Search for Extra-Terrestrial Intelligence, that's a laugh. We're not a part of their network, we don't take their money, not even their newsletter. I mean, we're scientists, right? We just happen to chart stars."

Max could see where this was going. "Right."

"I've never been interested in the fruitless search for intelligent life elsewhere, when we have enough problems finding it right here."

"Okay, okay, Annie. I thought it was a reasonable question. I didn't mean it as an insult."

Max backed off, but he was glad he had asked. The Colonel would want to know if she was going to act. It would be a security breach.

He watched Annie run a hand through her hair and shuddered. He knew very well what Wesley did to security breaches.

SIX

Annie stayed inside the shell of the music for a long time and quickly lost any sense of time in the heat of her concentration. The strange feeling of familiarity stayed with her.

After a long while of letting the music take her where it wanted, she finally put one cautious tendril of thought outside the cocoon of concentration she'd been wrapped in and started to think a little like a scientist again.

She began to run a few tests on the sound, checking the frequency, the shape of the waves, even making a sketchy start on a way to ask the mainframe computer to think about the sounds.

"Wake-up call for Annie Katz."

She looked up, startled. "What?"

"Good. You're showing real improvement," said Max. "Soon you'll be eating with a fork, leading a normal life."

She shook her head with irritation. "What are you talking about, Max? I'm busy—"

"I know. You've been busy for four and a half hours. So busy you haven't seen or heard anything—"

"How long?"

"—and your husband is on the phone now and wants to know where the hell you are and why, which is not in my job description, so why don't you talk to the poor guy?"

She punched the tape recorder off and, in the sudden stillness, mumbled, "Thanks, Max," as she reached for the telephone.

"Hello, Stan." Annie was still a little distracted but was brought crashing back to reality as Stan launched into an angry blast. He finished with a demand that she come home immediately. "I'll clean up and start for home within a half hour," she said. "Love you."

Annie hung up. Then she saw the tape recorder. She spun the tape back to the beginning and inserted a blank cassette in the deck to make a copy.

The sky seemed perfect to Annie when she stepped outside into the parking lot. The air was chilly, and this night was clear and rich and intoxicating, like wine is supposed to be but never is.

Annie paused to look up into the sky at the stars that

seemed so close and tangible. Even though she spent her whole professional life looking at the stars, it was still the first thing she did when she stepped outside.

Since childhood she had felt drawn to the stars. As a young girl she would slip out of the house and run to the fields, where she would lie on her back looking up at the stars for hours, and she would feel a kind of combined kinship and hunger that she could never explain, even to herself, but which surely drove her to her choice of careers.

She was tempted even now, at the age of thirty-four, simply to lie down on the pavement, still a little warm from the day's sun, and let the heat soak into her as she gazed up with a fascination that never grew old. *Sirius, Aldebaran, Rigel, Betelgeuse, Vega . . .*

But Annie knew Stan was waiting at home. He would have figured with his engineer's precision exactly when she should arrive home, plus or minus five percent, and started his countdown. So she didn't lie on the pavement and look at the stars. *Too hard on my back anyway,* she thought, and climbed into her ten-year-old Blazer.

As she started the car into the familiar rhythm of the road's curves, Annie's mind slid back to the extraordinary music she had taped, and she put the cassette copy into the player in the car's dashboard. The time was 1:13—plenty of time yet before Stan would start to worry.

Then the tape started to play, filling the car with its precise and eerie fugue, and Annie thought only about the music. She noticed nothing until, some ten minutes later, she was driving through a tunnel.

The tape had run out, and she reached to rewind it when lights flared ahead of her at the mouth of the tunnel, as though a large truck were heading in from the other side.

Annie started the cassette again and looked ahead to the mouth of the tunnel. Another fifty feet and she was out of the tunnel. The music began to play again. There was no sign of the truck, but the lights were still there. Bewildered, she looked around. She noticed the shape of the shadows the light was making. *But that's impossible,* she thought.

The light was coming from above.

Not sure what was happening or what she was doing, Annie slowed the car. She turned off the tape player so she could hear better and stuck her head out the window. But the music was still playing.

Annie looked back inside the car at the tape player. It was 1:23. Below the dim gleam from the clock the cassette was half-ejected, dangling out of the mouth of the tape player and definitely turned off.

But the music was still playing.

Annie leaned out the window and looked up. There was a light directly above her, so bright she couldn't make out any details. A hot wind whipped at her. She thought it must be a helicopter hovering with its searchlight turned on, but she heard no sound of rotors, only the music.

Startled, Annie pulled her head back in the window and glanced through the windshield at the road ahead—

just in time to see a large owl flying straight at the windshield.

For one long, strange moment the owl seemed to hang in the air inches away from impact, outstretched claws taut, wings spread wide. Every detail of the owl seemed unnaturally clear, as though she were looking at a highlighted illustration in a textbook. She could see each tiny piece of every single feather, every line and ripple in the owl's coloring.

But Annie was overwhelmed by the eyes, those strange dark swirling pools of reptilian intelligence that seemed to hint at terrible secrets beyond human understanding. The eyes, the deep whirling owl eyes, seemed to reach out in this frozen moment of time and wrap Annie in a total envelope that said the world was unimportant, all you were and thought and hoped for was unimportant, there was only the owl and the deep secrets of its eyes, and Annie found herself lost in the depths of the owl's eyes for an impossibly long moment with no sense of time until with a jolt of pure terror she remembered she was driving a car on a mountain road with an owl about to crash into her windshield.

Annie hit the brakes hard and swerved the car onto the shoulder, and the owl whipped upward and away without a sound and was gone.

Shaken, adrenaline roaring through her bloodstream, Annie took a deep breath. *That owl was really*— She flexed her fingers to work out the tension in them—a lot of tension for one owl, she told herself—and restarted the car. She glanced at the dashboard clock. *That can't be right,* she thought.

The clock said 2:58 A.M.

If it was right, almost an hour and a half was missing.

SEVEN

You've got a genuine mystery
all right. . . . Looks like
some kind of ancient symbol.
—Frank Cassidy
MUFON investigator

In the desert, above the hangar, a small craft hovered. A blue light shot out of the hangar, and the craft slid down through the light and disappeared inside.

Captain Crouch stared at it, glancing at his watch, and then went quickly inside.

"They're back, sir," Crouch said, coming to attention.

"What's the duration, Captain?"

"Two trips tonight—"

"Two!" exploded Wesley. "They've never done two in the same night before."

"No, sir."

"How long?"

"Twenty-three minutes the first time, sir. Back on site for fifty-six minutes. In that interval the guard said the only sign-ins were you, Major Andros and an experimental. He noted also an escalated activity in the genetics lab, after you signed out.

"They left again soon after. Away for forty-four minutes and then back just now."

Wesley spun his chair away, looking at the dark square of the window. *Escalated activity . . . Andros . . . the observatory signal . . .* He spun his chair back to face Captain Crouch.

"This thing has major shit-storm potential, Captain. Things are changing too fast. There are too many variables; I want them distracted. Turn up the juice on the subsonics. Give 'em a migraine that will pop their little bug-eyed heads off. And bring me Andros."

"Sir!" Crouch marched out.

Wesley threw his feet up on his desk and closed his eyes. He could feel another one coming on. That blinding pain behind his eyes, followed by another playback of memory he had no control over. He forced his breathing to remain deep and slow. He tried to remain calm. . . . He felt violated, in a way most men could never know. And the hardest part for him was knowing he was helpless to stop it.

He leaned his head back and took a deep breath—

—and he was inside the ship again. A double handful of gray figures moved rapidly around the cabin with jerky efficiency that underlined how very different they were from him. He could see a few definite features of the craft; smooth, gray walls curved around the enclosed space, and an even light seemed to come from no specific source.

At the far end of the room stood a row of glowing, blue, liquid-filled glass tanks. He could see the group move about the tanks, doing something. . . . He knew their actions were to protect the tanks. But although he had no idea what might be in the tanks, or what they were used for, he knew they were the whole purpose of the trip, and that what they were to do was very important.

There was the first hint of sound now, a hiss of air against the ship's skin. He turned back to the window and watched.

The surface of the planet, a great deal closer, lurched crazily as the ship entered the atmosphere at a tremendous speed—a speed he knew was much too fast even for this ship. Behind him, the movement of the crew remained calm, rapid but without panic.

The hiss grew to a roar, and in the window he saw the inevitable crash come closer at a dizzying speed.

Wesley turned to watch the crew work. Their movements remained calm but quick. Perhaps they would be in time, perhaps not; it did not appear to concern them very much. They simply continued to work, as though the idea of a crash at a speed of several thousand miles per hour was nothing to cause panic.

Seconds now and they would crash; and still the only sound was the screech of the air outside, growing louder and higher.

Wesley turned back to the window and saw the ground rushing at him. It was dusty, dry, reddish ground, nearly bare of life except for a few scrubby plants. He recognized it as desert Southwest.

The crash was only a second away now—did the ship re-

ally slow slightly? The impact was tremendous . . . any possible slowing didn't seem to matter. The window darkened as it smashed into the ground and splintered with tremendous noise.

Wesley gasped; he could almost feel the smash, buckle and twist of the ship as it broke apart under the tremendous impact.

And then . . .

Captain Crouch stood next to Major Andros.

The Major saw the Colonel's eyes flutter open. "Are you all right, sir?"

Wesley blinked, still struggling to clear away the awful clarity of that vision.

"To hell with you, Andros. You know damn well what they are doing to me."

"Sir?"

"Cut the crap, Major," Crouch demanded.

Wesley waved Crouch off and stood up, gaining control of himself again.

"Major, they are up to something and you're in on it. We had a report of an intense low-frequency radio emission at twenty-three hundred hours. They've taken two extended flights tonight and escalated activity in *your* genetics lab."

"Colonel—" Andros began.

"No, Major, you listen up. If I thought I could prove you have aided them in any way with their plans to leave, your life would be over. I don't mean that in a career sense. Understood?"

Andros nodded. "Is that all, sir?"

"No, it's not. I want to know: Where the hell are JOSHUA's specs, Major?"

"I'm pleased to say they've been downloaded, sir."

"Why the hell didn't you say so? Who has them? Just when were you going to tell me this, Major?"

"Sir. You made it clear that I was to answer you when asked. I have now done so. In addition, sir, I was not present at the time of downloading to their subject."

The Colonel stared at Andros coldly. "Dismissed."

After Andros left, the Colonel turned to Captain Crouch. "Start checking every man on this base for that download. I want that data!"

❋

Andros wasn't really worried, not yet. He was, however, surprised. *How did Wesley already know about the signal?*

The response came back: *Patience.*

Andros nodded. Wesley obviously hadn't made the connection yet. There was still time.

❋

"Where in the *hell* have you been?"

Annie was surprised to find him standing in the doorway in his battered bathrobe. "At the observatory, Stanley—really, what's wrong with you?"

"What's— Honey, do you know what time it is?"

"Why don't you let me in, and I promise to look at a clock first thing."

Annie pushed past and gave him a peck on his cheek.

"You're acting as if nothing has happened."

"Nothing *has* happened," she said patiently. "I came straight home after you called. For God's sake, you're being hysterical. You must have dozed off or something."

Stan's jaw clenched. "My pregnant wife vanishes for two hours and when I ask her what took so long she says it didn't. Says I fell asleep and lost track of time—and *I'm* hysterical?"

"Stanley, for God's sake!" Annie, fully exasperated, was on the verge of tears.

Stan raised a hand to ward her off. "All right. Fine. Forget it. I already have." He stalked away.

Annie kept hearing the space music in her head as she got ready for bed. But she snapped out of her trance-like mood when she got to the bed.

Stan had pulled the sheet up to his ears. His back was to her and the muscles along his spine and shoulders looked so tight with unrelieved anger that Annie hesitated. "Honey, I'm sorry. I guess I just lost track of time. The thing I found tonight was—"

She paused, because in all the arguing she hadn't even mentioned the music. She didn't know how to describe it or what it might mean.

She said, "Tonight I saw the most amazing . . ." But she found it too hard to continue that thought and instead finished, ". . . owl."

In the morning, Stan was no longer grumpy but his head felt as if it had been stuffed with old newspapers and leaky pipes. He had a big meeting at ten o'clock at the Aerocorp conference room, and since he had been up until almost four, he was not at the top of his form when the alarm smashed him out of sleep and onto his feet at seven o'clock.

He looked in on Annie before leaving. She was still asleep, her fists curled tight and a frown on her face, as though she was having bad dreams. Stan bent over the bed and planted a kiss on her forehead without waking her, and slouched groggily out the door.

Each major Aerocorp project began with a formal presentation by the military liaison for the project. Stan was relieved to see he knew the man from the Pentagon, had worked with him before and found him amiable and efficient.

Stan watched as the officer approached the podium and waved to his assistant at the computer.

"Lights, please," said Colonel Wesley.

The first image on the wall-sized high-resolution computer screen showed an etching of a bearded man in a robe blowing an ancient ram's-horn trumpet.

"The Bible tells us Joshua fit the battle of Jericho," said Colonel Wesley, "and the walls came a-tumbling down. Joshua blew his trumpet, and the sound caused the city walls to crumble."

The next image showed a stylized high-tech weapon design in 3-D. A long stainless-steel barrel led to four large black power packs. The whole thing was strapped to a heavy-duty military tripod with a virtual-reality targeting system. The image rotated, displaying the weapon from all angles.

"We think we can go Joshua one better," Wesley said. "Using our emerging technology, we can take a hard look at the SDI research we have done on directed-energy weapons and come up with a working prototype of the future of weaponry.

"In Project JOSHUA we will amplify the sound waves and focus them into a tight beam that's then accelerated with massive electromagnetic forces so what it appears to fire is a straight line or beam that then disrupts the target at a subatomic level. We believe JOSHUA will have an estimated effective range of two kilometers."

The next image was comic-book style and showed a computer-animated sequence of a tank and a row of soldiers hit with a beam of light and disintegrating.

"Project JOSHUA," Wesley continued, "will cause complete disintegration of all known materials, organic and inorganic, natural and synthetic, by entering the target at the molecular level and vibrating until the elemental bond of proton and electron is broken. There is no known or anticipated defense."

The picture of Joshua with his horn appeared again, but this time the bearded figure was surrounded by an aura and a stylized hydrogen atom.

"Ladies and gentlemen—welcome to Project JOSHUA."

Wesley moved on to the technical specifications. Stan followed these with some interest and found something that didn't quite make sense. He started to raise his hand to question Wesley on the point, but hesitated.

From the row right behind Stan, Dennis Albright, in his lab coat and power tie, saw Stan's hesitation. In fact, for the whole presentation he had been watching Stan instead of Wesley. He leaned in and said, "Isn't this great? It's right out of *Star Wars*."

"Yeah, great." Stan nodded, then looked down at his notes.

"You know, I'm so pleased to be working with you. I think it's really terrific that they finally made you project leader."

"Thanks."

"I mean it, Katz. It's a real pleasure."

"Great." Stan stood up as the presentation ended and followed after the Colonel, winding through the dozen glad-handing technicians.

"Colonel?" Stan called to him as they stepped into the hallway. "Colonel Wesley!"

The Colonel pivoted sharply on his heel. A smooth smile slid across his face and he advanced toward Stan with his hand held out.

"Dr. Katz, I can't tell you how pleased I was when I

saw you were free to head up this project. Congratulations. It'll be great to work with you again."

"Colonel—I couldn't help noticing a few gaps in the specs for the final stage."

Colonel Wesley continued to smile. "Yes?" he said.

"Well, I didn't want to say anything in open meeting in an area that might be, ah, sensitive, but it seems to me that with that kind of final plate voltage and no way to focus it we could have a very sloppy situation on our hands."

The Colonel's smile faded and he glanced up and down the hall. He lowered his voice.

"Dr. Katz—Stan—thanks for saving that comment for a private moment. And I'm glad you brought it up. It's the reason I selected *you* to head up this project. I've had top people working on this and they will continue, but so far they all have failed to give me this final stage."

Wesley raised a hand, then lowered it onto Stan's shoulder. "Now, I believe in JOSHUA. In fact, I'm counting on it. So while I could have had any of the senior engineers at Aerocorp, I picked you. You're young, hungry and you have an extensive background in quantum mechanics. Dr. Katz, my people tell me I need a project leader who can fill in holes, make theories realities. You're the one. This is your chance—and I can assure you, JOSHUA will be the kind of project that makes or breaks careers."

His hand tightened on Stan's shoulder. Stan winced slightly at the pressure.

"Well, thanks, that's, I really—but most applications

of quantum theory are still concerned with energy eigen-states of matter. And what we're looking for is a physical technology that does not yet exist, I mean, so far as I know. For JOSHUA to work, I would have to figure out quantum states of the configuration of the molecules and—"

"Dr. Katz. In English?"

Wesley's voice had the sound of a warning in it. Stan backpedaled. "I mean—I'm looking forward to the challenge, and, uh, I'll give it my best shot, Colonel."

Wesley clapped a hand on Stan's shoulder. "I know you will. Now—I don't have to tell you to keep this quiet. We'd hate to lose our funding or, more importantly, the team's morale behind a project that needs to be in proto-type within eight weeks."

Eight weeks! "Yes, sir."

Wesley shook his hand again, giving him an automatic smile. "Good. Great to work with you again," he said, and turned, clipping off down the hall.

Stan watched him go, then turned back in to meet with his team. He was surprised to see Albright standing in the doorway. But he shrugged it off when he saw that Albright was just grabbing a smoke.

EIGHT

Annie awoke a great deal later than usual, feeling like she had been beaten. She took a long hot shower and felt a little better, but the more she thought about it the more she worried and the more she worried the more she thought about the owl that had flown at her windshield the previous night. But no matter how she tried, her thoughts couldn't get around that owl to anything coherent on the other side, so she gave up and called Carol.

"Come on over," Carol said, "I'm clear until three o'clock."

When Annie got to Carol's house she found the front door unlocked. "Hello?" she called, sticking her head in the door.

From the back of the house there came a terrible screech and Annie gasped. "Carol!"

"Come on in. I'm in the back room."

She found Carol crooning over a chimpanzee in a cage. "Hey, Sonny. That's my boy. Come on, sweetie. Eat the nice food."

"Good lord, it's a monkey."

A yellow mush abruptly sailed through the cage bars and splattered on Carol's face. An empty purple Barney bowl clattered to the floor just inside.

"A chimpanzee, actually." Carol backed up a step before she wiped her face and turned to Annie. "I moved him here so he wouldn't know he was an experiment. But I'm not sure it was such a great idea. He's got a genetically enhanced IQ. But so far, aside from the fact that he does *not* like my cooking, I have yet to see any street smarts."

Annie reached for a roll of paper towels on the desk.

"Hold still," Annie demanded, pulling a chunk of smooshed banana from Carol's dark hair.

"Of course, I didn't say this to the cute Major who dropped him off. Ouch, don't pull."

"A Major?" Annie successfully distracted Carol from the growing mess in her hair.

"Well, he was not the usual. He's got a dynamite butt, a nice personality and great eyes. God, I could really fall into those eyes."

"Well, listen, I know this great beauty shop . . . nothing like a new haircut to turn a guy on."

"Stop already," Carol said. "I hardly know the man."

Sonny shrieked again, catching both Annie and

Carol's attention. "Oh, forgive me, Sonny." Carol gestured grandly to the cage. "Annie, this is Sonny. Sonny, Annie."

"How do you do, Sonny," Annie said as she took a step closer. A long brown arm reached out from the cage toward her. "Does he bite?"

"Probably, but only if you piss him off."

"Uh-huh. What might piss him off?"

"Haven't a clue." Carol shrugged.

Sonny slowly turned his palm upright in a submissive way. Annie found herself compelled to touched his warm leathery palm. *So gentle,* she thought.

She looked up and found herself staring straight at the four-foot-tall, hairy, reddish brown chimp, with his large dark eyes. Sonny gazed back. *There was something about him. An understanding . . .* Both seemed caught in a trance. Then suddenly the chimp pulled back his protruding lips, gave a wide grin, showing all his teeth, and let go another high shriek.

"Oh, good, he likes you," Carol said.

Annie smiled back. "Yeah, I guess so."

"Of course he does. Did you know a chimp's brain is about half the size of a human's, but proportionately to body size, it's about equal? They even match us with the same number of logic gyri-ridges. This little guy, however, has twice the number of gyri-ridges. Or so Major Andros says." Carol turned on the AM/FM radio. "Seems to really like music."

"Soothes the savage beast?"

"Something like." Carol shrugged. "Major Andros suggested it."

Sonny pulled his arm back and moved around in his cage. His attention was focused on the floor, as if he was looking for something.

"He's cute. I like him," Annie said, rising back to her feet. "In fact, he's probably the most charming guy you've ever lived with."

Carol laughed. "Sad part is, doll, you're absolutely right. Let's get some coffee."

Carol and Annie left the room just as Sonny found his Casio electronic piano in the small pile of toys. Had they stayed they would have heard him slowly working through an interesting melody.

It sounded surprisingly like Annie's space music.

In the kitchen Carol finished washing off the mush and took her time brewing some excellent decaf in her Melitta drip coffee maker.

Annie stood in the doorway, leaning against the frame, and tried to gather her thoughts. She wanted to say it right, with precision and scientific detachment. But what came tumbling out was neither scientific nor detached.

"Carol," she said, "something happened last night."

Carol looked up. "You are so lucky, honey. For me, *nothing* happened last night. Or the night before, or the night before . . . but I'm not without hope."

"Carol. This is serious."

Carol looked at her again, with an eyebrow raised this time. "Oh." She put down the pot of water. "Okay. Sorry. The doctor is in."

Annie opened her mouth, closed it, looked away. "I— Last night at work . . ." She trailed off and frowned at the wallpaper.

"Yes? Something happened?"

Annie nodded. "I found something very significant. It was new. Completely different. But—on the way home—it took me a lot longer than ever before to get home, Carol, and I don't—"

Carol nodded and poured coffee into two mugs. "Uh-huh. And Stan figured you and Max were fooling around?"

"No," Annie snapped at her, then sighed. "I mean, maybe. But that's not the thing."

"I bet it is for Stan."

"Carol. Please. Me and Max?"

Carol shrugged. "Just asking. I would—in a heart-beat. He's a sweet guy. Great sense of humor and tight buns."

"Look," said Annie, "as far as I know I just went straight home. But it took . . . I was . . . This morning I hurt all over. My head, chest, jaw, everywhere." She did not specify the raspy pain in her vagina. "Is it possible for me to, I don't know, blank out or something? I mean, just shut down, lose some time? And not know it?"

Carol shrugged. "Sure it's possible. You're overloaded right now. Emotionally, physically, spiritually; did I leave anything out?"

"Well, uh—psychically?"

"Sure, that too. And if you add in a big shot of adrenaline from something happening at work—" She shrugged again, holding the palms of her hands up.

"So it could happen?"

"Yeah. It could happen. Stop worrying. Of course, if it happens again, you can worry. So keep an eye on yourself. One symptom doesn't always mean you got the disease."

"What disease?" Annie interrupted anxiously.

"A figure of speech, for Pete's sake. But let me know if other stuff happens, all right? Like anxiety attacks or severe depression or stuff like that, okay? Otherwise stop worrying. It's the worst thing for you."

Annie sighed. "Stop worrying? *Me?*"

"Ah, give it a try. You never know."

❄

As the day wound down toward dusk, Annie found herself driving to work along the same road; the only road that led to the observatory, or she would have taken another way.

This time she unconsciously sped up as she passed the spot where she had paused for the owl the night before, and a cold shiver ran from the base of her spine to the top of her head and came out as small drops of sweat on her forehead, but again she could not say why.

NINE

It was dusk out in the desert around the hangar labeled Area 51. Small reptiles, insects and animals scurried through the sparse scrub, making ready for the night. Some of them went deep into their hidey-holes in hope of sleeping through the night without being eaten.

Just as invisibly, the Black Berets prepared for their night. A handful blacked their faces and roamed silently across the area, looking for anything or anyone that didn't belong, so quietly that even most small animals were unaware the soldiers were passing.

Other troops sat in front of electronic consoles in darkened rooms far below the hangar and scanned in every possible spectrum—not just for activity, but for anything scanning them, too.

All these preparations were routine, needing only a

signature from Captain Crouch. At random intervals he made changes in the lists for added security. Not tonight.

"Damn it, Crouch!" Colonel Wesley said. "The project is starting and the nerds at Aerocorp already know it's incomplete!"

"Yes, sir," Crouch said, still standing at attention.

"The whole goddamned project is a heap of junk without those final specs! I want 'em now, and I mean pronto!"

"Yes, sir. But sir—The Major says they've downloaded the specs. I've screened every man on the base and all were negative, sir."

"Well, God damn it! Where else could they download it? Who else has been on this base?"

"Sir! No one, sir!"

"No one? No one at all?"

"Just the experimentals, sir—but they're in no condition to do anything. Besides, the bugeyes would never download into somebody who wasn't connected. They can't afford that risk any more than we can."

Wesley sighed and sat at his desk. He reached for two cigars in his top desk drawer. "Sit down, Captain." Wesley flipped him a cigar. "First we helped them, then they helped themselves—there's no control here. We don't have a vehicle that can catch them or a weapon that can stop them. But I don't have to tell *you* that, do I?"

"No, sir."

"Captain," Wesley said slowly, "I want your suggestions."

"Colonel, none of us have a clue where to look for this thing."

Wesley took a slow puff. "That's not true. One of us does."

"Colonel, permission to speak freely?"

"Granted."

"Colonel, I suggest we quit pussyfooting and put the screws to Major Andros. He knows a lot more than he's saying."

Wesley rubbed the end of his cigar in the ashtray. "True enough, Captain. But the Major has his own orders, under a separate command structure."

"Orders to do what, Colonel?"

"Propagate a fair and open exchange of ideas, is how it reads. What that means is, grab all the technology he can and damn the torpedoes.

"Now, the bugeyes like him because he is a genius in genetics, and because they like him, Washington and all of MJ-12 have to put up with him. This does *not* mean we have to like him, only that we can't eliminate him. Unless, of course, we could prove a security breach."

"Yes, sir. I see, sir."

"Captain," Wesley said slowly, "I think it might be time to consider finding a security breach involving Major Andros."

"I understand. I'll get right on it—" Crouch turned his head to blow the smoke off to one side and stopped in mid-puff.

Wesley saw the look of surprise on Crouch's face. "What is it, Captain?"

Captain Crouch stared at the hangar wall behind Wesley's head. He raised a finger and pointed without taking his eyes off the wall.

"Jesus Christ!"

The wall—all the walls in the hangar—were showing a very faint shimmer of color, a color like mother-of-pearl. The range of light colors was pulsing through the spectrum as if to unheard music.

Wesley stood and held a hand out to touch the wall. When his fingers came into contact with the wall he heard a very faint music. It was as if the wall carried the vibration of sound—something like a classical fugue made out of telemetry sounds.

Wesley jerked his hand away. For a moment he stood stupefied. Then he roared out of the office and down the hall, Captain Crouch trailing behind.

✤

The two soldiers hurried through the corridor toward the gleaming steel door at the end of the hall, guarded by one Black Beret and labeled:

GENETICS
STERILE AREA!

Behind the door was a large laboratory. On one side of the room stood a glass DNA containment unit. A chimpanzee sat inside, content as a child playing house. He moved his toy furniture around and seemed happy. He was about four feet tall, but had a larger head and lacked most of his hair, and his eyes were strangely darker. He let out a screech when he saw Wesley and Crouch enter.

"Shut up, you half-ass hybrid," Crouch growled, and the chimp scuttled backward.

Dressed in hospital scrubs, Major Andros faced a wall that looked like a huge fish tank and was filled with deep blue liquid.

Inside this tank and illuminated from below were hundreds of smaller glass tubes, each holding what appeared to be a human fetus.

They ranged in size and development from about 1.1 inches long, three months old—with fingers and toes just becoming differentiated and the external genitalia starting to show and the head growing disproportionately large principally because of development of the brain—to a much larger size, nearly twenty inches and seven pounds: almost full-term humanoid babies that were developing in a thin leathery sack.

All were alive and breathing the blue liquid. Each took its sustenance from filaments that ran from their stomachs to a main panel.

The Major's hands moved quickly about a small fetus he had out on the table. It was about the size of a hamster and had large black eyes and light skin—so light the skin color was almost grayish. He rechecked a bank of monitors, then returned the fetus to the blue water of the main tank. He grabbed a clipboard and moved to study a new readout coming up on the computer.

With all the sounds from the rhythmic fetal heartbeats, air bubbles and the hum of a mainframe, Andros had not heard the warning cry of his chimp or Wesley and Crouch as they moved toward him.

"God damn it, Andros," Wesley began, "what in the name of *hell* is going on?"

"Sir," Andros protested, "this is a sterile area."

"Answer me, Major."

"I assume the Colonel is not referring to my work with chromosome spectrography?"

"You know damned well what I'm referring to, Major!" He jabbed a finger at the wall, which rippled faintly with pulsating pearl color. "That!"

Andros looked up at the wall. "Oh. Good, it's working."

"Good? *Good?* You know what that is?"

"Why, yes sir. Of course, sir."

Wesley fought hard for self-control. "Would you mind sharing that information with me, Major?"

Andros allowed himself a small smile. "It's just a simple test. At this stage they only need to know a few basics about the new equipment and, as you know, they find expression of these ideas works best along the following lines: first—"

"That's enough, Major. As long as you are willing to state, *for the record,* that it represents no overtly hostile or threatening action on their part."

"Of course not, Colonel. Simple equipment test, that's all. I'd tell you if it were anything else, sir."

Wesley gave him a hard look. "Would you, Major?"

"Of course I would, sir."

"You know, Major, if I believed you, I'd say we had

a fighting chance. But I see what you do in here and I know whose side you're on—and it isn't ours."

"It's not a matter of choosing sides, Colonel. It's not a win-lose situation. It's a win-*win* situation. Both sides want the same things, sir."

"I'm glad to hear it, Major. Then suppose you tell me what's happened to the missing JOSHUA data."

Andros shrugged. "They say they downloaded it, sir."

"Captain Crouch has screened every single man on the base. He's found nothing."

"Perhaps Captain Crouch has made an error, sir."

Captain Crouch smiled slightly.

"You know he didn't," said Wesley. "If they say they downloaded it, they're lying."

"And you know they're not lying, sir. They can't."

"Then where in the bloody blue fucking hell did they put it?" Wesley said, moving within an inch of Andros's face and shouting.

Andros barely blinked. "With all respect, Colonel, that's not my department."

Wesley stared hard at Major Andros. Finally he let out a long breath. "All right, Mike, I'll give you that. But you occupy a very special position here. They'll talk to you. Do us all a favor and find out where they put the data, all right?"

"Colonel," he said carefully, "I'm not sure—"

"Listen, Mike, I could make this into a political showdown, but I'm not. I'm *asking*. For now. Okay?"

Wesley turned and glanced at the wall of floating

baby fetuses. God, he hated them. Just looking at them turned his stomach. It just wasn't natural. It wasn't right. They weren't ours and they weren't theirs—they were hybrids, they had no right to exist. He didn't care what deal had been struck. Washington was wrong. Dead wrong. And with JOSHUA, he could put an end to them. He shuddered and marched out.

TEN

Stan reached across his desk past a brightly colored baby-toy catalogue to pull out one of several books he had taken from the Los Alamos Technical Library. He thumbed to an article about a group of German physicists who had worked on an idea for turning sound waves into light waves nearly fifty years earlier.

The group had discovered that sound waves traveling through water could vibrate bubbles in the water until they suddenly burst into a blue visible light. They had named the phenomenon "sonoluminescence."

It wasn't until the early 1990s that this phenomenon was more fully explained by a couple of American physicists. They theorized that the light was caused by miniature sonic booms inside the bubbles. The bubbles reverberated until the surface was moving faster than the speed of sound. A shock wave or sonic boom occurred within, causing the bubble to disintegrate in a burst of light.

Compressed air produced the light as it heated to more than a hundred thousand degrees—almost ten times hotter than the surface of the sun—before exploding. The heat was the effect of electrons shattering loose from atoms. Billions of charged particles resulted, flying around at high speed, giving off electromagnetic radiation that appeared in the form of a visible blue light.

Of course, blowing up air bubbles was not the same as vaporizing the walls of Jericho. But it was a start. And most importantly, it proved the core of his theory that sound waves could indeed be turned into light waves.

Stan reached for the pastrami sandwich on top of his workbench. He ate while he looked at the blueprints and schematics spread out across the top of his desk. He didn't hear Dennis Albright slip into the room, and he jumped when the voice behind him said, "Dr. Katz, how's it going?"

"Hi, Dennis. Did you locate an energy recoil and Kevlar turret?"

"Just finished the paperwork. Needs your signature."

Albright put the parts-requisition papers on the table.

"Great." Stan grabbed a pen and signed. Dennis busied himself studying the JOSHUA blueprint. After a moment he whistled.

"Boy, you've got your hands full."

Stan sighed. "Tell me about it."

"Well, I'm sure you'll do a great job."

Stan handed Albright back his papers. "It'd be a piece of cake if we didn't have this little problem." Stan shook his head and tapped the lower right-hand corner of the blueprint. "Fine-tuning the wave output."

Albright blinked at Stan. "Gee, I would have thought that part would be a cinch."

"That's what the Pentagon thinks," said Stan, rubbing his temples. "But look at the final plate specs, and look what we can do so far."

Albright bent over and whistled again. "Holy mackerel, I wouldn't even know where to start."

Stan stepped to the green chalkboard. "Well, I was using the Schrödinger equation as a starting point. It should be a good approximation for our wave base, but it's well known that the resulting integration procedure is unstable. The least trivial part of the operation is the kinetic propagation."

Stan began writing. "Kinetic energy becomes simply $E(k) = (hk)^2/2m$ where k is a transformed variable conjugate to x. See what I mean?"

"Dr. Katz, that's terrific. I never would have thought of that. I guess you've got it under control. You're going to be a great project leader."

Stan barely heard him. He was frowning at the equation.

Several minutes passed before he noticed that Dennis Albright was gone.

On the floor below, in Colonel Wesley's office, Dennis Albright was in full swing.

"Honestly, Colonel, I don't know why you picked him. He seems obsessed with the smallest details instead of the overall picture. If time is a consideration, perhaps I should step in and take over."

Wesley shook his head slowly. "Dennis, you really are a charmer. I'll keep your offer in mind. Let me think on it." Wesley stood up and showed Albright out.

Two minutes later, Colonel Wesley stood in Stan Katz's lab. "Dr. Katz, what is this?"

Stan was still working at the chalkboard. "Well, sir"—he turned to the Colonel—"I'm exploring possibilities. I have a working hypothesis for JOSHUA. It treats sound waves like light waves. The missing design circuit will have to act like a lens to force the waves into a tight enough focus to permeate at a molecular level. The problem is, we're not looking at a lens, but at an electromagnetic circuit, the design of which I'm not sure about . . . yet."

"Dr. Katz, what I need from you now is not lines on a chalkboard but a working model. We're on a schedule."

"Yes, sir, I know. But if we built it right now as the design shows, all JOSHUA would do—well, it could take a sound and make it louder for range, no problem. Pitch?

Turn it to high-end beyond human hearing for stealth. But focus? Forget it. I'd say Uncle Sam just spent a couple million bucks on the world's largest dog whistle."

"Dr. Katz, I'm notifying Aerocorp that you have until the end of next month to get this prototype up and running, understood?"

Stanley's stomach knotted. That was two weeks earlier than the already insane deadline that had been set. "Yes, sir."

"And Dr. Katz, project engineers don't make funding jokes."

"Sorry, Colonel. But look, time restrictions aren't going to solve this. We're still talking about applying technology that simply does not yet exist."

"Let me tell you about the last A-o-One engineer who said that, Dr. Katz. He kept us waiting eight months while he tried to sell the Stealth design to the highest bidder. Now, I know talking about national security has gone out of style—"

"No, no, that's not what I—"

"Since I feel I know you well enough, I'm certainly not going to question your loyalty after all these years. But: Money is just as dangerous as foreign ideology." He looked down and saw the baby-toy catalogue. "Especially for people who suddenly find they need a little extra money."

Wesley gave him a long hard look and left.

Stanley looked at the toy catalogue.

What the hell am I doing here? Why not go back to teaching? The extra money isn't worth it.

He sighed. Whatever he did, he had to finish this first.

Inside the observatory the sound of the space music was floating through the room. Annie had been playing it almost constantly as she ran test after test.

She pulled her chair up to the table with the oscilloscope, an older gray model, all the observatory could afford. Its beat-up case stood twenty inches high, and it had a green circular nine-inch screen. A keyboard and cables connected the oscilloscope with the observatory's mainframe computer, bringing it almost up to date in its applications.

Using the oscilloscope was a shot in the dark, but Annie was running on hunches and this one seemed reasonable—or no less reasonable than any other at this point. She fed the musical signal into the mainframe and punched up the Vega sector coordinates.

Vega was twenty-seven light-years away. The star's color revealed its mass and age, measured by the percentage of starlight emitted from calcium atoms in the star's atmosphere.

The so-called calcium emission line reflected the magnetic activity of the star which, in turn, reflected its age. It was much younger than our star, too young for any of its planets to have evolved sentient life. But the signal was definitely coming from the Vega region.

The small screen before Annie showed an instantaneous visual display of Vega. Annie typed in a code to enlarge the quadrant. Now the oscilloscope should find any trace pattern of the space music's signal in electron motions in the star's corona.

A highlight appeared on the upper right hand third of the screen. *Good,* Annie thought, *Positive identification of where the signal was deflected. Now, maybe I can get a fix on where you came from.* She typed in the command, SEEK ORIGIN.

The mainframe kicked in, working with the oscilloscope to take the fix from the position of deflection, its velocity and angle of trajectory to compute the space-line coordinates of the signal's origin.

Annie's heart raced. She waved to Max as he returned from a systems check on the parabolic dish. "Max, we may never know *what* it is. But we're about to find out where it came from!"

"Great!" he said.

Max moved to the coffee machine, glancing at the clock above the door. Twenty-one hundred hours. If they were successful in analyzing the signal, Wesley would expect a full report.

Max felt like his heart was being shredded. What he should do and what he wanted to do were completely different. Although he had started this job as one of Wesley's men, he had taken on a very real cover of a happy family man with a secure job. He did not want this to change, but he now saw no way of stopping what he knew Wesley was about to set in motion.

Annie watched the screen, her heart pounding. Secretly she wanted something wonderful, like discovering a small moon. But in her heart she knew that the signal, whatever it might be, was *not* a natural planetary electromagnetic sound wave, or the low-frequency radio emission Voyager 1 had discovered late in '92 that proved to be electrically charged gases or plasma from the sun interacting with the cold gases from interstellar space at the edge of the solar system.

Whatever this signal might be, she believed it was far more.

What the specifics of that "more" might be she refused to guess. Her mind shied away from ideas like "contact" and "intelligence"; they were just too hard for her to take seriously. But still—

Max came up behind her. "Annie?" he said softly.

Without registering what the sound was, Annie turned, and saw—

The owl was coming straight at her, its huge wings spread impossibly wide, its claws tense and sharp, its eyes—its endlessly deep and dark eyes, so full of an intelligence unlike her own . . .

Annie was not aware of fainting. Or that when she fell, she hit the oscilloscope, sending it crashing to the floor. She simply saw and heard everything as though she were suddenly at the far end of a long tunnel and the world was on the other end. She heard Max's anxious voice calling her name and then his gentle hands supporting her and, still at the far end of the tunnel, she took a very deep breath—and slowly came back.

"Oww," she said. "I think I hit my head."

"Jesus," said Max. "I'll say you did. What happened?"

"I don't re—" Annie started, and then she remembered. "The owl! There was an owl coming at me."

"Is there something . . . wrong with owls, Annie? I mean, what's wrong with owls?"

"I—don't know. Nothing, I guess. I just, I suddenly saw one and—I don't know."

"You're still very pale. Let me get you some water." As he stepped away, Annie saw his coffee cup on the table. Sure enough, there was the owl. It was a cute, cartoony owl and not the frightening, cruel owl she thought she had seen, but— *That must be all it was,* she thought, *just Max's coffee cup.*

Nevertheless, she reached a still-trembling finger out and turned the coffee cup around so the awful thing was facing away from her.

Max returned with the water. "Sip it slowly."

"Really, Max, I'm fine,"

Annie turned back toward the oscilloscope and saw the scattered pieces of the machine and the glass from the scope on the ground. "Oh damn! Did I do that?"

"Yeah, I had a choice of catching you or the oscilloscope. Even with our budget, you're harder to replace."

"Thanks, but next time, save the oscilloscope." *We*

were so close— "Max, where are we gonna get the money to replace this?"

Max grabbed a garbage bin and started picking up the pieces. "You know, for a smart woman, Annie, you worry about the wrong things. Go home, get some rest. I'll clean this up." Max frowned. "Hey, you smell something?"

"Yeah." Annie sniffed. "Something burning." Annie and Max walked around the room sniffing for a moment.

"Over there!"

Against the wall, the cables running from the oscilloscope to the mainframe had slowly begun to melt. Smoke rose from the short in the wire.

Max grabbed a fire extinguisher and rushed toward the smoking wall. With three short blasts the flames were out.

"That was close."

What worried Max was not the foamy mess from the fire extinguisher or the broken oscilloscope, or any damage that might have been done to his precious, irreplaceable mainframe computer. For Max, it came down to a much simpler question.

How was he going to tell Wesley of their delay in analyzing the signal?

Max knew Wesley. And he knew the sort of thing that happened to people who did not live up to Wesley's expectations. Max did not want to be one of them.

And yet—

If he could persuade Wesley that this delay was unavoidable, and that he, Max, was necessary to fix it . . .

He smiled. The delay was good. Life could continue, as it had, if he could keep up the delays. It might work, if . . . if Wesley didn't suddenly order everything terminated. It was a gamble, yes.

It was also his only choice.

ELEVEN

And so we build JOSHUA, and
what do they build that's bigger,
better, even *more* threatening?
—Major Michael Andros
Head of Genetics MJ-12

Tom Jr. opened the door of Frank Cassidy's office. The
big man had not slept much since meeting Frank Cassidy. He didn't mind doing without sleep; just one of the
many hardships of the farmer's life. But this—

It was winter, the slow season for farmers. He
should have been resting up, relaxing a little bit. Instead,
he lay awake, turning over in his mind the conversation
with Frank Cassidy, trying to justify staying away, trying
to imagine driving down to the city to the meeting.

In the end, what had drawn him on this long drive
was Frank's last words. *You are not alone.*

Were there really others? Had they seen the same
things? Had the same experiences? He found it hard to
believe.

A large friendly black woman showed Tom Jr. to the

conference room. Five men and fifteen women, ranging in age from teens to seniors, sat inside: black, white, Spanish, Oriental, rich, poor—the most diverse group Tom Jr. had ever seen, but they had one thing in common. They were all victims.

Frank stood to greet him. "This is Tom Jr., a friend."

Tom was about to learn that the word *friend* meant more than friendship. It meant a shared experience, a communion with the unknown.

Tom Jr. twisted uneasily in his chair. Everyone sat in a circle around a young Chinese-American woman, Lisa Chung. Her voice calm, her eyes closed, she was fully hypnotized.

"I'm looking past the *taller one* at these fragile babies, they're not really human, I don't know."

"What are they doing?"

"Just sitting there. *He* says they are playing, but they're not playing. They are just sitting in this pool of light. *He* wants me to like them. I— Oh, *he* is leaning closer."

"How close?"

"Real close, maybe inches from my face. Oh, God, those eyes—" Lisa's face tightened.

"What is it?" Frank asked. He glanced at the rest of the group. Two of the women looked teary-eyed.

"*He's* telling me over and over; these are the *children of the future.* Our children, your children."

"Do you believe him?"

"I don't believe it. I think *he's* lying. Testing me. I hate *this*. I hate *him*. I want it to stop."

"All right," Frank says, "we'll stop. But you will remember and not be frightened."

Tom Jr. let out a deep breath, unaware that he had been holding it. Lisa Chung sat up and rubbed her face. Tom was surprised that he had become caught up in a stranger's nightmare, one that was nothing like his own.

"How do you feel, Lisa?" Frank asked her.

"Better," she said.

"I know these things aren't easy for any of us, but each time we meet, we gain a better understanding. However, I want to stress that we do not have enough information to warrant any conclusions. Several times women have seen unusual babies, but we don't know their purpose. They may be the logical conclusion to their extreme interest in our sexual reproduction."

Tom Jr. looked up. *Sexual reproduction?* The images were vague, but it did not stop a flush rising to his face. Tom's neighbors had judged him a sexual deviant or suggested he had been a victim of child abuse. In either case, the painful memories were socially and personally unacceptable. It was time to learn the truth. Tom Jr. stood up.

Frank turned to him. "Are you okay, Tom?"

"Yeah. I, ah, I think I need to, uh—to do this now."

"Are you sure? I didn't want you to rush into this. There are a lot of pros and cons to memory collection."

"I want to know—no, I *need* to know."

Frank nodded. "Okay."

"After this blue light hit you what happened?" Frank asked. Tom sat in the overstuffed chair next to him in a light hypnotic trance, eyes closed.

"I'm floating. Kind of horizontally across the field, toward the barn. I hear some kind of sound, maybe, I'm not sure—*weird music?* My stomach is hurting real bad. I think I'm gonna throw up. I can't move. Oh, Jesus, this can't be happening."

"Can you see what you're approaching?"

"Sort of, the bottom is roundish—no, maybe oval. The light's pretty bright, but I guess if it had a color, it would be like the color of pearl. Mother-of-pearl. Oh— it's opening, right in the center, oh no, I'm going in. Boy that light is bright. I'm scared. Never seen anything like it. Oh, no . . ."

"What is it?"

"*They're* waiting for me."

"Who?"

"*Four of them.* Short, gray, those eyes. *He's* looking at me. I can't turn away, I'm kind of falling into his eyes, like black pools. It's—they're . . . doing something."

Tom's upper body jerked in short twists, as if he were struggling with unseen bonds. Frank reached out and put a hand on Tom's shoulder.

"*They* can't hurt you, Tom. Do you understand?"

The uneasy twisting slowed, then stopped. Tom seemed calmer.

"Can you tell us what is happening?"

"It's embarrassing." Tom shifted uncomfortably. *"They're* down there. . . . My pants are off and *they're* hooking up this . . . machine."

"What kind of machine?"

"A tubelike thing . . . runs from the wall to a silver funnel thing. . . . Oh, God. It's like the milking machine I use in the— Oh. The *taller one* is looking at me. The other ones put it over—ah, Jesus, I, um, ejaculated. I'm angry. *They* shouldn't have done that. I'm very upset—*they* don't understand. The *taller one* is looking in my eyes again. I get the feeling he wants me to like him. But I don't. What is that? What are you doing?"

"What do you see, Tom?"

"It looks like a BB, a round ball on the end of a long thin—they're putting it—owww, my ear."

Tom Jr.'s whole body jerked in pain.

"All right, Tom, I'm going to bring you out. When I do, you will not be afraid. What happened to you has happened to everyone in this room. What happened was real. But you are not afraid. Do you understand?"

"Yes." Tom nodded.

When Tom Jr. opened his eyes, he remembered clearly. He didn't know what any of it meant, but he remembered and that was a start. He knew he had taken the first steps.

Like everyone else here, he had needed to know the truth. Now he knew it—but was he really better off?

Tom Jr. rubbed his face and wiped a tear. "I was so sure it was—a bad dream. Or something was wrong with me."

Frank nodded. "Tom, that night the light hit your barn—did anything happen to your animals?"

"Yeah—around noon, the Sheriff called me. Said they had found one of my Holsteins, down in Dexter, about thirty-five miles away."

�֍

When Annie got home she could hear the TV blasting, meaning Stan was home and working on something. He had tuned in a nature program, loud enough to rattle the windows. Annie ran to turn down the volume as the announcer rhapsodized about the use of tranquilizer darts on Kodiak bears.

"These enormous creatures soon fall asleep like two-ton babies," the announcer said. "They are then tagged with tiny radio transmitters so we can track them."

Annie stared at the picture of the helpless bear being tagged in the ear with a tiny transmitter. She reached unconsciously up to brush the hair back from her own ear, her eyes fixed on the stainless steel of the bear's tag. Suddenly her chest felt tight and it was hard to breathe.

"You all right? You're home early." Stan came in and put a hand on her shoulder.

"The oscilloscope broke and Max needs to shut down the mainframe." She shrugged, not wanting to worry him.

"You look pale."

"I'm fine, Stan, really."

"Let me get you a cup of tea."

Annie sighed and settled back into the heavy cushions of the chair. She realized she wanted, *needed*, Stan's opinion on her fainting. So when he came back with two cups of herbal tea she told him how the owl had frightened her into a dizzy spell.

"An owl, huh? It's probably just pregnant nerves. You know, you get your hormones all bent out of shape."

After a moment Stan continued quietly, "Uh—you know that offer to go back to teaching? The position is still open if I'm interested."

Annie put her tea down, confused and angry. "Isn't this kind of sudden? Yesterday you were in love with your job. You got the big promotion. I mean, teaching is a whole lot less money."

"Less money," Stan admitted, "less guilt, less pressure. Good medical benefits. And Syracuse is a great place to raise a family."

"But will there be a position for me, Stanley? I didn't intend to give up my career to be a full-time mother. This is not my hormones speaking. I'm very attached to my job here. Stan, this isn't because of my dizzy spell, is it?"

"Uh—nnnno." He set his cup down and moved over beside her. "Look, it's not that I wasn't thinking of you. I was thinking of us. Weapons systems design just doesn't seem so important now." He leaned over and gave her belly a kiss, then gently rested his head on her lap. "Truth is, my priorities are changing."

Annie stroked his hair almost automatically, as he trailed off.

"Anyway," he said after a minute. "Just rest, honey. Just rest. We're going to have this baby. We are." He kissed her belly again and she closed her eyes.

Annie was in a tunnel again, but not in her car. She was flat on her back and could not move even though her arms and legs did not seem to be tied.

She was nauseated and dizzy. Her body trembled with fear. She was moving, not walking, but floating, feet first.

Somewhere nearby she heard the music again but this time it frightened her, even though now she remembered where she'd heard it before and as she tried to turn her head to see what was going on, she couldn't.

In her peripheral vision she saw what looked like several small people walking beside her. She fought with all her strength simply to turn her head enough to see who it was. One of them turned to her and she realized it was not a person at all—but an odd gray OWL! And as she watched with hatred and loathing the owl spoke.

"Annie?"

She screamed.

"Annie?" Stanley shook her awake. For a moment she just gasped for breath. "Oh my God," she finally said, still trembling.

"Hey—hey, wake up. Are you all right?"

"I, I think so," she said, still panting. She sat up and pulled the comforter around her.

"That was quite a nightmare you were having. Are you sure you're okay?"

Annie rubbed her eyes and shook her head slowly. "It was just a dream, Stanley."

"Uh-huh. What kind of dream makes you sweat and scream and kick your beloved husband so hard he almost falls out of bed?"

She gave him a half smile; the panic of the dream was starting to fade now, along with most of the details, but some of the images stayed with her and she was still shaken up, although she was no longer quite sure why.

"It was just a nightmare. Everybody has them—especially when their hormones are in an uproar. It's nothing to worry about," she said.

"You want to talk about it?"

"There's really not much to talk about. Just—" She shook her head and went on.

"I was in some kind of tunnel, I don't know where, but—something about it, or somebody who was there, it felt like I *knew* them or something. I know that doesn't make sense. But there were these, these *owls.* . . ." She said the word with such fierce loathing that Stan studied her before he spoke.

"Is that so bad? What's wrong with owls?"

"I don't know. I don't know. They're just so— I don't know."

"But you never hated owls before. This is kind of a new thing with the owls, right?"

She blew out a breath. "Forget it. It was just a nightmare, Stan. Talking about it is silly."

But the dream stayed with Annie and the more she tried to shake it off, the more it came after her, waving its owl face and whistling uncontrollable panic into her veins.

And when morning finally climbed up the walls and peeked in the windows, Annie was still awake.

The three times she had miscarried, she had had no bad dreams, and so she found herself clinging to the idea that, because she felt bad this time, the baby would come to term and be healthy. Good feelings in the miscarriages, bad feelings for a healthy baby.

She knew that was stupid and was probably symptomatic of something or other, so she sat heavily in the chair by the telephone and called Carol.

"Hey, doll, how're you doing?"

"Um, I'm not sure," said Annie.

"Something wrong?"

"I don't know."

"Well hey!" Carol said. "How about if I decide?"

"Okay." Annie swallowed hard. "If you have a few minutes."

"For you I can find it. Hmm—two o'clock okay?"

"That would be good, Carol. I really—"

"Forget it. Let's say the Astro Coffee Shoppe? That way I can get my lunch at the same time."

TWELVE

C arol was sitting in a corner booth, tucked neatly be-tween two plate-glass windows, when Annie came in. Annie sat down as Carol smiled and waved out the window to the parking lot.

"Who is it?" asked Annie.

"Sonny. I've been taking him into work, then home again. You know, I think he really *is* smart. He's already got my TV remote figured out. Loves anything with buttons. A regular guy. Tell Stanley I finally found a male I understand. Of course, don't tell him I have to keep him locked up."

"Oh, Carol, and I came to *you* for help?"

"Doctors get colds, too. So—what can I do for you, doll?"

"Well, remember you said to let you know if anything else, um, unusual happened? To me, I mean?"

"I remember. What've you got?"

Annie looked out the window. "Is it unusual for people to have weird dreams? And then not really remember them?"

"Do *you* have weird dreams and not remember them?"

"No. Well, yes. I mean, not until just recently. I mean, as far as I can remember. Except I don't really remember them, so—"

"Have you had a weird dream recently, Annie?"

"Well . . . yes. Last night."

"Mm-hmm. What was weird about it?"

"I, uh, I don't remember too many details." Annie couldn't meet Carol's eyes. "Just—this tremendous sense of panic. They were doing something awful to me and I couldn't do anything."

Carol nodded. "Close your eyes." Annie did. "Now without thinking about it, just blurt it out. Who are 'they'?"

"Owls," said Annie, and opened her eyes, embarrassed. "I'm sorry if that's—"

"It's not anything, good or bad. It's what you feel about it that matters. How do you feel about the owls?"

"Oh, my God, I *hate* them." And she said it with such heat that even Carol looked a little startled.

"Why do you hate the owls?"

"Because, they—they . . . I don't know. . . ."

"Mm-hmm," Carol said, and then she said nothing.

"Well, what am I supposed to say? How should I know why I hate owls? I never used to."

"Mm-hmm."

"I mean, up until the other night when I almost hit one on the road, I never thought about owls."

"Mm-hmm."

"Will you stop saying that?"

"Did you used to hate onions, Annie?"

"Onions? No, of course not, you know that. I only hate onions now because I'm—" She stopped abruptly.

"Because you're pregnant. Because your whole body, and your mind, is changing, and some things seem a little different right?"

"Y-y-yesss," Annie said reluctantly.

"And if something threatens you, and threatens the baby, then you might hate it now, right?"

"Well, yes."

"Didn't you almost have an accident because of that owl the other night?"

"Yes—but that's not the whole thing, is it?"

"My God, of course not. They'd have my license if I said you were okay after ten minutes and a glass of juice. It'd take me ten years just to figure out what you *really* mean when you say good morning. But—listen, doll. Can I give you a quick fix and you won't report me to the AMA or anything?"

"Really, Carol." Annie doodled on her napkin with a ballpoint pen.

"Okay, here goes. In the first place, there's a lot going on with this pregnancy—emotional, your childhood, it's not just physical. And you're over thirty, there's some extra anxiety about that, and about your miscarriages. I think your worrying is perfectly natural. You want to protect your baby. That owl that you almost hit probably triggered your subconscious into believing all owls are a threat. So the truth is, this fear is based on one of the primal needs of motherhood: to protect your child. It's perfectly natural—"

Annie flung down the ballpoint pen. "Oh, Lord, you had me going, Carol, but every time something horrible happens, you or Stan tell me it's perfectly natural. If this were all so natural nobody would ever have babies!" Annie picked up her pen again and resumed her furious doodling on her napkin.

"Why do you think this really bothers you, Annie?"

"Oh, I don't know. Why do you have to talk like a shrink?"

"I *am* a shrink." Carol placed a large slice of tomato, and then a large slice of onion, on top of her bagel.

"Yeah. I guess—I'm just scared, Carol. I'm afraid I'm going to lose this one, too."

"What's your OB's name?" Carol asked, and took a giant bite of the bagel.

"Dr. Dolan. A wonderful lady who drums it into me every time I see her that I should not take this pregnancy for granted. I think she's being a bit scary."

"Mmp," said Carol. Annie looked up at her.

"Onion on top? You never change, do you?"

Carol swallowed hurriedly. "Oh, damn, I forgot. Let me get rid of this—"

Annie waved it off. "Forget it, I don't mind, it reminds me of Manhattan."

This startled Carol. It hadn't been more than a few days since she had seen her friend turn green and run from the room at the mention of the word onion, and now—

"What's that you're doodling?"

"What?"

"What's that you're drawing," Carol repeated, "on the napkin?"

Annie blinked. "Um—I don't know. You know. It's just a doodle." She looked down at the clear lines of her sketch. "Why? Is it significant?"

Carol winked. "Everyzing is zignificant. Und alzo— nothing is zignificant."

"Well, go for it." Annie shoved the napkin across the table to Carol.

Carol smoothed the napkin. Its center, a series of spokes like a wheel, ended with odd geometric designs. She couldn't tell if it looked more like an ancient symbol or some kind of circuit schematic.

"Does this mean anything to you?" Carol asked.

"No, you know," Annie shrugged. "It's just a doodle."

"Mm-hmm."

"Oh, lord, that 'mm-hmm' again. Tell me, Doctor, what does it mean?"

"Simple. You're completely nuts."

"Right, I take it 'nuts' is the professional jargon for 'fruitcake'?"

"Honey," Carol said, turning serious again, "all by itself this doesn't mean anything, any more than the dreams do, or when you thought you blanked out. But what we're getting here is a pattern. You have some powerful anxiety, and under the circumstances I think that's okay. But why don't you go see Dr. Dolan. Maybe she can give you a safe sedative. If you're sleeping okay, everything else will feel a lot better."

"Uh-huh. Okay."

Carol shrugged. "After that if you're still flipping out we can talk some more."

"There you go again," Annie said, with a stab at humor. " 'Flipping out'—is that Freud?"

"Of course not." Carol laughed. "You know me, always Jung at heart."

Carol was worried: about the dreams, and Annie's uncertain emotions—and the fact that the onions hadn't bothered her at all.

She dropped the doodle-on-a-napkin into her purse and got up to go.

For two hours after her meeting with Carol, Annie sat in her kitchen thinking. There was just too much going on and it had unleashed the quiet huddle of worry that had been lying in the back of her mind. So Annie methodically began to examine each small piece of her dream.

The feeling of floating, dizziness, fear, the music, a blind-

*ing light. The treetops receding—stars coming into view?
What does it mean?*

She thought back over her talk with Carol and could
not really do much with any of it except, *Go see Dr. Dolan. . . . a safe sedative . . .* The idea flitted in and out of her
head too rapidly to hang on to, but finally she called Dr.
Dolan.

"It's not really an emergency," she told Cheryl, the
receptionist, on the telephone, "but it's kind of important. . . ."

Unknown to Annie, Dr. Dolan kept a trouble list. On
the list she put the names of patients at risk for problems.
Cheryl scanned it quickly, saw "ANNIE KATZ," the
sixth name down, and smoothly and sweetly told Annie,
"Dr. Dolan has a cancellation in a half hour. Can you
come in?"

"Annie?" Dr. Dolan flipped open the folder. "You were
just here. What's the problem?"

"Well, I'm sure it's really nothing, you know—"

"Good," said the Doctor, moving in with her stethoscope at the ready, "then I can get out of here and back to
my patients with *real* problems." She placed the stethoscope on Annie's chest and listened for a moment. "You
sound okay. Let's hear Junior."

Annie leaned back, flat on the table.

Dr. Dolan moved the flat metal disk a little lower,
over where the baby was. "Hmmp."

"It's silly, I've just, felt very nervous lately, and—"

"Hush." The Doctor moved the stethoscope around Annie's belly and listened at several places for a long time.

Annie found she was holding her breath. She let it out with a nervous whoosh as Dolan straightened and let the stethoscope drop, to dangle around her neck.

"Is it—" Annie sat up and began, but Dolan stopped her and picked up the jar of contact jelly.

"Lie back again, please." Numbly, Annie leaned back on the table. Dolan smeared on the jelly and then rolled over the ultrasound monitor. She flipped it on and ran the wand over Annie's belly.

"I, um— Didn't we just do this? I thought . . ."

The Doctor stared intently at the screen. She shook her head and moved the wand back slowly over Annie's belly again.

Dolan stood in front of the monitor, without moving, for what Annie considered much too long.

Finally Annie felt sure she heard the doctor mutter, "Shit," and tap the side of the monitor a few times.

Dr. Dolan turned back to Annie with a spasmodic smile. "These damned machines. They never work. And you wouldn't believe what they cost."

"What is—"

"I'll be right back," Dolan said, and disappeared out the door.

Annie blew out her breath and slumped back on the table, closing her eyes. *I'm all right,* she tried to tell herself. *My baby is all right.*

Annie heard voices outside the door and opened her

eyes. She had leaned back and straight above her was the examination light. Too quick for her to pinpoint, it reminded her of something and—

There were owl eyes bending over her, doing things to her, and they were about to—

The door opened and Annie gasped for air.

Dolan and Nancy wheeled in another machine. They hooked it up and Dolan threw the switch. She and Nancy moved together like a team, all with an air of emergency-room calm, and soon an image took shape on the monitor.

Dolan sighed heavily, turned off the machinery and nodded to Nancy, who wheeled it all back out of the room.

"Shit," Dolan said.

Annie knew exactly what that meant, had known all along, and now realized she could no longer hide from it.

THIRTEEN

I think we've found our missing
JOSHUA data.
—Colonel John Wesley
Head of MJ-12

Stanley turned away from the blinding sparks of the arc welder and looked around the engineering room. Pieces of JOSHUA were being put together, from the ground up. *The Colonel will have his hardware,* he thought wearily. Of course having it and using it . . . that was a different matter.

Stanley chatted with some of the men and women who were part of his team, doing the actual construction of the prototype. Morale was good; Stanley was a little startled at how much they all seemed to trust that he would find the answer. It made it a pleasure, and at the same time a strain, to talk to these loyal and bright people.

Stanley missed speaking to the lone figure in the corner by the coffee machine.

Dennis Albright smiled and admired his creation. On the side of a milk carton he had covered up the picture of a missing child with a picture of the lost Voyager probe. *Missing since September 1993. Last seen in the dark of space, wearing antenna cluster and heat shield. If found, please call JPL, Pasadena.*

It was not really a waste of time. He viewed it as a private moment to gather his thoughts on his pet project: How to get rid of Stan Katz.

Back in his lab, Stan went to work on the unspecified final plate voltage circuit.

He had studied the latest, still unpublished quantam mechanics research papers and the phase of the wave function to determine what potential a semiclassical Wentzel-Kramer-Brillouin formula might have to combine with the Landau-Zener treatment to get an analytic model for the interferometric oscillation.

If it worked, he could see the effects of the phase change induced. And it should eventually bring him one step closer to a more defined wave pattern—something he could focus.

Stan was just beginning to feel like he might salvage something of this project. Then the buzzer sounded on the intercom.

"Your wife is here to see you."

"What?"

"Your wife is here to see you," the voice repeated. "She's waiting in the lounge."

"That's, ah—" He wanted to say "impossible." "Thank you."

Annie sat slumped on a vinyl sectional chair. It had an ashtray built into one arm, and Annie's elbow was lumped down on top of cigarette butts and old chewing gum. When Stan saw her, he stopped dead.

Once when Stan was ten the neighborhood bully had smacked him in the gut so hard that for several long terrifying minutes Stan had been unable to breathe. He felt like that again.

Annie looked so devastated that Stan knew at once something horrible had happened.

"Annie?" The sound was a dry croak, and she looked up at him with such a terrible expression of loss that his legs felt like jelly.

"We—I, lost it, Stan," she said. "It's gone."

Stan knew exactly what she meant, had known since he saw her sitting there, but still he said, "That's, what are—you *lost* it?"

"The baby, Stan. I lost the baby."

"How? How did it—"

"I don't know. I really don't know. The doctor doesn't even know."

"The doctor doesn't—what?"

Annie shook her head. "Dr. Dolan says it's not a miscarriage, Stan. I know it wasn't a miscarriage. I mean, after three miscarriages I should know and I know I didn't have one this time, Stan, I'm sure of it. I would have noticed, if—"

"What did Dr. Dolan say?"

"She says the endometrial material is still there. That can't happen in a miscarriage. She. She said—she said there's no sign I was ever pregnant at all."

Stan blinked at her. "But that's not possible."

"I know."

"But we saw the ultrasound of the baby. You were pregnant."

"Yes," said Annie. "I know."

"If you could just wait at reception for just a minute, I ah, I have to put away the classified stuff. And then I'll drive you home," Stan said, leading his wife into the corridor.

Down the corridor, behind Annie's back, Colonel Wesley stepped into the hall to look.

Wesley waved at Stan.

"Dr. Katz, is something wrong?"

At the sound of his voice Annie felt her whole body turning into a cold soup, and she turned to see him standing there, twenty feet away, hand braced against his doorway.

It's really him, she thought before she even knew what she meant by that.

And then her mind whirled her away—

—and she once again lay flat and helpless on the examination table. Now she was no longer moving along the dream-

hallway, but just lying motionless. Above her she saw several shapes—doctors! And she struggled fiercely, with all her being, to make out the faces of the doctors and could not.

And now a face joined the ring around her: Colonel Wesley, beyond any doubt. He paused, glanced down at her casually . . . their eyes met. . . .

. . . And she stood in the corridor of Aerocorp, looking into those same eyes.

For a frozen moment both of them stared.

And more shocking to Annie than seeing this man from her dreams was that she could tell from his stare: *Wesley recognized her!*

A gray hand reached out and touched Andros's arm. He turned and looked down into a set of deep, dark eyes. "He knows? Already? Then we better move up the program."

Annie dimly heard that Stanley was speaking. "We've had some bad news, Colonel."

Wesley took a step closer to them; Annie flinched. He spoke without breaking his stare at Annie.

"I'm sorry to hear that, Dr. Katz. If I can help in any way, please let me know."

He took one more step closer. She could feel her bile rising. "And this must be your—wife?"

Annie's heart hammered in her throat now, but she stood and stared back. *He's connected to the dream. He's connected to the owls.*

To Annie's horror Wesley reached out and took her limp, sweating hand in his. "Mrs. Katz, I really mean it, you know. If I can help in any way, please call me."

Annie slowly removed her hand from the Colonel's and took a step back without speaking, without taking her eyes from his.

"Annie . . .?" Stan said.

Annie ripped her gaze away from Wesley and looked to her husband. "I'm sorry." She looked around her, catching Wesley's eye again for a moment, then turned away.

"I'll be at reception," she told Stanley. As she turned the corner with a quick glance back at him, a very small, very triumphant smile appeared on Colonel Wesley's face.

During the ninety-minute flight from Aerocorp to Groom Lake, Wesley tried the smile again, more than once.

He passed through the last regular checkpoint, and walked into his office, slid into his oversized wooden swivel chair and picked up the phone, still smiling.

"Crouch? Colonel Wesley. Get over here on the double. I think we've found our missing JOSHUA data."

Captain Crouch arrived in moments, which meant he must have run most of the way.

"Here it is, Captain. The bugeyes said they downloaded the missing data. We knew they wouldn't dare break security by giving it to somebody with no connection to the project.

"And they didn't, Crouch. They didn't. I almost have to admire those sneaky little triple-jointed bastards. They've downloaded it into one of their experiments."

"Sir?"

Wesley smiled again. "That's right, Crouch. Into one of their experiments—the wife of Stan Katz, project engineer for the JOSHUA project. See the way their minds work? Like everything else they've 'given' us, they need this too. They can't build it, so they give it to someone who can, then they move in and take it. And before we know it—we're hit."

He took a long pull on the cigar and then pointed it at Crouch. "Do you realize what this means, Captain? They're not passive, they were never passive. They intended all along to make the first strike against us. And with their hybrids coming on line—they really could recolonize Earth."

"Jesus," said Crouch. "I never knew they were that devious."

Wesley puffed his cigar with tremendous enjoyment. "Captain," he said as he let the smoke trickle out of his mouth, "if you think that's devious, you ain't seen nothing yet."

He blew out a large cloud of smoke, already enjoying his triumph.

"There may be casualties, of course—but one A-o-One engineer and his wife stacked up against our whole civilization? I think that's a good trade."

FOURTEEN

S tan parked the car at their house after a painfully silent drive. *She's going to snap this time,* he thought. *It's
just too much.* And so when he got her settled he took a
deep breath and went to the telephone to do something
alien to his nature.

He called Carol Blum.

Stan paced anxiously as Annie poured brandy down
her throat. It was a little less than ten minutes when the
doorbell rang.

"Come on in." He unconsciously blocked Carol's
way with his body. She gave him a quick hug and
brushed past. Stan followed her into the living room,
where Annie was slouched on the sofa with a glass of
brandy. She didn't look up, so Carol knelt in front of her,
gently trying to pry the glass out of Annie's hand.

"Hi, kiddo," Carol said, "how's it going?"

Annie still refused to make eye contact, either with Carol or Stan. Carol looked up at Stan, who shrugged, more miserable than he'd ever been before.

Carol touched Annie's cheek gently. "What happened, honey? Can you talk about it?"

"Something—really—weird," mumbled Annie, already half-drunk.

"What kind of something, Annie?"

"I don't know. The doctor doesn't even know. I don't know. It's just gone. The baby's gone, Carol." Annie's simple, lost quality came close to breaking Carol's heart.

"Annie, we should try to find out how it happened, and—"

Annie dropped the brandy glass to the floor. "Shit," she said, and leaned over to recover the glass. "It doesn't matter how it happened. It just matters that it happened. It happened *again*. It just keeps happening. It's going to keep happening. That's all that matters," she said, and she stood and weaved into the kitchen to refill her glass.

Carol looked up at Stanley, who shrugged helplessly. "It's—that's how she's been since—" He shrugged again.

Carol stood and moved in front of Stan, her eyes searching his for a moment. *He's hurt*, she thought, *maybe hurt worse than ever before. But he's okay for now.* "Stan, I know this is just as hard on you. But Annie needs the kind of help only I can give her."

"I know," Stan said quietly, not looking at Carol. "That's why I called."

"Can you give me a little time alone with her, Stan? Maybe a half hour? I need to see if I can talk her down, you know. Find out what's going on."

Stan hesitated.

"I'll wait in the hall," he said, and turned stiffly away.

Annie stumbled back from the kitchen holding the bottle of brandy in one hand and her tumbler in the other. It was one of those man-sized transparent glasses with the small air bubble in the middle of its wide base, and Annie had not bothered to put any ice or water or soda into it.

She didn't stop or even slow down as she saw Carol sitting on the couch waiting for her, professional face firmly in place. Instead she fell back into her chair, took a large slug of her drink and went back to staring at the floor.

After a moment Carol spoke gently. "Annie, we need to talk."

Annie didn't look up.

"Something bad has happened to you, but we have to find a way to go on," Carol said.

There was still no response from Annie, nothing that even showed she knew Carol was in the room.

"Can you talk about it, Annie? I think it would be good for you."

Annie sipped from her glass and looked at the floor.

"Annie." Carol showed just a trace of exasperation in her voice for the first time.

"The doctor says there's no sign I was ever pregnant. It was all a lie, Carol." Annie looked up and met Carol's eyes. "But it wasn't. The doctor knows I was pregnant. And I haven't had a miscarriage. I've had three miscarriages and I would know if I'd had another and I haven't. Not this time. I would know it if I had."

"What do you think happened, Annie?"

Annie hesitated, then shook her head. "I don't know," she said. "Something."

"I think you do have some idea what happened," said Carol. "Why don't you want to talk about it?"

"Because," Annie said. Carol gave up after ten minutes and stepped out of the room to talk to Stan.

He was looking out the window by the front door. "How is she?"

Carol sighed. "Basically okay. But I think she has to find out what happened this time. Something about it really bothers her."

"Can we just let it be?"

"I don't think so. I think it's going to come out sooner or later, and it's better if it comes out with supervision."

"What do you mean come out?" Stan demanded, upset at the clinical sound of this. "What's going to come out?"

Carol hesitated. Her mind raced with thoughts of Annie slipping into manic depression, or a catatonic state or even a waking state of psychotic episodes involving owls in visual and auditory hallucinations. She shook off these thoughts and focused on Stan.

"I can't be sure. That's why I want to hypnotize her."

Stan blinked, totally caught off guard. "No," he said.

"You don't want this to just lie there and fester, Stanley," she said softly. "There's no telling when and how the dam will burst."

"But you don't know what the problem is, and she won't say," Stan argued.

"Yeah," Carol admitted, "that's about the size of it."

FIFTEEN

Annie woke up early the next day with a blinding headache. She wished there were some way to crawl to the bathroom, without standing, but she had to get to the bathroom, and she had to get there by standing up, so she finally did, clenching her teeth against the rush of her stomach and the thundering pain in her head.

When she came out of the bathroom, Stan stood by the chair where he had slept, rubbing his eyes. "I, uh . . . I'm going to take the day off, stay at home with you," Stan told her.

Annie shook her head and quickly wished she hadn't. "Go to work, Stan. I'm going to."

He blinked, still too stupid from the bad night to talk very well. "Uh, yeah, but. Are you sure?"

"I'm sure, Stan," Annie said a little snappishly.

"Yeah. Well—" He was unconvinced but didn't know what to do about it.

While he got dressed, Annie continued her mechanical preparations for the day. She tried hard not to think, but everything she did reminded her of what she was trying hardest not to think about. She made Stan and herself bag lunches automatically, because she had been doing that for the past four months, and then remembered the idea had been to save money for the baby.

Still, she finished the sandwiches and put them in brown paper bags, determined to follow routine as much as possible.

After Stan left, with a weary "Love you" and a muted hug, Annie went outside and worked in the garden.

Carol called and Annie managed a half-decent imitation of somebody coping. It didn't fool Carol, but at least she gave the impression of trying.

"Going to work is fine," Carol told her, "maybe even a good idea. But Annie—"

"I've got to go," Annie cut her off, "I'll talk to you later." And she hung up.

As she backed her car out onto the road and headed for the highway and the observatory, a late model off-white Buick that had been parked across the street from her house started its engine and followed her.

He was there again, at that terrible moment.

The ground shook, the ship splintered with a tremendous

noise. The crash became real again. Not as a memory, since it had happened/was happening to someone else—and yet not someone else exactly since he felt it just as if it were happening to him, now.

The ship skidded to a stop without sound, and a calm filled the ship—or what was left of it. He felt a sharp pain race down his leg. He saw his foot pointing in the wrong direction. A bloody mess blossomed around his thigh. The bone pushed through the skin in a compound spiral fracture.

He beat back the pain and moved to the more important job at hand, crawling out of the wreckage. He pulled clear of the grayish hull and lifted himself to see better the flat reddish brown surface. It amazed the Wesley part of him to find that large pieces of this shattered craft were moved so easily. He could lift a chunk the size of a formal dining table with one hand.

Although the core of the ship was intact, he knew the tanks—the precious tanks, the only hope for the future—were gone, shattered. So was the main drive unit of the ship. The wreckage littered a quarter mile of the desert. Still, the damage could have been much worse.

Among the crew, the destruction was critical. Two-thirds were dead outright. Five more were probably going to die. Most of those were simple crewmen and didn't matter.

But four of the dead mattered very much. They were the two engineers, the navigator and the pilot. They were the only ones who would have been able to fix the drive unit.

Fear, pain, hopelessness unlike anything he had ever felt engulfed him. He tried to regain control of his mind but the harder he struggled the stronger the feeling of terror became. But just when he knew he would go mad, it stopped.

His mind held the image of the small scout ships, and he sensed hope. He knew they could travel short hops over the surface of this small, dim planet. But without the drive unit, the mother ship and all who had survived would remain marooned.

The planet was inhabited; they had known that before the crash. He felt sure the inhabitants would come, and that they would want to help. He even felt amusement connected to the idea.

And help did come. It was not possible to say how soon, since time was not important. The bent leg got better, whether from time passing or from superior medical technology was impossible to say. But the leg was fine when the first strange pink face arrived.

He was startled to recognize that face as his own of forty years earlier.

And as the strange gray hand reached to touch his temple with a long thin silver rod, the "he" from the ship was surprised to see the adverse reaction of the "he" who was young Wesley. The look of fear, terror, madness on his young soldier's face as the pictures began to flood into him was unexpected.

But the rod touched his temple all the same and he knew he would scream, because—

Wesley came to on the cold floor of his office, his hand still gripping his leg. His face felt wet with tears, and when he reached up to touch them his eyes filled with anger.

"You bastards," he whispered. ". . . I won't crack. I won't!"

A knock came on the office door.

"Colonel? Are you okay?" Crouch asked.

"Yes, Captain. Just a minute." Wesley wiped the dampness off his face onto the sleeve of shirt, and stood up. He tucked his shirt back in and opened the door for Crouch. "What is it?"

"Sir," he said, avoiding direct eye contact with the Colonel. "Surveillance has followed the subject to her place of employment."

The screams, he thought. *The bastards made me scream—Crouch heard me.*

"Good," said Wesley. "Here's what you're going to do, Captain."

❖

A half mile from the observatory the off-white Buick that had followed Annie parked by the side of the road.

After a long stretch of silence, the man in the passenger seat leaned forward to tune the receiving dial slightly.

A faint sound came through the small speaker on the console, dry, slightly raspy, and the man cocked his head as he tried to identify it. He turned another dial, bringing the sound closer, and the two men exchanged a glance as they recognized it: the sound of a sob, a soft unwanted and partially stifled cry.

The man sat back in his seat again, apparently satisfied.

The take-up reel on the small Nagra tape recorder continued to turn steadily, recording a series of very small crying sounds.

"Delta One, any change in our subject?" Wesley's voice came from the military TWIXT radio. The driver lifted the microphone to his lips and said, "Negative, Colonel."

"Stay with it, we may have a change of plans. Out." Wesley signed off and looked across his desk at Crouch.

"Okay," said Wesley. "Even if we tie Mrs. Katz to the alien signal and to the bugeyes, we still don't know what the signal is. Or how it effects them, or us, or . . . Mrs. Katz."

"Sir? It seems like they would be placing an awful lot of eggs in one basket, if she is really the subject of their download."

"Maybe they're not as bright as we thought. Or maybe they are damn bright, and the signal was meant for her. To do something, somehow . . . It may be connected to JOSHUA."

"If that is the case, sir, Project JOSHUA may have been compromised. And we should consider assembling a wet team."

Colonel Wesley nodded.

Annie sat hunched over a stack of graph paper from the oscilloscope test the night before, trying desperately to work hard enough not to think.

As she had feared, the test had ended before the mainframe could compute the signal's origin. It had seemed to come from within the gas cloud.

With her luck, it was probably a once-in-a-lifetime find, maybe as wild as the discovery of a new planet hidden within the cloud, but she knew no way to confirm it or find it, or figure out what the signal truly had been or why it had been sent.

Annie's depression came and went like waves on a beach. She couldn't seem to stop the tears and she let out a few more quiet sobs.

She turned and saw Max across the room working on the broken mainframe. "I've to get some things from my car," he said, and went out the door, avoiding her eye.

Depression, it seemed, had become contagious.

❄

Outside the observatory, the beauty of the high desert sunset seemed to breathe some life back into Max. The red clay of the mountain range seemed almost purple now, and the sky came alive in a pink-red glow. Sunsets like this restored your belief in God and life, thought Max, until he saw a flash of light reflecting from the car down the road.

He knew who was out there. He knew when he picked up the phone that they would be coming and now they were here.

Wesley's men. No doubt the "wet team." There was

no way to talk them out of doing their job, and no way to stop them.

He had seen them in action in East Germany, just before the Berlin wall had come down. The Russians, fearing a brain drain to the West, had sent in special security teams to kidnap scientists and engineers and bring them to Moscow.

A team of four Black Berets had been sent to counter the Soviet hit squads. Only four. But when it was over, forty men of the top Russian security forces lay dead in their well-guarded station house.

If four Berets could take out forty elite Soviet killers, two could certainly handle a depressed astronomer and a guilt-ridden military computer engineer. But how could he let them come in and kill what had become his life? And possibly one of the best people he had ever known?

He did have a loaded 9mm automatic under the front seat of his old K-car, but how to make the best use of it . . .

A few minutes later, Max found himself creeping down the hillside with his gun in his hand.

If I get past the parabolic dish without getting spotted and if I can climb the embankment to the road without being spotted, and if I can get up to the car, and if I can bring myself to kill—

Yes, kill. He would have to kill them, both of them.

And then what? He could warn Annie. Then race to his wife and son and grab the first plane out . . . to? . . . no place was safe, not if *they* were after you.

. . . Maybe New Zealand. He had always promised himself he would see it before he died. He'd heard they had great fishing. No doubt because fools like him waited until they were about to be killed before they thought of going there.

His hands shook as he pulled back the slide on the automatic. From the edge of the embankment he could unload the eight-shot clip—but chances were he would only hit one of them and piss off the other.

His face felt wet with sweat. His eyes stung and his head pounded. The only way to get a good shot was to go right up to them and pull the trigger.

"Hit 'em in the head," he remembered Wesley coaching him before his trip to Germany. *"Never shoot the body, too many ways to fix it. Unload on gray matter and no regrets."*

On the face of the embankment leading up to the road now, Max tightened his grip on the thick desert root and pulled himself up the sand and rock ridges toward the paved road. He could see the heads of Wesley's men in the car just twenty feet ahead.

No wait, only one head in the car? Then where—

There was a muffled click in his ear. Max felt something cold and hard, something very much like a gun barrel, pressing into the side of his head.

"Dr. Berger. Sir, Colonel Wesley would like to speak to you."

Using all of his remaining courage, Max turned his head, slowly, to see the second Black Beret. There was no emotion showing on the man's face. There never was

with these men. But Max thought he could see a gleam of
amusement in the trooper's eyes.

The soldier helped Max to his feet and led him to the
car, gripping Max's arm with fingers that felt like steel.

The door of the car opened. The driver held the
radio's microphone toward him.

"Sir, Colonel Wesley."

". . . Of course, thank you," Max said, trying to recover. He took the radio's mike from the driver. "Colonel?" he said.

"Max. Good to hear your voice again." Wesley's
voice crackled over the radio.

"Sir?" The cheerfulness in the Colonel's voice surprised him. The driver pulled the clip from Max's 9mm,
then disassembled the gun neatly into six pieces.

"Max, you're a key player here. I need to know everything about that signal you found."

"Colonel, the mainframe is down, but I'm working
on it."

"Good. You've got four weeks. I want results,
Max. . . . How's that partner of yours?"

"Annie? Colonel, I'll need her expertise to crack this
one."

"Easy son. We're here for each other. Don't go soft
on me. My men are there for *our* protection."

"Yes, sir. I have the highest confidence we will find
the source of the signal."

"I know you will. You're a good man. And I know
you will do as ordered if we have a security problem.
Wesley out."

The driver handed Max back his 9mm reassembled. "Same team, the winning team." He winked. "Don't get traded."

Max started back to the observatory. He knew if he ran, or did anything suspicious, it would be certain death. He had to toe the line, do his job.

There was a German phrase for this: *Arbeit Macht Frei*—Work Makes You Free.

It was a lie then, as it was now. But he had no choice.

SIXTEEN

Annie arrived home totally exhausted. She could barely keep her eyes open long enough to stretch out on the bed. She drifted off quickly into a heavy sleep.

And then it began . . .

She was lying on the table again. She was not strapped down, but she couldn't move.

Once again the circle of faces bent around her. Odd faces—the owls! She felt a coldness, a breath of frosty air below her waist, and knew they were doing something terrible.

She saw a long black instrument with a cup on the end of it move between her spread legs. A burning sensation replaced the cold of the instrument. They were tearing out something from deep within her. It hurt, but she couldn't stop them. Terror, hatred and pain filled her. She opened her mouth to scream—

—And a child-like hand touched her face.

Although she could not turn her head, she knew whose hand it was and she didn't scream. She was suddenly, almost magically, calm again.

Maybe it will all be all right. . . . After all, look who's here. . . .

But she couldn't quite remember the name, or why he made her feel so much better, and as the thin hand withdrew again, it struck her that something was a little wrong with the hand, although she couldn't really say exactly what. . . .

She tried to turn and look but couldn't quite see, and then the owls were there again, doing something, and the cold air was blowing hard at her, and—

"Annie!" Stan shook her awake. "Annie, sweetheart, are you all right?"

Annie sat up, struggling against his grasp, gasping. "Oh, my God," she said at last. "Oh, lordy."

"Are you okay, honey? I came in and heard you moaning."

"I'm okay," she said, and took a deep breath. "It's just that dream again, it was . . ." And she shook her head.

Stan held her again. "It's okay," he told her. "It was just a dream."

"It was different this time, Stan. The owls were there, and that part was awful—but somebody else was there, somebody I knew well, and just when it got most awful . . . I don't know. Whoever this was . . . touched me. And I felt okay, even though I knew something awful was still happening."

Annie frowned, and repeated it as if it had to mean something. "I actually felt *good*, Stanley, like it might all turn out okay." She shuddered. "I guess maybe that's the scariest part of it all."

"Well, it will turn out okay, honey. You just have to—"

"Mr. Boojum," she interrupted, excited.

"What?"

"Mr. Boojum. I know I told you about Mr. Boojum," Annie said impatiently. "When I was little and didn't have any friends? I apparently made one up. Mr. Boojum—my imaginary friend."

"Oh, and he was in your dream, uh-huh."

"Please don't look at me like that, Stanley," Annie said. "I'm not crazy, not yet. I don't think . . . Yes, Mr. Boojum was in my dream. Just when things got so bad I couldn't stand it and was going to scream, Mr. Boojum was there. . . ."

"And he, uh, he said it would be okay."

"Yes, that's right. Of course he didn't *say* that. Mr. Boojum doesn't talk."

"No, of course not."

"He always knew what I was thinking and I didn't have to say anything. And I knew what he wanted me to do, so he didn't have to say anything, either," said Annie.

"And he was there in your dream, and he made you feel, um, good?"

"That's right," she said, "and I believed him for some reason. I actually started to feel . . . good . . ."

She was quiet for a minute and Stan pulled her against him, rubbing her neck with one hand.

"It's going to be okay, honey," Stan told Annie softly. "It was just a dream."

She turned her head sideways and looked at him, so earnestly and so hurt.

"Is it?" she asked just as softly.

"The details don't change," she told Carol the next day at the Astro Coffee Shoppe, where they met for lunch.

Carol sipped her coffee and nodded. "Recurring dreams are very common, Annie," she said. "Lots of people have 'em."

"Not me." Annie shook her head. "Not before this."

Carol shrugged. "So now you have. Why do you think that is?"

Annie drummed her fingers on the Formica tabletop. "I don't know. It must mean something, but—I don't know. Unless I'm totally nuts."

"Would you prefer that?"

Annie looked startled. "Uh—I don't know. Maybe," she said slowly.

"Why do you think you'd rather be nuts than have these dreams mean something?"

Annie fidgeted with her spoon. "Do you think my dreams mean something, Carol?"

"Dreams always mean *something*, Annie. Quit stalling. Why do you want to be crazy?"

Annie looked out the window.

Outside, a man with a crew cut and exceptionally clean running shoes was doing his best to look down and out by poking through a wire trash container for tin cans. It didn't strike Annie as odd, but then she could not see the skin-colored wire running up the man's neck to the monitoring device in his ear.

"Because," Annie said, "if I'm *not* crazy . . . if all this means something—you know, not just symbolism or repression or any of that stuff—I mean, if it really, means something, then . . ."

"Go on," Carol said softly.

Annie sipped her coffee. "Then . . . if this isn't all just weird dreams . . . then—then something definitely . . ." She put the cup down, exasperated. "I don't know, Carol, Jesus. I thought you could tell me."

Carol shook her head. "I can show you how to figure it out—I can't figure it out for you."

"I know. I'm just not ready for ten years of analysis."

Carol nodded. "Good. So why don't we take a short-cut here, with hypnosis?"

Annie let her breath out. "I don't know, Carol."

"Why not?" Carol pressed her. "These dreams are trying to tell you something. Even if it's just your subconscious saying, I Hate Owls!"

"I don't know."

"Let me tinker, Annie, I'm good at this. I'm pretty sure we can make you feel a little better."

Annie started to doodle on her napkin again. "I really—I'd just feel so—"

"What," Carol demanded with her old acid amusement. "You'd feel naked? Doll, we were roomies for three years. You'd feel stupid? I'll let you hold your diploma. Come on, Annie, what do you say?"

"Let me think about it, Carol, okay? I just—I need some time to think." She pushed her doodle-covered napkin away from her and stood up.

"All right, Annie." Carol signaled for the check. "But if you have the dream again, I'd like to hear about it, okay?"

In spite of the warmth of the day and the cheerfully ridiculous decor of the Astro Coffee Shoppe, Annie shivered. "I'm sure I'll have the dream again, Carol," she said. "I almost don't have to sleep to have it."

Carol started to shove a couple of dollars under the napkin holder in the middle of the table when she saw Annie's scrawled, defaced napkin. She picked it up.

Funny, she thought, frowning. *It looks exactly like the other one. But with a few more lines, like a picture developing.*

This one, too, she popped into her purse.

Annie arrived home without noticing the panel truck that had come off her street and onto the main road only moments before she turned toward her house.

The truck's two crew-cut passengers had left a few small but sophisticated pieces of equipment in Annie's house, leaving as they got word that Annie was turning onto her street.

Annie parked her car in its usual spot and went in, noticing nothing out of the ordinary.

Part of the reason was that Annie was preoccupied. All that day at home and into the evening at work, she had dreaded the time when she would have to go to sleep. She knew the dream would come again, all its details the same, and the thought made the sweat start on her upper lip. The more she thought about the dream the more she dreaded it, and soon she couldn't think about anything else.

And when she came home from the observatory it seemed like a struggle against the clock. She wondered how long she could win and keep her eyes open.

Stan watched and worried about the way she sat stubbornly in her chair, drinking coffee, refusing to come to bed. Eventually Stan went off to sleep alone, leaving Annie still grim-faced in her kitchen chair.

In the morning Annie had won a small victory. She'd stayed awake all night. Already numb and bone-weary from her grief, she was now almost paralyzed by fatigue, too. She knew it couldn't go on, not even for another day. She would have to sleep and have the dream.

So as soon as it seemed decent, she called Carol.

"Come on over," Carol told her. "I don't have my first session until ten." A hideous sound of screeching suddenly drowned out Carol's voice on the phone. Annie's look of concern turned to a halfhearted smile as she heard Carol yell at her chimp, "Sonny, knock it off. Or I swear, no more Game Boy!"

❈

It was just a quarter after seven when Carol, still wearing her threadbare pink velour robe and tattered fuzzy slippers, opened the door for Annie. She had worn the same thing in the morning for all the years Annie had known her, and there was comfort in the familiarity of the ridiculous costume.

"Want some coffee?"

"Yes, please." Her stomach still churned and the inside of her mouth felt puffy from the stuff, but she needed something to keep her awake, and coffee had worked so far.

From his cage in the back, Sonny could see the light blue car as it pulled up and parked across the street and a few doors down. He saw two men inside and the fur on his back began to rise.

Danger!

His eyes were wide as he moved against the cage door and put a hand through the bar.

He had to get out.

"Where's Sonny?" Annie asked, rubbing her eyes.

"You thought you had trouble sleeping? Ha! I moved him to the back of the house so we could have some quiet. Fur-brain is out of here in two weeks, and not a moment too soon. The Major called, said he was ending the experiment, said the schedule had been moved up.

"So tell me, doll," said Carol, "how was last night?"

Annie looked away, a little embarrassed. "Well," she began, and took a deep breath. From the neck down she felt as if she'd been savagely beaten, and from the neck up she felt packed with dirty sand. She rolled her head to ease the dry creakiness of her neck muscles, and finally looked up and met Carol's eyes. "I didn't go to sleep last night."

"Oh? Why not?"

"I was *afraid* to. To go to sleep and have the dream. So I stayed awake."

"Mm-hmm."

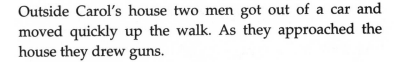

Outside Carol's house two men got out of a car and moved quickly up the walk. As they approached the house they drew guns.

Andros pushed a needle into the back of the head of a small pale fetus. It looked more human than hybrid. In the middle of this very delicate procedure, Andros looked up and mouthed one word, "Sonny."

Annie leaned against the kitchen counter. "I can't begin to tell you what this is doing to me, Carol," she burst out. "It's not just losing the baby, it's—either something else or I'm totally losing my mind. I'm beginning to think it might not be a dream. Does that sound crazy?" Annie watched carefully, but Carol's poker face gave up nothing.

"Annie, you've had a tough time. It's going to get tougher before it gets better. Grief is hard work, but with hypnosis—"

Suddenly there was a CRUNCH-SMASH behind them in the hall. Annie and Carol both looked up, terrified. A young cop in a crew cut whirled into the room at a half crouch, pointing his revolver at them.

"Freeze!" he said, and as Annie gasped he pivoted to cover her. "I said freeze!"

"We're frozen already," Carol said, holding her hands in the air and staying remarkably calm. "So what do you want?"

A second, older cop passed the door and headed for the rear of the house, his gun at the ready. A moment later there was a savage screeching and the second cop backed quickly into the kitchen. "Danny, there's a fucking gorilla loose back there. Call Animal Control!"

Carol cleared her throat. "That's Sonny." They turned to her with expressionless cop eyes. "My chimpanzee. He must have gotten his cage open and hit the alarm. He loves buttons." She looked at them with amusement, eyes lingering on the younger cop.

The older cop holstered his gun. "We're responding to the silent alarm," he said, and consulted a scrap of paper. "Is either of you Carol Blum?"

"I am," Carol said. "If you can keep your partner from shooting me, I'll show you some ID."

"Don't shoot her, Danny," the older man said. While

Carol rummaged in her handbag for her wallet, he said, "I'm Sergeant Nuñez. This is Officer Briggs."

Carol handed her license to the sergeant. "Thank you for getting here so fast. It's good to know the system works."

"Yes, ma'am." He handed her license back.

"Can I get you some coffee? Soda? Beer?" she asked, smiling shamelessly at Officer Briggs. "We can send out for doughnuts." The young man blushed.

"No thank you, Ms. Blum," Sergeant Nuñez said. "We're going to have to ask you to keep that animal locked up better. I believe you may be in violation of zoning ordinances."

"I'll get right on it." Carol swished to the back of the house, where they could hear her crooning to Sonny, coaxing him back into the cage.

Briggs smiled self-consciously at Annie. They could all hear Carol soothing Sonny.

"It's all right, they're our friends," Carol said. There was a rattle that meant she was locking Sonny's cage. "That's a boy, much better."

❋

Andros suddenly breathed easier. He looked back down at the small fetus in his hands and smiled. "It's okay."

❋

"Sorry for the false alarm." Carol batted her eyes at Officer Briggs. "Are you sure I can't get you something?" She smiled.

The young man turned beet red. "We appreciate it," Nuñez said, "but we'd better be going." As they turned to leave, he looked back at Carol and shook his head. "Shame," he chuckled.

"You really are a hussy sometimes," Annie said.

"Darling, you don't know the half of it. If I'd realized they had cops as cute as Briggs, I'd have set that alarm off months ago."

Noticing that her friend's mood had lightened, Carol asked, "Feeling better?"

"A little. But I don't know about this—hypnosis."

Carol gave an elaborate shrug. "What's to know? Listen, I know you think it's ooga-booga, some kind of New Age voodoo, but it's not. I can't do anything you won't let me do. I can't make you dance like a chicken or any of that Hollywood crap. What I can do is help you get out of your own way and see what you're hiding, and why."

Annie looked away and a thought flitted across the back of her brain. It was quick and powerful but it was gone too fast for Annie to recognize it. All she could say was that it was a powerful and compelling reason *not* to submit to hypnosis.

But all she could remember of it was, *They won't like it. . . .*

SEVENTEEN

JOSHUA could send a wave at a
molecular level and cause the
atoms of the target to vibrate
until they simply lost their
bond. The split would cause
such heat that the target would
appear to vaporize.
—Dr. Stan Katz
Head engineer of Aerocorp

Two weeks had passed, and Stan had not given in to his grief. He felt wrapped in a giant bolt of flannel that kept him from feeling and was grateful for this. He had continued his work on his office computer, a chalkboard and any available paper—napkins, phone books and gum wrappers.

Wherever he was when an idea hit him, he wrote it down and then took it to the office and thumbtacked it to the wall behind his desk. The wall now looked like a collage of formulas, diagrams and an engineer's scrapbook collection. But the result— He stared at the final diagram that had just come up on the computer, and smiled.

He had investigated a single vibrational motion that could be set off in molecules consisting of two atoms or more. The vibrations combined in a simple harmonic oscillation until the atoms were forced apart. He could achieve this with an ultrasound wave.

While Stan had worked on theory, his crew had spent the time welding together something that at a distance looked like a sleek brontosaurus skeleton. But on closer inspection, the neck became a Kevlar turret. The body, more U-shaped, was constructed of boron-carbide armor. Positioned inside this energy-absorbing mounting was the heart and soul of JOSHUA: a precision voltage generator, a reprogrammable multichannel waveform amplifier, an onboard TX military computer and an image digitalization system for the heads-up 3-D acrylic targeting visor.

The visor worked on the same principle as its domestic cousin, the virtual-reality headset and glove. The only major difference in the military application was that the viewer displayed a heat-sensitive image and on the left side a column of continuous readout of targets: location, movement and armament. It had become mandatory for all advance tactical weapons systems to have this kind of system built in.

For now, Stan had simplified the heads-up visor to a pair of acrylic glasses. The trigger glove was just a couple of pads for his fingertips.

He had not received any new information on the final stage and doubted that he would. It was going to be up to him to finish this project, and he promised himself that once it was done he would get out, go back to teaching or whatever else, anything but weapons design.

"We're here for the primary test?" Dennis Albright said, wheeling in JOSHUA.

"Set it up over there," Stan said, pointing to the center of the room. Albright wheeled JOSHUA to the center, then turned it around.

"The point of this will be to transfigure a simple note into the high-end ultrasound. We know ultrasound moves cleanly through organic matter. After that, the only obstacle is how to bring it into focus so the wave breaks down the matter."

"Stick 'em up," said Albright, aiming the clumsy thing at Stan.

"Very funny," Stan said.

"Who's kidding?" Dennis shrugged, but then he smiled.

Stan grabbed the fish bowl off his table and set it up on a chair in front of JOSHUA. The small Japanese fighting fish darted about inside.

"Very nice. Fighting fish, isn't it?"

"Yeah, a nice healthy one. Okay, let me in," Stan said, moving toward the controls.

Dennis stepped down. Stan moved in and opened a back cover on the TX computer. He looked at the crude circuit board he had designed. It was kind of a wagon-wheel layout of multicolored wire leads that ended in HD silicone chips. After a minute of rechecking the slew rate and gain bandwidth of the circuit board, he stepped back.

"It's as good as I can make it." Stan screwed the cover back down. "Let's give it a try."

"Okay," Dennis said.

Thin fiber optics ran from the glasses and two finger pads to the keyboard of JOSHUA's TX computer. Stan powered it up and placed the trigger pads on his right pointing and middle fingertips and put the dark acrylic glasses on. The computer-generated image of the room seemed surreal. A look around produced a swatch of cool blues and grays. The only hot color came from the window, bright yellow, the fish, a light orange, and . . .

"How do I look?"

Stan turned to Albright, who was fiery red and dark orange. "Like the devil himself."

"Cool." Albright grinned.

Stan turned to the fish and tapped his middle finger. An overlaid targeting grid came on-line. As he turned his head to aim, the hydraulic servos on JOSHUA's body automatically adjusted.

A tap of his pointing finger and he was locked on and firing. A soft humming sound filled the room, sliding up the scale as the circuits completed their internal checks and moved up to operational mode.

The sound disappeared off the high end of the scale, although a dog could have heard it, and certainly Stan's hair was standing on end and Dennis ground his teeth.

But ten feet away, at the receiving end, the fish didn't seem disturbed. It hovered in the exact center of the tank, darted to the surface, then drifted back down when it failed to find food.

"You're supposed to die," Stan told the fish.

"So much for cell walls rupturing," Dennis chuckled.

Stan pulled off the glasses and lifted the cover of the circuit again. Dennis watched with pleasure. Both had their full attention on the inside of JOSHUA and missed seeing what happened across the room.

JOSHUA was still running. Its invisible beam passed through the optic lenses of the water, the glass, and came out the other side, where it hit a small potted philodendron on Stan's desk.

The bright green leaves drooping over the side suddenly moved.

Five leaves vanished.

Stan typed a command on the TX terminal. A second later, the small LED screen began a series of diagnostic functions.

"Okay, we were within operation parameters of voltage—waveform—amplification—"

The final graph came up showing wave focus. Here the level of performance dropped dramatically.

"—and a big NG on the wave diffraction intensity."

A fountain of sparks and smoke suddenly came from the failed board in the TX computer.

"Ooow. Geez," Stan said, jumping back. He switched off the power and waved a hand to clear the smoke hanging in front of him.

Dennis was coughing as he reached to open a window. "Ahhh, an air of disappointment," he said, comically exaggerating his coughing.

"Damn." Stanley stood and turned to the workbench to consult his schematics. He stared a full five minutes before he finally snapped his fingers and said,
"Yes!"

"Dr. Katz, either you're in shock, or you just had an
idea."

"Well, it's just a different way of thinking about it. It
might actually be the key to making it work." Stan pulled
a chair up to his office computer. Typing in commands
for Autocad, he retrieved a computer-generated design
for his failed circuit board. He moved two of the microchips using the mouse, then ran it through for analysis.
The screen filled with the readout.

"See, we've been working under the belief that
JOSHUA was set up to fire sound waves. I think it's
doing just that. But this circuit that defines the diffraction
intensity is not working. Now, if we were to replace the
sound waves with particle waves . . ."

Dennis looked at Stan. "A particle wave?"

"Yes." Stanley pointed at the readout. "Particle
waves start out like sound waves—they are emitted or
absorbed in packets, or quanta. They only differ in how
they travel. A particle by nature moves without definite
position. That's just what JOSHUA needs in order to
work."

"Whoa." Dennis grinned and took a step toward
JOSHUA. "Not only could it work, but it would maxi-
mize the firing spread. This is *elegant*."

Firing spread? Elegant? An alarm bell sounded. Stan's

mind raced. He had been so busy solving the problem, he had forgotten why he was solving it, the classic dilemma of weapons research. Yes, he could easily convert JOSHUA into a working particle-beam weapon. The SDI hotshots had been trying to design this for the last twelve years, and he had just stumbled on it.

The downside was just what Dennis had said, the maximized firing spread. That was how particle beams worked.

Particles are the basic unit of the atom. They are the building blocks of which we, and everything around us, are made. A sound wave, or even a light wave for that matter, is much larger than an atom. So the difference in using a particle beam would be that it would destroy at a subatomic level, a level where the chain reaction of molecular destruction continues behind the initial target.

In other words: Shoot a soldier and the tank behind him melts. Shoot the tank and the city behind it melts. Shoot the city, say from a satellite . . .

Stan grimaced. This was too ugly, too effective. He couldn't imagine a time when the world would need a weapon like this . . . or when any good could ever come from it.

"So what's the first step?" Dennis asked.

Stan spun on his heel. "Step? I, ah, I've got to do more work on it."

"Nonsense."

Dennis opened up the back of the TX computer and pulled out the failed circuit board.

"Wait—what are you going to do?"

"Oh, not me, you." Dennis handed it to him. "You know how to make the changeover. We all do."

Yes, Stan knew, but he didn't want to do it. The question was, what would Dennis do if he didn't—tell Wesley? Stan took the board from Dennis but dropped it. Microchips slid across the floor; the wires came loose from their solder.

"You did that on purpose," Dennis accused him.

"No, this is your fault," Stanley countered. "Take JOSHUA back to engineering. I need those wires and chips replaced."

Dennis was gone only a few minutes when Wesley knocked at Stan's door. "Dr. Katz! Don't let me interrupt," he said. "I heard the good news, you've got some new ideas to get JOSHUA working."

Stan shook his head. *Damn Dennis.* "Well, I'm not sure," he hedged. He flicked a finger at the plans on the workbench and lifted his shoulders. "I'm still trying to get the flaws worked out. It's not ready—yet."

Wesley moved in and put a hand on Stan's shoulder. "How is your wife doing, Dr. Katz? It's Anne, isn't it? How is she?"

Stan looked up and blinked. "Uh, fine. She's fine," he said, and then, feeling like this wasn't the right answer, "That—I mean, you know. It's hard."

Wesley nodded. The hand he had placed on Stan's

shoulder now kneaded the muscles. "Stan, I've been in the service a long time. All my life, really. A long time," he repeated. "And I've seen some damned good men lose their concentration and then fall by the wayside. Because of domestic matters."

Stan could only blink. Wesley's almost Victorian tone of voice and phrasing had thrown him for a complete loop. He felt as if he were back in high school, on the receiving end of a guidance lecture on the perils of masturbation.

"It's a damn shame," Wesley continued. "But there it is. Career shot. Because they could not keep their personal problems out of their professional lives.

"I would hate to see that happen to you, Stan. No matter how bad it is for you right now, I'd like to see you hang on, get through this, without screwing up your career. Because you will get through this, Stan. You will. And when you do, you'll want your career to be in one solid piece, won't you?"

Wesley kneaded Stan's shoulder extra hard. "Until then, I want you to know you can come to me."

Wesley looked searchingly into Stan's eyes. Stan could only nod and look away.

"I mean that, you know," Wesley said relentlessly. "You can count on me. Talk to me. I'm here for you. Because you are important to this project, and nothing is more important to me than this project." He finished up his shoulder-kneading with a vigorous slap on the back. "Okay?"

"Uh, sure. Okay," Stan finally managed.

"Good man. Now, are we going to get this thing finished up in time for dinner?"

"Well," said Stan. "I've been trying—"

"I know you have." Wesley beamed. "And I believe in you. You're a good man. Sometimes solutions to problems come from odd places. Never be afraid to act on them." He leaned in for one more hearty clap on Stan's back and then marched on out.

Down the hall, the Colonel thought about Stan Katz. He even chuckled at a mental picture of the brilliant Stanley running to him and announcing that his wife had dreamed this design and JOSHUA was now operational.

And he would congratulate Stanley and make a quick call.

Nothing fancy—car accident maybe, or a gas leak at the house.

EIGHTEEN

M ax, hearing Annie come in, pushed himself out from around the thin plastic shell of the Cray XMP and tightened the last screw in the outer casing. "Well, that should do it," he said in a tired voice.

Annie looked surprised. "I thought you said it would take a few more days." Max smiled and flipped a few switches. The lights of the old Cray computer came back on. "We got lucky. I bypassed most of the wiring damage to the DT3801. Those are our acquisition boards of the real-time signal processing. With them clear, we're back on-line."

"Great." She took a deep breath and slowly let it out, as if now, finally, real work could be done. "Max," she began, "I've been thinking. What if, you know, this *is* a signal of some kind? Could you download a SETI diagnostic? We could just run it through to, uh—just to be thorough."

Max paused before he answered. He knew the chances were good that Wesley's men were rolling tape. "Annie . . . you don't want to send this out. What about your reputation, the hard-core scientist and all that?"

"Okay, okay. I know what I said . . . I just wanted . . ." For no reason she could name, Annie felt the tears coming again. "Damn," she muttered. "I can't seem to get control . . . hold on."

She wiped a tear from her cheek. "Look, I think about this signal, you know. There's something to it. I can feel it. I don't know how. But where it came from doesn't seem that important anymore—not if—if I can just figure out what it is."

Max recognized Annie's determination, and the Colonel did want it fully analyzed. The downside, of course, was that if they found something Annie would become an instant security risk. But at this point, if they *didn't* find something they would meet the wet team anyway.

". . . Okay, but we keep this quiet," Max said, his voice filling the room. "We'll do the diagnostic right here on the old Cray. Nobody sees it but us."

"Agreed," she whispered, and went to her desk.

"Max, remember my friend Carol?"

Max, loading the programs to get the Cray back online, looked up.

"Um, the psychologist?"

"Psychiatrist," she corrected him. "She, uh, she wants to hypnotize me."

"Why?"

"Well, I've had some very odd dreams and she thinks it's my conscious mind repressing what my subconscious won't let out."

"Uh-huh. Maybe it's just, you know. Stress."

She gave him a pitying look. "Of course. That must be it. Gee, I can't imagine why a trained mental-health professional like Carol didn't think of that."

Max winced. "Okay. What's so weird about your dreams?"

"The details. They never change." She frowned. "I just remembered something. I've been hearing our music in the dreams, too."

"You can't be serious."

"I am. And I know I've heard that music before. When we first taped it, I said I knew what it was, and I do."

"So what is it?"

"I don't know."

"Wait," Max said. "I'm missing something. You know what it is, but you don't know what it is?"

"Yeah. But I know I'm right about this—I've heard it somewhere before!"

"Listen," he said, "maybe you should let the psychiatrist hypnotize you, I mean. Because, you know. You're not really—" And his words trickled to a stop as he saw the expression on her face. "I just mean you should talk to your friend."

"I thought I was." Annie turned away.

"Please, Annie. I was only trying to say—"

"Don't patronize me, Max! You think I don't know the difference between a dream and, and something that really happened? Something really happened, Max!

"Something happened to me and I don't know what it was or how it happened, but god *damn* it! *Something happened!*" And she kicked the chair, turned on her heel, and stomped out of the observatory.

Outside in the night air Annie stalked blindly across the paved parking area to the edge of the lot, where the high desert soil met the blacktop.

The hell with it, she thought, *I am right. I'm not losing my marbles. Something definitely happened. And I'm going to find out what.*

Filled with new resolve, she started the car and drove home. She felt better than she had for several days and didn't even feel a twinge when she passed the spot where she had seen the owl, although she did unconsciously press her foot down slightly harder on the gas pedal.

She didn't notice the slight increase in speed, but the tan Buick a half mile back did notice.

"She's speeding up," said the crew cut behind the wheel.

"Give her a ticket," answered the slightly older crew cut in the passenger seat, and the driver gave him a small *huh* of laughter.

They didn't speak again at all until Annie pulled into her driveway, and then the passenger lifted the radio microphone and said, "Eagle—this is Beta. We're home."

In the middle of the night Annie awoke drenched with sweat. This time some of the details were wrong and it felt like it really had been a dream.

The owls bent around her as she lay helpless on the table, and they were speaking! But that's wrong, *Annie thought,* the owls can't speak. *The head owl leaned over and opened his beak. A clicking sound came out and Annie recoiled in horror.*

And as she did she found that she could move now, for the first time in the dream, and this too told her that it really was just a dream this time.

Move she did; she got off the table and ran down the low, dark hallway. But owls jumped out at her from every shadow, clacking their beaks at her with a horrible dry clicking sound. And just when she was running into the light, away from the owls—

—she sat up in bed with her nightgown plastered to her body and her breath coming in hard, raspy pants. For a moment she breathed, and then, just as she started to slow down her racing heart, she heard the clicking sound again.

Annie's heart stopped cold. Her dreams had crossed over into her waking. She had never felt such terror. Heart pounding so hard it hurt her head, she reached for Stan.

His place was empty.

Slowly, using every bit of her willpower, she slid out of bed. The sound came again, from the back of the house. More scared than she'd ever been before, Annie walked slowly toward the sound.

A small dim puddle of light spilled out into the hall from the family room. The sound came from there.

Inside the room, crouched on the floor with his back to the door, Stanley carefully took apart his elaborate, lovingly overdone train set. As the pieces of track hit each other, they made the clicking sound Annie had been hearing.

In her already fragile state this was more than Annie could bear. Silently pushing the door closed again she walked back down the hall.

By the time she came to the door of the nursery, the tears rolled down her face. She paused just inside the door, unable to walk past and unable to bear the pain of seeing it: the cheerful wallpaper, the stacks of baby equipment—unassembled crib, playpen, car seat—and, balanced on top of the stack of gifts from the shower, presiding over the dismally happy room, Gruffy Bear, sitting in judgment, a reminder that she had failed yet again at the most basic human task.

Annie stood in total misery in the doorway of her nursery, tears sliding down her cheeks, a half-formed sob caught in her throat.

And then rage broke the walls of her emotions and she kicked the boxes, flinging the car seat, smashing the unassembled stack of crib and playpen.

With a last blast of soul-searching anger she grabbed up Gruffy Bear, intending to shred his ears, gouge his one button eye, and instead, as quickly as it came over her, the rage simply drained away, and with it all of Annie's remaining energy. She slumped onto the floor and sobbed into Gruffy Bear's battered fuzz.

Stan looked in on her, having heard the noise of her rage, but, with the same delicacy that made Annie leave him alone to disassemble the train set, he left Annie her private moment of grief in the nursery and returned to bed.

In the morning Stan came into the kitchen to find Annie already there at the table. He had surfaced from a dreamless, motionless sleep that subdued the aching feelings of the night before.

"Good morning, sweetheart," he said with a smile. "How are you this morning— Oh, damn it, look at the time." He splashed coffee into a cup and fumbled with his tie. "Why am I always late? It must mean something. Don't tell Carol I said that."

Annie looked up at him and met his eye. There was something at the back of her gaze that almost made him back up a step. Glowing out of the red-rimmed fatigue, the weary pain and heartache in her eyes, was something new, a feeling of determination, an indication that a line had been crossed and Annie had had all she would take.

"I've had three miscarriages, Stan," she told him. "This time was not a miscarriage. The other times it was hard, but I could deal with it. This time—I wanted this baby more than anything else in the world, Stan, and something happened that wasn't normal, and it *wasn't* a miscarriage—"

Stan knelt beside her and put an arm on her shoulder. "Honey, don't you think I'm hurting too? But you've got to let it go—"

Her hands slammed down on the table. "I do *not* have to let go! Not until I know what is going on! Something is happening to me. I don't know what it is, but it's happening. And I am going to find out what it is, and what happened to my baby, even if I have to, to—"

"Honey, please, you have to—"

"Because I can't take it this time, Stan—the not knowing what happened and nobody believing it *did* happen, or—"

"Honey, Annie, listen to me." But she jerked free of his grip and slammed her coffee cup down so hard the handle broke off and the coffee spilled down the table.

"And if you're going to tell me I've been under a lot of strain and I need to take it easy, Stanley, so help me God—!"

"Aw, geez," he said, taking her hand in his, studying it carefully. The breaking coffee cup handle had made a small but deep cut on her hand and it was bleeding. "I'll get a Band-Aid," he told her. "Sit tight."

He came back to see her holding the two pieces of the broken cup. He touched her cheek. "I can fix it," he said. "It's okay."

"I'm going over to Carol's this afternoon," she told Stan as he put the Band-Aid on. "I'm going to let her hypnotize me."

NINETEEN

I t is dark on the small two-lane road and there is no sign of anything human anywhere nearby; no lights, no power lines, only the blacktop stretching in front of her.

The air coming in Annie's window has a chill to it, as it always does at night in the high desert. Besides the rush of the wind there are a few faint noises outside the car. Some night-time insects chitter and far away a coyote wails.

But Annie is really aware of these sounds only as background. Her concentration now is all on the car's tape player.

The cassette is playing the space music, the pulse she recorded from the Vega region that seems to be a fugue composed of telemetry sounds.

Ahead, Annie sees the tunnel. Her car approaches and then enters through the stone arch and all the desert sounds are abruptly cut off.

At the far end of the tunnel a light is coming closer. She is still concentrating on the music, but the light . . . Something is not quite right. . . .

And then she knows—it's the angle of the light. That must be a very large truck, she thinks. Its headlights are so high off the ground. But as she comes out of the tunnel, the lights are still too high: It's not a truck.

Whatever it is, it's above her.

She turns off the tape player, but the music continues from somewhere outside her car.

That's impossible, *she thinks.*

She leans out the window to look. She sees nothing but a bright light above her. No sounds of engines or rotors spinning, only telemetry sounds.

She feels a hot blast of air from the direction of the light and suddenly, for no reason she can really put into words, Annie wants more than anything to mash her foot down on the pedal and race away as fast as the ten-year-old Blazer will take her.

Instead, she eases off the gas, brakes and steers her car off to the shoulder of the road.

She doesn't have any idea why, since she wants to do just the opposite, but she moves the gear shift lever to Park and turns off the ignition.

"Now what do you see?" asked Carol. Annie was stretched out on the couch in her living room. Although her eyes were closed and she was in a hypnotic trance, she started to fidget. Whatever she was seeing, Carol decided, she didn't want to see it. "What is it, Annie? What do you see?"

"I— It's just right there," she said.

"What is, honey? What's right there?"

The light is moving closer, and although it hurts her eyes Annie stares at it.

The light begins to take on a blue tint. It has a physically compelling effect on her. Suddenly Annie is floating up off her seat and heading directly through the windshield, as if there were no substance to the glass or even the steering wheel blocking her way.

She has the sensation of being on an invisible elevator, moving up toward the light. She's weak, nauseated and, most troubling, she is totally unable to move.

Panic fills Annie as the light comes closer. She has no idea what it is—and yet it is so familiar. . . .

"No," Annie said, "please, no, please . . ."

Carol recognized the symptoms of a traumatic event so profoundly disturbing that it had been blocked from her conscious memory.

Carol's experience and intuition told her the first session was too soon to go very far into something that bothered Annie so deeply. The important thing at this point was to realize it was there.

She leaned forward and stroked Annie's hand. "Okay, Annie," she said. "Now, take it easy, take a deep breath, it's okay. It can't hurt you now. You hear me, Annie? It can't get to you. You're all right."

Annie's look of closed-eye panic shifted slightly down the emotional spectrum. "It . . . can't get to me . . .?" she said with a trace of puzzlement.

"That's right, honey. It can't get to you."

Annie sighed and shifted her weight slightly. Her features were composed now. "All right."

"Okay, Annie. It's a little later now. You're okay and nothing will hurt you. All right?"

"Yes. I'm all right," said Annie.

"Good. It's later now, but the same night. You are okay. You're not scared, nothing can hurt you. Where are you?"

Annie frowned. "It's . . . the tunnel?"

"The tunnel? You're in the tunnel again? Are you sure, Annie? It's later now."

Annie is flat on her back and limp. She wills herself to move but can't.

She is on a low-lying table, in a narrow gray fog-filled tunnel, propelled by figures on both sides she can't quite see. And in spite of Carol's reassurance she is scared.

She wants to shout, "No, stop. Why are you doing this? Stop now!" But she does not shout; in fact she can't move her lips, tongue and mouth. Whoever, whatever, is pulling her along pays no attention to her terrified look or her silent pleas.

"Where are you, Annie?" Carol asked. "Are you still in your car?" The reference to the tunnel had confused Carol and she needed to make sure Annie responded to her suggestion about time and place and safety. If not, it would be better to bring her back out of it, before something truly frightening happened. Carol knew very well that the mind could be a hostile foreign country when traveled without maps.

"Car?" Annie sounded puzzled. "No, not my car. It's . . . I'm on the table . . ."

"A table? You're on a table?"

"Yes . . ."

"What kind of table?"

Now she is approaching a circle of light and Annie tenses and thinks with weary horror, "Oh no—not this."

Annie grimaced as she relived what she saw.

"What kind of table, Annie?" Carol repeated.

"It's—medical. Medical table. A . . . gurney?"

"You're on a gurney. In a tunnel."

Annie nodded. "Yes . . ."

"Okay," said Carol. "Nothing bad will happen, Annie. Tell me what you see."

The gurney moves quickly up a slight incline toward a pool of light in a large room.

Although Annie can't move her head to look, can't really see anywhere but up, the room feels like it might be round, domed, but she gets no sense of the scale. The room could be the size of a coat closet; it could be the size of St. Peter's Basilica.

What she can see is the ceiling. Besides the dominant metallic color, there are also gray ribs that bend out from the center, like spokes on a wheel.

Annie is now placed under that center. The light above her becomes brighter; she recognizes it as some form of surgical or dental light.

"Where are you, Annie?" Carol asked, gently but persistently. "Tell me what you see."

"It's—an operating room?" she said. After a slight pause Annie giggles.

"What is it, Annie? What's funny?"

"It's just—this table is too low."

Annie feels her blouse being unbuttoned and thinks,
"Stop! Stop it, you can't!" But it's no good, the blouse comes
off. She wishes she could see who is doing this, but she can't.

If only she could lift her head, she would tell them off—
that is, if she could control her limbs, neck or mouth. Only her
eyes work and while they can move, nothing is in her field of
vision now, nothing but the light.

She works hard to stay calm, to think, to get some kind of
control. She tells herself to pay attention, think, remember—
whatever happens, no matter how horrible, she must remember.

And suddenly she feels her jeans and underpants being
jerked down her legs.

"Oh!"

"What is it, Annie? What do you see?"

"They're taking my clothes off. I want them to stop
it. I'm telling them to stop."

Carol put a calming hand on her. "It's okay, honey.
They can't hurt you now. But we need to know what
they're doing. You're safe. They can't do anything now.
Just tell me what you're feeling."

Annie's bare skin is touching the surface of the table, and
her whole body shudders.

"It's cold, I'm shivering." Annie's face tightened, her
lips quivered as she lived through the moment again.

Carol scribbled a note, then asked, "What is it,
Annie?"

"The table," Annie said with a puzzled look, then
added, "It's—too smooth? Not . . . wood, or—I don't
know, kind of silky."

"Okay, the table is silky," said Carol. "What else? Can you hear anything from where you are?"

". . . it's—quiet. No, wait. Now I hear something. Kind of—clinking sounds, and—feet shuffling. Someone's coming. It's more than one. I can't—oh."

Carol leaned closer and whispered, "Who is it? Who do you see?" Annie took in a deep, gasping breath. Her face twisted into a grimace. "Doctors . . ."

Standing over her are four short figures that look like doctors. They work fast, on specific areas of her body. They start on the soles of her feet and work their way up to ankles, calf muscles and knee joints.

She's pushed on her side and they examine her back. She feels fingers prodding each vertebra in her spine from neck to coccyx.

Annie is rolled back over, like a big limp rag doll. Her arms are lifted above her head and suddenly she feels a painful squeezing of her nipples, as if the doctors expected to express fluid.

Annie wants to scream. But the doctors move their concentration on to her head, probing her eyes, ears, nose and throat.

"What are the doctors doing, Annie?" Carol asked.

"They're examining—checking me."

"For what?" Carol demanded.

"I, ah—oh, no." Annie tensed up. "Not that!"

"What?" said Carol. "What Annie? What is it?"

Annie feels her legs spread and her feet raised, as the table molds itself to the shape of OB-GYN stirrups.

From across the room a much taller doctor moves to Annie's side. He seems different from the others. It's not just his surgeon's cap and mask. But Annie doesn't have time to think about it; she feels something very cold below her waist.

The taller doctor picks up a thin black rod with a tiny suction cup on the end.

"No. Oh, please, no," Annie cried out, her tone and expression heartbreaking.

"Annie—" Carol began, but Annie's terror became suddenly intense.

"No! Stop that. You can't do that. You *can't*. Oh, please, they're—don't let him do that, please!"

Annie is trying with every fiber of her being to run, to escape, just to move an arm, but she can't. She is trapped, helpless.

And suddenly Colonel Wesley enters her field of vision.

Wesley glances at Annie briefly, without any real interest, and then says something to the taller masked doctor. The doctor shakes his head and says something back. Wesley seems angry and moves away.

Carol watched Annie's writhing stop for a moment. She looked puzzled. "Colonel Wesley?" Carol leaned forward. She wrote down the name on her pad and said, "Go on, Annie."

Annie again feels the burning deep inside her. The cold intensifies, builds until there is a sharp cutting sensation and— "NO! DON'T YOU DARE! GOD DAMN YOU! DON'T YOU—" *A small, childlike hand touches her face and Annie is instantly calm.* "Oh. All right. I guess so."

The shift in Annie's mood was so abrupt and so complete that Carol recognized it as artificially induced. "Annie! Where are you, Annie! What's going on!"

An expression of peace, even contentment, settled on Annie's face. "It's all right. They're not going to hurt me. It's all right, really."

Carol shook her head. If ever there was a time to worry it was now. Who or what had that kind of power over absolute terror?

Carol held Annie's hand. "That's right, doll. Nobody's going to hurt you. Now it's a little bit later, okay?"

Annie nodded again. "Yes. —Oh!"

"What? What is it? Annie?"

One of the short doctors leans forward in a quick, jerky way and raises his hand. A cold metal rod touches her head just behind her ear and there is an intense burst of sparkles. Lights whirl and settle into spokes of a wheel. At the end of each spoke is a geometric pattern.

"Oh, wait. I don't think I . . ."

"Okay, Annie. What's going on now? What is happening?"

"I, it's, some kind of . . . it's—"

The patterns of light settle into something very regular, very familiar, and now Annie is sure she knows what they represent. It's a—

"Okay, then," said Carol. "We won't push it for now, let's move on. Okay? You're not on the table now. It's just after you get off the table."

Annie relaxed. A hint of a smile flitted across her face. "Yes," she said.

"Good. Now where are you?"

Annie is dressed again. She looks to her side. Clasped in her hand is the small hand that comforted her earlier. The hand leads her across the road and back to her truck. She knows it's time for her to leave, but she doesn't want to go.

"What is it, Annie? What's happening?"

"Oh," said Annie, "It's—time to go. I have to get in my car and go. But I don't want to leave without— Wait. Wait. It's mine!"

As her voice started to climb the scale Carol leaned forward and took her hand. "Annie, it's okay. They're not going to hurt you. Do you understand? They can't hurt you."

Annie relaxed, nodded. "Yes. Yes, that's right. They don't want to hurt me. I'm just not supposed to— It's just time for me to go. They're taking me back . . . I'm in my car and— That can't be right. . . . That clock is wrong. Oh, my, Stan will be so mad . . ."

"It's okay, honey. You're coming home, all right?"

Annie smiled. "Yes."

Carol looked at her watch. For a first session this had been very intense and she suspected it had gone long enough. Also, she had formed a few new ideas about what had happened to her friend and needed some time to work with them.

"Okay, when I snap my fingers you're going to wake up. You'll remember what you just told me, but it's all right, do you understand? Everything is going to be all right."

"Yes."

"Okay, here we go then. One, two—three," she finished, and snapped her fingers.

Annie opened her eyes, blinked. "Oh, my God."

Carol gave her a smile. "Welcome back, Annie. How do you feel?"

Annie stared at her friend for a long moment. "Feel? How do I *feel*?! What in God's name is going on?"

Carol gave her a small, professional smile. "Let's take this one step at a time, before we go handing out a diagnosis, okay?"

Something in Carol's tone made Annie sit up and look hard at her. "You know something about this, don't you?"

"Why don't we decide whether to go on with this first?" And she glanced down at the notebook in her lap. At the bottom of the page she had written "*COLONEL WESLEY*," and under that, "CALL FRANK *TONIGHT*!!"

Carol's aloofness irritated Annie—but the session they had just finished felt like the first step in the right direction.

"Okay, but I want to get Stanley to come along," she told Carol.

Carol shook her head. "It's hard enough to have another person in the room when we do it, but Stanley—"

"Now, don't you start," Annie warned her. "Besides, Stanley *needs* to hear this."

Carol cocked her head to one side. "Needs to hear it? What do you mean?"

Annie gave her a smile with absolutely no pleasure in it. "Stan works for a guy named Colonel Wesley."

TWENTY

There's no way I'll go," Stan said that evening when Annie told him about it. "Hypnosis is witchcraft, pseudoscience for half-educated yabos who can't do algebra. It's not a legitimate investigative tool."

"Legitimate or not, we uncovered some remarkable things today—"

"That's just your subconscious mind playing tricks—"

"How can you believe in the subconscious mind and not believe in hypnosis? Do you realize how stupid you sound, trying to be logical?"

"It's like vitamins or astrology, Annie—it preys on people's fears by encouraging them to believe in something half-smart."

Annie gave him a thin smile. "And who's half-smart here? Me? Or Carol? Or both of us?"

He groaned.

"Because I already know more about what happened than I would have without hypnosis. I never would have understood about your Colonel Wesley otherwise."

Stan blinked. "What about Colonel Wesley?"

"He was there, Stan. Whatever happened to me, he saw it. He was there!"

Stan was appalled. "Annie—" he said. "Honey, that doesn't make any sense. You're making up a story for something that hurt you very deeply."

"Stop it, Stanley. Stop and listen. Did your Colonel Wesley act normal when he met me? You *saw* him. Did he act like a man meeting somebody for the first time?"

"We were all a little upset that day—"

"He wasn't! He acted like he'd seen me before and wasn't supposed to let on. At the time, all I knew was that he seemed familiar and frightening—I didn't know how or where we had met, but *he* did!"

"I think you might be reading a little into that. Colonel Wesley is—"

"Stan, I saw him there. When Carol hypnotized me and took me back to that night, he was there."

"I, uh—no. I'm sorry. It's, it's too— I mean, you're asking me to believe in a dream, a, a, a *vision* from under hypnosis, and that's—I mean, I've known Colonel Wesley for ten years."

The thin smile came back to Annie's lips. "And how long have you known *me*, Stanley?"

The phone rang in the other room. It rang four more times before either moved. "I'll get it," Stan said, and marched to the kitchen counter.

"Hello? . . . Hi, Max. Yeah, hold on." Stan turned to Annie, still fuming in the dining room. "Max. For you."

"Hi . . . The SETI program . . . Wonderful. No, no. Wait. I'm on my way. Oh stop. It's a forty-minute drive. . . . Thanks."

Stan held up a pleading hand. "Come on, Annie, please. Let's talk this over."

"What do you want to talk about? You're not going to listen."

"All I'm saying is, you need some proof, more than just something that came to you in some kind of trance. Your subconscious mind is mixing fantasy and reality—like, Wesley—an authority figure, a real one. You place him in a nightmare, and—I don't know—"

"Is that what you think? I'm so far gone I can't tell the difference between fantasy and reality? So what do you think happened to our baby, Stan? Or did I dream that, too? Did Dr. Dolan's ultrasound dream it? Or doesn't that count? You don't want proof unless it fits the answer you already have."

"Annie, you're not being fair."

"Oh, I'm not being fair. The logical thing to do is to sit on my butt and pretend it never happened. You're right, Stan. I'm unfair."

"Annie, please. Come on—"

She spun on her heel and stared at him. "No, Stan. *You* come on! I am going back tomorrow. No more mysteries, no more nightmares. And Stan—I will find out how your Colonel Wesley fits in." She stormed out the house.

"Annie!" he called after her, but the heavy front door slammed shut and she was gone.

"Ready to move out," said the driver of the light blue Buick across the street. "I'll transmit direct to the Colonel."

Annie had backed out of the driveway by the time Stan got out the front door. He ran after her for half a block before he had to stop. His legs cramped and his chest hurt. He considered how out of shape he was—and then he saw the blue Buick speed by.

Like most people with clearance as high as his, Stan existed in a constant state of mild paranoia. The blue Buick had just triggered his alarm.

Have I seen that car before? Have I seen other cars following me recently? He wasn't sure—but he knew that by the time he was sure it would be too late.

Even if it was just his imagination, he'd had it drilled into him; you only have to be right once.

He decided to go to the Colonel about it in the morning.

Colonel Wesley rolled the tape ahead for a moment, then slowed it to speed. Annie's angry voice rose again, "No, Stan. *You* come on! I'm going back tomorrow. No more mysteries, no more nightmares. And Stan—I will find out how your Colonel Wesley fits in." Wesley stopped the tape.

"That tears it," he said.

"Yes, sir," Captain Crouch agreed. "Should we move in the wet team?"

Wesley shook his head. "You're too damn eager with that wet team, Crouch. We can't kill her yet—we need what she knows. Annie Katz is not a threat to us at the moment."

"Yes, sir."

Wesley blew out a large breath between his teeth, making strong cords stand out on his neck. "Only one thing can make her a threat, and that's if she gets the data to the bugeyes—" He narrowed his eyes. "The computer," he said softly.

"Sir?"

Wesley's hand slammed down on the desk. "*Damn it, Crouch, of course! The bugeyes are pulling an end run on us!*"

"How, sir?"

"That mainframe computer at the observatory. She's been fooling with that and the signal. We know the signal is from the bugeyes—it has to be the key to this thing."

"Yes, sir."

Wesley shook his head. "I don't know how—but she's using that computer for the bugeyes." He shifted his eyes to the thin Captain, who was watching like a tethered hawk. "All right, Crouch. Move a team in. Blow the computer. Hell, blow the whole observatory. We have to be sure the bugeyes can't get the data."

"Yes, *sir!*"

"And Crouch—JOSHUA is now priority two. Priority one is keeping the bugeyes away from the data. If it looks like Annie Katz is going to have a chance to leak the data, kill her."

As Crouch leaped up there was a knock and Colonel Wesley's door opened. A Sergeant stepped in and saluted crisply.

"Sir," he said. "We've been unable to locate Major Andros."

Wesley stared hard at the Sergeant and thought, *That's not possible. Andros can't just disappear, not from this base. Not unless . . .* Wesley turned to Crouch.

"Seems our Major has finally chosen sides. Find him—*before* he gets to Annie Katz."

Carol picked up a file labeled ANNIE. Leaning back in her chair, she flipped through the meager contents: the two napkins and a few pages of notes.

Carol smoothed out a few wrinkles on the napkins and compared the doodles; they each depicted a wagon-wheel design with each spoke ending in a geometric image.

But the most interesting thing about the two napkins, Carol realized as she placed one on top of the other, was that the doodles were identical, right down to the length and placement of each line.

Next Carol flipped through her notes. When she reached the end of the final page, she saw, "CALL FRANK *TONIGHT*." She spun her chair away from the desk and reached for the phone. But the doorbell rang.

Sonny screeched from the back room. "Oh right, I'm sure it's for you, Sonny boy." She laughed and opened the door.

But it was for Sonny.

Major Andros stood framed in the doorway. "Dr. Blum." His smile seemed to melt her. "I've come for Sonny."

"Of course you have. Come in, come in. And call me Carol." She pulled on his arm. "Sonny has been an absolute delight. Can I fix you a nice cup of coffee? How about tea?" She led him into the kitchen.

"No. No thank you. I really don't have much time. Carol. I need to see Sonny."

"He can wait, he's fine. Trust me, Major. He's not going anywhere." Carol pulled two mugs off the counter and poured the dark coffee. "Fresh. Just made it. Take anything?"

"No, black is fine, thanks." Andros picked up the steaming mug, but didn't drink it. "I really do have to be running. But I wanted to thank you . . ."

"The pleasure is all mine," Carol interrupted. "May I say, you've got a real winner there. You know, he settled right down. Been kinda my watchdog." She laughed, then brushed the hair from her face, and wished like hell she had kept her makeup on.

"My protector," she continued in a forced sultry voice, "good with people and charming . . . just like his daddy."

Andros blinked as he realized Carol meant him.

"Yes, well . . . Carol. I'll never, ah, be able to thank you enough, I'm sure. Could we go see Sonny now?"

He didn't wait for the answer, but started off toward the back room.

"Oh, sure. Duty calls, don't I know it." She rolled her eyes, and moved toward the back room wondering how such a beautiful guy could be so insensitive. "You know the way, Major."

Andros smiled when he saw Sonny. He sat down next to the cage and Sonny reached out to him. His rough fingers brushed the Major's cheek.

"See, he's fine. Told you," Carol said.

"Yes, fine." He stared into Sonny's eyes in silent communication.

Carol watched for a moment. *That's a little spooky*, she thought. She reached down and touched Andros's stiff shoulder. "You okay, Major?"

Andros looked up. He gave her a warm smile. "Of course." Sonny looked at her with an identical expression. But before she could really register that, Andros pulled an odd-looking silver rod from his jacket.

"Hey! What's that?" Carol asked.

It was the last thing she remembered saying. The

wand touched her temple and she couldn't be sure if she was looking into the Major's eyes, Sonny's eyes, or someone altogether different. The only thing sure was that the eyes . . .

The eyes were wrong.

They were so dark, so liquid, so near. She tried to turn away, but couldn't. She felt herself falling deeper into the eyes.

He's in me. He's flooding me. I can't stop him . . . he's spreading into my brain. . . .

Annie? . . . What about Annie . . .? You can't have her. Danger . . .? What kind of danger? Annie?

Carol came to standing at the front door.

"Good-bye, and thank you, Dr. Blum," Andros said.

"Call me Carol," she said automatically, and blinked. What had just—?

But Major Andros, carrying Sonny like a small child, turned and walked away, and the question died in her mind, half-formed. Something was not quite right, but— *It doesn't matter* came to her, and she went back inside and closed the door.

Carol sighed. There was something she had to do. She was going to do it, right before . . . never mind.

She moved back through the house. She glanced toward Sonny's empty cage, and a shiver ran from the top of her head to the tip of her spine. . . . A phone call. She had been about to make a phone call. She flipped through her Rolodex and found the card that said:

FRANK CASSIDY
(513) 555-0742

Carol stared at the card for a long moment before she picked up the telephone and dialed.

"Hello, Frank? Carol Blum. What? No, how the hell would I know what time it is in Ohio, for God's sake? Well then, you sleep too much. Yeah, that's Manhattan for I'm sorry. Listen—I think I got something here you might be interested in. No, it's for a good friend. How soon can you get here?"

TWENTY-ONE

Max had been very busy.

Right after calling Annie he had gone to work with the computer, getting the program set to run when she arrived. It was working, he told himself. His small series of stalls was actually keeping Colonel Wesley away, keeping his life here safe. He was winning, for once, he was sure.

Of course he was wrong about that.

❄

Only a few minutes after his call to Annie, Max had heard a chuffing sound outside, which faded, slowed and stopped. It didn't really register until a minute later when the door opened and swished close on its pneumatic hinge. Without looking up from his work, he frowned. It was too soon for Annie to be here, so—

"Dr. Berger," said a soft, cold voice.

Max jerked his head up.

Two Black Berets were standing there. They stared at him, as if measuring him for a coffin.

"We have new orders for you, sir," the shorter man said.

And as simply as that it was over.

Max had already wired in a lead from the main power box. The heavy-duty jolt would make sure the explosion was fast and hot.

His hands shook as he wired in the positive lead from the napalm incendiary and C4 explosives to the Cray's internal digital clock. He knew they had had only forty minutes before Annie arrived, and thirty were already gone.

He glanced over at the Black Berets. Wesley's men had just finished putting a gritty green Play-Dough-like crown of C4 with number-twelve blasting caps on the half-dozen twenty-pound military napalm tanks.

The tanks stood next to equipment and files. Each looked like a small scuba tank, but was filled with the jellied gasoline that became liquid hellfire. The only beauty of the military, Max thought, is in the high quality of the destruction.

The C4 crown on top of the napalm added to the

high brisonce, or shattering effect, and the result would be an effective fireball flash that would do more than merely level the place.

It would leave nothing but a crater.

The Black Berets moved to the door. "Ready."

Max tightened down the last lead and started the Cray's digital clock. The blue screen on the monitor displayed the countdown. "Three minutes, mark it—*now*," Max said, and the men synchronized their watches. 03:00, 02:59, 02:58, 02:57.

One of the Berets swung open the door, but Max didn't move. Instead he looked around the room a last time. *God damn Colonel Wesley,* he thought. But he did not say it out loud.

"Sir. Now."

He nodded and stepped toward the door. The taller of the Berets grabbed Max roughly and pulled him on out.

The sky was bright and peaceful as it was every night, but this was not every night. *It's over,* Max thought. *My work, my family life, my happiness. Wesley will send me off on some new assignment with some new identity. The only comfort in any of it is that no one has been killed, which is better than the last assignment.*

Max and the Berets had just passed the huge parabolic dish and headed down the hill about three hundred yards to a black jet helicopter when the lights of Annie's Blazer cut through the dusty night.

The truck had a familiar rattle as it came down the gravel driveway. Without even turning to look, Max knew it was Annie.

"Jesus, not now." He spun around and started sprinting back up the hill. He had to warn her. He had to reach her. But something hit him hard from behind and he fell face forward into the sandy soil.

"Can't let you do that, sir," the taller Beret whispered from on top of him. He made no apologies, simply squatted there as Max crawled to his knees, spitting grit from his mouth.

"You son of a bitch. She's done nothing wrong. That's murder." He glanced at his watch. "I've got a minute thirty, I can still reach her. She doesn't have to die."

"She's a security risk," said the other Beret as he knelt down next to Max.

"To hell with you—both of you. I'm going back," Max said, and forced himself to stand. But before he could take a step he saw the red dot from the laser sight on his chest.

He looked up. The taller Beret was holding a steady bead with his .357 magnum Desert Eagle.

"We have our orders. So do you, Dr. Berger." Max heard emotion for the first time—a faint sense of disgust, disapproval. "You are staying with us, dead, or alive. Your choice."

The shorter Beret stood up again, looking down at his watch. "Fifty-seven seconds. We need to clear the area."

Max looked up again. He could see Annie sitting in her Blazer. *He had to warn her.* He took a deep breath to shout, but instead only grunted as he hit the sand again.

The taller Beret shook his head. "You know, Dr.

Berger, you're the ungrateful type. Probably won't even thank him for saving your life." The Beret shoved the .357 magnum back into his leather holster. He grabbed Max by the shoulder and dragged him toward the helicopter.

❦

Annie sat in her Blazer. Her jaw ached and she realized she had been clenching it for the whole drive from her house. She was embarrassed to catch herself so angry, but that didn't stop her from slamming her car door and stomping toward the observatory.

She'd have slammed the door there, too, if she could have, but it had a pneumatic door closer, so she made do with flinging herself into her chair, shoving a large pile of paperwork to one side and simply fuming. She did not see the computer's monitor continuing its countdown: 00:23, 00:22, 00:21, 00:20, 00:19 . . .

Annie took a deep breath and drummed her fingers on the desktop. The sound echoed around the room and she looked up.

Where's Max?

She looked around the room. It seemed very quiet, too quiet, no sound but the hum from the mainframe. *Well, if it's running, he's here,* she thought, trying to calm herself.

"Hey Max?" Annie called out. "Come on, we got work to do."

No response. Annie moved toward the bathroom,

the only other room in the building. "You in there?" She knocked; no response.

She swung the door open and saw that it was empty.

"Oh, great. He's outside." She marched toward the front door, but caught from the corner of her eye the lit computer screen. "What's he up to?" She spun on her heel, grabbed her chair and rolled right up to the terminal.

The screen showed the digital count at 00:09, 00:08, 00:07 seconds.

Annie called, "Max, is this the SETI program?" No answer. She bent over the keyboard to type in a query. But as she touched the first key the room went black. She gasped and jumped back.

It was pitch black.

"Power failure. Great. Well, just find the door."

She reached down and felt the heavy oak worktable. Hands outstretched, she took a step, feeling her way to the door.

The Black Berets and Max reached the helicopter just as their watches ticked off 00:00.

"Now!" said the short one. Max ducked to shield his head, but there was no boom. He closed his eyes and whispered thanks.

"Either she stopped it, or it stopped itself," the taller Beret said, looking back at the silhouette of the observatory.

"I'll go," the other said, pulling the slide back on his .45-caliber Glock automatic.

"No, wait," Max said, regaining his courage, "Annie couldn't have done it. She doesn't know enough to disable it. It must have been a failure in the Cray's digital system. I'll go. I'm the only one who knows it."

The Berets exchanged a look and then the taller nodded. "Okay—and do it right."

"Of course." Max started back up the hill. This was his last chance to help Annie.

The two Berets sat down on the carriage of the helicopter and watched him go. When he was out of sight the shorter Beret spoke into the radio.

"Eagle, this is Gamma. We have a situation."

The reply sounded cold, even on the radio. "Report, Gamma."

"Primary subject is at Ground Zero. Request instructions."

"Has she had time to access the computer?"

"Yes, sir."

There was no hesitation in the reply. After two clipped sentences, the short Beret said, "Understood, sir." He replaced the radio and raised an eyebrow at his partner.

The taller man shrugged and pulled a McMillan high powered .308 sniper rifle out of the cockpit and loaded it.

Annie's left shoulder pressed against the cold concrete wall. She inched forward. In her four years of working at the observatory, there had never been a power failure quite like this.

Not that power failures didn't occur. They did, but usually in late January or early February, caused by heavy rains. And always the backup generator came on.

Well, she thought, *I'm sure Max can fix it in the morning.*

Another step ahead and she felt the cold steel door handle touch her arm. She jumped before she realized what it was. "Oh, Lordy."

She pulled down the handle and the door opened.

Max had made it up to the parabolic dish when he saw Annie step out. He glanced back toward the Black Berets. They were too far away for him to see what they were doing.

"Max?" She called and waited for a response. "Are you out here? . . . Max?" She continued, "The power's off."

But Max did not answer.

Annie glanced around the grounds and still did not see him. "All right, you're on your own. I'm gonna go home," she called into the silence.

Off behind the dish, Max watched her go. *Good. Go home, Annie, go fast.* He glanced again down the hill at the Black Berets. He saw nothing but shadows, shadows and . . . movement?

The taller Beret raised the McMillan rifle and centered the crosshairs of the night-vision telescopic site. Inside the scope the magnified starlight gave a bright grayish green tinge to the observatory surroundings. He could clearly see Annie walking toward her Blazer. "Looks good, stand by," he said.

Annie pulled open the truck's door, just as the Beret tightened his finger on the trigger.

But no shot came.

The second trooper moved toward his taller partner.

"What happened? It jammed?" the other Beret asked. He heard Annie's truck start and saw her backing to turn around.

The tall trooper toppled over, still clutching his rifle.

The other Beret exploded into a run up the hill. He had seen this before. Only *they* had that kind of control. He knew he had to move fast to preserve the mission.

The target had to pass over the drive before turning onto the paved road. He never blinked, he never showed anger. He showed no emotion at all as he pulled out his .45-caliber sidearm. His powerful strides brought him right up to the ridge. Annie's truck passed above him. He took aim.

He felt the strange half tingle spread over him and had time only to think, *Damn. . . .*

Then his fingers, hands, legs, body, all froze. The last thing he saw before collapsing to the ground was Annie turning safely onto the paved road.

From Max's position he could not see the Berets. What he did see was the Blazer's taillights disappear over the next ridge. That was all he needed. Annie was safe. He turned and plodded into the observatory.

Down the hill the taller Beret stirred, then snapped up onto his feet, weapon in his hand. He scanned the darkness until he saw the off-color mound that was his partner.

As he reached the shorter Beret's side, the man stirred, and then snapped up, alert, as had the taller one.

The taller one looked up and scanned the night sky, then the ground. "It must be *them*. But we can't compromise the mission." His partner nodded.

In the observatory Max stood looking down at the computer, a flashlight in his hand. As he suspected, Annie's curiosity had shorted his clumsily wired circuit.

He felt glad he had been hurried, had rigged the timer so badly. Had he thought someone might disturb it, he would have wired it so nothing would stop the count. But as it was—he was glad it had worked out this way.

He sighed. His options were limited at this point. He had to go through with it. But at least Annie was safe now.

Max bent to the keyboard. Once he restored power,

the countdown would resume where it left off. Impossible to tell how much time was left, but it felt like a good gamble. He only needed six, maybe seven seconds, to type in the command override and begin a new count.

He stepped to the small closet containing the power box. It took only a moment to get the power back up, and run for the keyboard.

But as he came out of the closet he could see the screen across the room: 00:04, 00:03—

Not such a good gamble after all, he thought and ran for the door.

The jet black helicopter whipped up a reddish dust cloud as it passed over the parabolic dish. The pilot maneuvered to get directly over the observatory. "When Berger comes out, get a clean shot and then we'll intercept the woman." The taller man nodded and leaned out with the rifle and took aim.

As the count hit 00:02, Max lunged for the door. He had never been a sprinter. He wasn't now.

At 00:01, he was still four or five long steps from the door.

At 00:00 he dove.

The blast lifted his body as if he were a rag doll and flung him straight up at the ceiling. He was burning like a torch before he got halfway there.

Mercifully, he was dead when he slammed into the ceiling.

BOOM.

The flash-fire explosion caused a superheated thermal updraft. That, coupled with the burning napalm on the undercarriage, sent the helicopter pitching uncontrollably. The final damage occurred when the first of the four rotors hit the ground and building debris. The stress cracks ripped through the fuel tanks and grenade ordnance.

"SHEE-IT!" said the taller Beret.

That was all there was time for.

Annie was in the tunnel four miles from the observatory when explosions lit up the night behind her. She did not see the spectacular fireball, nor hear the solid *whoompff* of the blast. She just drove home.

The devastation, however, was not without an audience. Well off the road and seemingly without any vehicle around, Andros, Sonny and an oddly childlike creature watched. Their reactions were more like kids on the Fourth of July.

"Wow," said Andros.

"What?" Wesley asked looking up at Captain Crouch, who had awakened him.

"We lost contact, sir. But we're sending a second team to investigate."

The Colonel sat up. "You do that. And send for the wet team."

"Yes, sir. They're at the Country Club, sir. They can be here by tomorrow night."

"Fine. Until they get here stay tight on her. No leaks."

"Sir." Captain Crouch saluted and left. The Colonel lay back in his bed.

Damn them!

TWENTY-TWO

A nnie awoke early the next morning. She had slept well for the first time in almost a month. Although there had been the mix-up with Max the night before, she felt sure they would have a good laugh over it, then solve the power outage and resume work.

When Stan finally dragged himself out of bed around seven, Annie said, "Better get the paper. Sprinklers come on in just a minute."

He stepped to the front door, rubbing his eyes. On the sidewalk he took a deep breath, enjoying the clean, crisp air. But as he picked up the newspaper and straightened, he caught sight of the tan Buick parked diagonally across the street.

Stan froze. From where he stood he could see the vague outline of a man in the car. The man got out and walked toward him. He wore a gray jacket and a blue tie and was bald with a dark goatee and an earring in a pierced left ear.

"Dr. Katz?" the man asked as he strolled toward Stan. He reached into his inside jacket pocket.

"What? I mean, who . . . who wants to know?" Stan took a fumbling step backward just as the automatic timer on the lawn sprinklers kicked on. In seconds he was soaking wet. So was the other man, who produced an official badge in a leather case.

"Dr. Katz, I'm Detective Chambliss. Is your wife home? I need to ask her some questions regarding last night."

Annie saw Stan through the stained-glass window, standing off the walkway, soaking wet with the soggy morning newspaper under his arm. Then she saw the man in the gray jacket.

"Dr. Anne Katz?" asked Detective Chambliss.

She hesitated. ". . . Yes?"

"Dr. Katz, I'm Detective Chambliss. I need a statement from you regarding the problem at your observatory last night."

"You mean the electrical outage?" she asked.

"No, I mean the fire and murder."

Annie blinked. She could feel the world lurching to one side, off into unreality. "I— Excuse me?"

"Murder," the detective repeated patiently. "May I come in?"

"Oh, Lord," gasped Annie. She just stopped her knees from buckling. "What was— I— Murder? Who?"

The detective pointed toward the house. "Why don't we go in and sit down."

❄

Down the street, a man in a light blue car picked up the radio mike. "The cop who was watching her house has moved in."

"Stay with it. She's got to be alone sometime today," Crouch's voice replied.

❄

Annie's legs finally gave way, and she sank deeper into the soft couch. Stan held her hand. Detective Chambliss sat in a straight chair beside the telephone. He rattled off the end of Annie's statement to his captain.

"Yeah, a power blackout. The generator failed and she left. Never saw anyone . . . No, doesn't seem to be." Chambliss glanced at Annie. It was the kind of professional cop look that fills a person with worry, whether she is guilty or not.

"Okay." He hung up. "The Medical Examiner appears to have gotten a positive ID on your coworker, ma'am. They only found two partial teeth, but there's no doubt. It's him."

"Oh, no," Annie whispered, the tears starting to flow. She leaned her head on Stan's shoulder. "I just can't believe—Max—oh God—everything—just gone?"

"Mrs. Katz, at this time you are not considered a suspect. So relax, all right? The area is still secure. But if you want to search for any personal effects, I'll escort you back."

As they rounded the little bend and turned onto the gravel driveway, there was no building silhouette peeking over the last rise. All Annie could see was a few tendrils of greasy smoke.

She stepped out of the car and felt sick. The three cups of coffee she had had for breakfast churned and roiled as she looked at what was left. For a moment it was all she could do simply to look and gasp for breath.

It was gone. All of it.

A large hook-and-ladder fire truck had parked at one end of the parking lot next to a nearly intact parabolic antenna. A small cluster of firemen stood beside it.

Almost nothing remained of the observatory itself. There were a few small heaps of blackened building blocks, one or two twisted girders, but for the most part there was nothing to see but steaming rubble.

"Dear God," she said, and for a few minutes she just leaned against the car door and let the desolation wash over her.

Stan stood next to her. He had watched the detective disappear into a group of firefighters. He had seen another group move off and start to work on a second pile of debris just off to the side of the observatory.

Stan studied it. The pile started to take form; he

could make out a metal skeleton of something. What was it? Long, narrow, fuselage shape but without wings . . . a helicopter?

"Why in the world would—" he started to mumble, but was startled by a heavy rap on the car's trunk.

Annie and Stan turned to see an overly muscular black fireman staring at them. "Lieutenant Mulder, Bomb and Arson from Albuquerque," he said in a tired but official tone of voice. "I need you to answer a few questions, Mrs. Katz."

"Could you tell me how this happened?"

The man studied her and Stan again, hard this time. "You got any enemies?" he asked finally. "A rival observatory or something?"

The question, only half a joke, took Annie by surprise. "You're saying this was *arson?*"

"Unless you guys use napalm with C4 for cleaning the telescopes or something."

Napalm with— Stan shook his head; did he hear that right? "C4?" he asked.

Lieutenant Mulder nodded. "Like Play-Doh, but with a bang."

Annie was too stunned to speak.

"No enemies?" Lieutenant Mulder paused to wipe sweat off his face. Annie numbly shook her head. "Well then, in that case I'd have to say it was probably arson." He smiled with no humor. "Just a guess."

Annie's head whirled in unison with her stomach, and she barely heard Mulder go on.

"Okay, we already have a positive dental ID on your partner, Dr. Berger. But we're still working on the other two."

"What other two?" Stan asked.

Mulder pointed toward the metal skeleton of the helicopter. "There were two bodies in that wreckage. I'm not allowed to go into the specifics but I can tell you, whoever did this was professional."

He turned back to Annie. "Your coworker is dead. I need to know if there was any reason for someone to kill him."

Annie shook her head. The idea was totally crazy. "No one would ever want to kill Max."

Lieutenant Mulder nodded. "Okay. Then think hard, Mrs. Katz. Is there anyone who would want to kill *you?*"

Stan knew that only the military could get C4. Whatever group had bombed the observatory had not only been professionals, but military professionals. There was a very short list of military units capable of this kind of work, with those tools. And Stan could only think of one that had any connection to him at all. So the thought had come at once.

Is Wesley behind this?

A small Northwest commuter plane touched down on runway B at the Los Alamos public airport. It was the only plane landing, from Cincinnati, and only one person waited to meet it.

"Yo! Frankie!" a voice bellowed, and Frank Cassidy turned.

"Carol Blum. It's been what, three years?"

"Come on, let's get your bags before the crowd gets there."

Frank looked around the airport. Seven other passengers had deplaned. "Crowd?" he asked with mild amusement.

"Yeah, I know. So I miss Kennedy. Now, there's an airport."

"Tell me more about this woman, Carol."

"She's my best friend in the world. And something screwy is happening to her which, I hate to say, sounds like one of your cases."

"Is there any physical evidence?"

"What do you want, a souvenir T-shirt or something? Come on—she was pregnant and now she isn't. Her doctor says there's no sign of a miscarriage and no sign she ever was pregnant. Except we got ultrasound pictures of the baby."

"What else?"

"Dreams," said Carol. "Except they're not dreams because they come completely clear under hypnosis. They're memories. No question. But they were hidden at first with, what do you call it? A fake memory about an owl flying at her car."

"Screen memory," Frank said. "An owl would fit the pattern."

At the baggage carousel, Frank picked up a battered leather bag. As they stepped out into the sunlight, Frank paused. "All this," he said, "just a few miles down the road from Roswell. How about that?"

❋

Colonel Wesley had had a bad night. The dreams were getting worse, and he knew that meant *they* were close to making their move.

So when he arrived at Aerocorp two hours early, he made it his first priority to check on the security of JOSHUA. He knew *they* had the technology to get past the most advanced military security. And while ready for and half expecting JOSHUA to be missing, he was not ready for what he found.

JOSHUA stood inside engineering room 114. Next to it stood Dennis Albright, working as he had worked through the night to complete the changes to turn JOSHUA into the first working particle-beam weapon. He intended to grab the credit.

Instead, Colonel Wesley grabbed him.

"What's going on, Albright?"

Dennis found it hard to speak with Wesley's hand around his throat. "Working—late—all night."

Wesley shook him. "You are not cleared for this unless your team leader is present, and you know it."

The blood was roaring in Albright's ears and things were getting dim, but he tried to explain. "Particle beam—conversion—"

Wesley had expected an enemy, so he found one. All

the man's sneaky, backstabbing tactics now made sense. *Never trust a spy. Even your own.* And Wesley had a pretty good idea who else Albright spied for.

He gave Albright a hard shake.

"I know how men like you operate, weasel. Just answer me one thing: What did Andros promise you?" Wesley's voice whispered into Albright's ear. He pulled Dennis hard against him in a lethal headlock.

"Please—I didn't—"

"But you *did.*"

There was a snapping sound, followed by the thud of a body falling to floor.

Goddamned traitor.

Colonel Wesley left the room.

TWENTY-THREE

S tan's day had been full of surprises. But none shocked
him more than finding Dennis Albright dead and
being wheeled out the door by military security.

"What the hell is happening, Colonel?" Stan de-
manded. His anger made his veins bulge in his temple.
Wesley looked up, a slightly surprised smile on his face.
"Dr. Katz, I was hoping you would stop by."

"Colonel, what the— Albright was murdered?"

"That's correct. And it is my opinion that this is only
the beginning."

"What—what do you mean?"

"Project JOSHUA is now at a stage where it has
raised some security questions."

"Like what?"

"Loyalty, for starters."

"Loyalty? Is that why you have me and my wife under surveillance?"

Wesley smiled. "Dr. Katz . . ."

"I have had top security clearance for almost ten years," Stan said. "My loyalty has never been in question. This is an outrageous breach of privacy, and I won't stand for it!" He took a deep breath to go on, but Wesley nodded and said, "You're absolutely right."

Wesley straightened his jacket, came around the desk and clapped a hand on Stan's shoulder. "Come on," he said, "let's go get a beer."

"A—get a *what?*"

"Beer, Dr. Katz. We drink it to relax." He stepped toward the door, half pulling Stanley. "Come on."

Wesley led the way past a pool table and an alcove holding a jukebox. He slid into the booth, nodding for Stan to take the seat facing him.

Stan sat. "Look, Colonel—what's this all about? I asked a simple question. If I could just get a simple answer . . ."

Wesley nodded to show how reasonable he thought Stan was being. "And you will get your answers, Dr. Katz," he said, holding up two fingers to the tubby woman behind the bar. "Your work on JOSHUA is important, probably more than you know. So what I have to say is very serious. All right?"

"Sure. But what the—"

"Dr. Katz—Stan—because we never really got to

know each other, we've had a misunderstanding. But it is just a misunderstanding, Stan."

Wesley stopped talking as the woman from behind the bar slammed two heavy mugs on the table.

Stan took a sip. "Colonel, the thing is—"

"Stan, we're off the base here. Call me Jack."

"All right," he said, "*Jack*. Look—I am being watched, followed, and I know damn well my wife is being followed. And this morning, her observatory was burned down."

"I'm sorry to hear that."

"I bet." Stan rolled on. "Look, what I'm saying is they used napalm and C4. This was not some college prank. Three people were killed. Now, I know in today's world it makes perfect sense to kill strangers, dismember and eat them, so we're not talking a big deal. It's one less small scientific station and—but that's exactly my point! It's not worth using napalm or C4 for Chrissakes."

Stan looked straight at Wesley. "The only people with access to that kind of ordnance is *our military*. So what I'm asking, *Jack*, is—did you order that arson?"

Wesley's eyes were like blue gemstones, hard and cold. "Are you accusing me of a capital crime, Stan?"

Stan opened his mouth but could not speak. When Wesley put it in those terms, it sounded impossible.

"Because that would be crazy, Stan. The U.S. military does not get involved in domestic civilian matters, particularly capital crimes. So I hope I didn't hear you right.

"I know you're under a lot of pressure, Stan, so I'll forget you said that, all right?"

But a streak of stubbornness made Stan say, "Colonel—Jack—*somebody* used C4 and napalm on my wife's observatory. And the only people—"

"The only people who have access to it are military? I think you're being naive, Stan."

"But I know that you— Have you been watching us? I have a right to know."

"Yes, you do," Wesley agreed. "So let me just put your mind at ease here. You *are* being followed. You are being watched, twenty-four hours a day, and it *is* at my orders. And you have done exactly the right thing by coming to me now."

"Damn it, Colonel—"

"I know. But let me add further that nobody is questioning your loyalty, Stan. You're a fine man, and a gifted engineer. But—we've had information that Project JOSHUA might be threatened from outside.

"We know now that information is correct. This morning we discovered Dennis Albright's body. He gave his life defending JOSHUA. But that doesn't mean the threat is gone."

"How do you mean, threat?"

Wesley nodded. "Stan, some enemies you never know about until it's too late. I am not at liberty to tell you where the threat lies, but it's real, you can see that now as well as I can."

Wesley sipped his beer and carefully let Stan see that

he was measuring him before adding, "To be honest, what happened out at your wife's place of employment was probably the result of these enemies, Stan. I want you to ask yourself what could be a better way to get to a man than by threatening his loved ones? The surveillance is our only way to guarantee your safety. It's for your sake, your wife's sake, and yes, for the good of the project."

"Wait a second. If what you're saying is true, then— the threat is still here. Annie could still be in danger?"

"That's right, Stan. Kidnapping, a hostage situation—we don't know, can't know. You see now the position I'm in? We can't afford to take a chance of leaving you or your wife vulnerable. You're just too valuable to this project. I have good men, dedicated men, giving you top security."

"Who?" Stan asked.

"Don't worry. These guys are the very best."

Stan looked up to see Wesley watching him closely. "I don't like this, the extra security, the danger to my wife—"

"I understand."

It was clear to Stan that at that moment he was in way over his head, and if he failed to do something, he would drown.

"You know," Stan finally said, "I've had an offer to go back to teaching."

Wesley's smile was thin and laced with warning. "You don't want to do that right now, Stan."

A small chill spread across Stan's back. "Why not?"

"Stan, we have a nice, tight family in our group. And when you're in a family you're in for life."

"I don't know," Stan said.

"*I* know," Wesley told him. "Forget about teaching."

"Colonel—Jack—I don't like the thought of Annie in danger."

"My men are watching out for you. Believe me. We're watching your wife around the clock."

For some reason that didn't make Stan feel a whole lot better.

Frank Cassidy laughed and looked across at Annie, who sat on Carol's overstuffed couch. Everyone seemed to be getting along, but something suddenly dawned on Annie.

"Frank, you still haven't told me what you do."

"Oh. You're right, I haven't."

"Well," said Annie, "what *do* you do?"

"I'm a UFO investigator," he said.

Annie had a moment of stunned, frozen panic. What was Carol thinking?

"Will you excuse me for a moment?" she said politely, and went into the kitchen.

"Carol!" Annie whispered fiercely. Carol turned from the stove top, where she was pouring hot water into the coffee filter. "What in the name of the good Lord God do you think you're doing?"

"Making coffee," she said with infuriating blankness. "Don't you want any?"

"You know damned well what I mean."

"Annie, I want you to listen to what the man has to say. That's all. Just listen, huh?"

"Listen? To flying saucer garbage? Are you nuts?"

"No, Annie, I'm not nuts. I'm a shrink. So tell me why you're having such a violent reaction to this?"

Annie had trouble breathing without panting. "I don't believe this. Now I'm crazy because I don't believe in flying saucers?"

"Lots of people don't believe in 'em. Most don't get as worked up as this."

Annie took a deep breath, unclenched her hands. "Look, I need to know what happened to my baby. I thought you were helping me, taking this seriously."

"I take this very seriously, Annie," Carol said. "Maybe more seriously than you, because I'm not ruling anything out until I've checked every possibility, no matter how unlikely it seems.

"That is a very serious guy out there. He gave a paper at a shrinks' conference a few years ago that about turned the joint on its ear, and he backed it up with plenty of evidence. So just listen to what he has to say. Then, if you still think it's a lot of garbage, okay, you tried."

Annie looked at Carol with a very hard, searching glare. "You're serious about this, aren't you?"

"Why not? I'm a Jungian. You ever read what Jung said about UFOs? He was serious about 'em, and he didn't have ten percent of the evidence we have now."

"Damn it, *what* evidence, Carol? This thing has been investigated time and again and there's just nothing to it!"

The soft sound of Frank clearing his throat came from behind them. Unseen, he had come to the doorway. "Actually, that's not quite true," said Frank apologetically. "It's never really been investigated with anything approaching competence."

"But I read about it—there was that, oh what was it, that report a few years ago—" Annie began.

Frank gave a deprecating shake of his head. "The Condon Report. Sorry, Annie, but did you read it?"

"There were some excerpts in the paper. Quotes from the conclusion. But no, I didn't read the whole thing."

"I didn't think so. I *did* read it, and what it said was basically this: After explaining away as many sightings as possible—sometimes in a very offhand, unsubstantiated manner—they were left with a body of thirty percent of sightings they couldn't explain, no matter how hard they tried. But then they went on to conclude, with no evidence outside of wishful thinking, that there was nothing to it. And people accepted that, even smart people like you, because that's what they wanted to believe. Now, *there* is your unscientific garbage."

"But . . ."

Frank nodded. "Yeah, I know. It's silly stuff; little men from Mars and all; really goofy bullshit. We all think so. We all *want* to think so, and all we hear from so-called responsible authorities is that UFOs are just wishful thinking by a lot of hysterical cranks under mass hypnosis.

"I never understood that one. Has there ever been a documented case of mass hypnosis on this scale? But people are perfectly willing to believe in that instead of the possibility of UFOs. That's because instead of investigating any of this, the government decided that if it was true we'd all panic and start a revolution or something. So they put all their energy into making people doubt the whole thing. They spent millions trying to make it all seem like lunatic fringe stuff."

He smiled. "It's nice to see the government can really do a great job once in a while, huh?"

"But—but you're saying that I . . . that, that they . . .? I mean, wouldn't I remember something like that?"

"The fact is, doll," said Carol, "you *don't* remember. That's what's really bugging you."

"And that kind of fits a pattern we've established," said Frank. "That if you have gaps in your memory, missing time, and maybe some disturbing dreams, that maybe you've had one of these abduction experiences."

Annie looked at the two of them for a long moment, and then shook her head. "I can't. I'm sorry. It's just too—"

She saw Carol and Frank exchange glances, and Frank shrugged. "Okay," he said. "I'm here to help, and I can't force you to take my help. But do me a favor? Just to humor me, since I've come all the way from Ohio and I'm so obviously off my rocker . . ."

"Of course. What favor?"

"Show me around a couple of places. I'd like to see where you pulled off the road and saw the owl, for starters."

Annie was unable to think of any reason not to go along, although a small part of her, buried deep in her subconscious, was trying very hard to find a reason. But finally she said, "Sure. Why not?"

TWENTY-FOUR

It didn't take long to reach the spot, and soon Annie slowed just in front of the tunnel. "Um, there. I think. Yes. Right there." She pulled the car onto the shoulder and they all climbed out.

"Where were you exactly, Annie?"

"Right here, I think. I'm pretty sure." She pointed with her foot to a spot on the roadside. Frank dropped to one knee and brushed at the weeds with the back of his hand.

Annie looked over his shoulder. "What are you looking for?"

Carol butted in. "Aw, come on, you've seen 'In Search Of,' 'Sightings,' all those shows. We're looking for depressions in the dirt, burn marks in the grass, radioactive soil, cattle mutilations. I mean, a beer can that glows in the dark would be a big help, right?"

"Is that sort of thing, you know . . . usual?" Annie asked.

"Not usual, no. Only sometimes. But think how stupid I'd feel if it were here and I didn't look for it. Anyway, it's nice to have some evidence."

"Sure, but—evidence of *what?*"

Frank sighed and stood. "Annie—three weeks ago you were very much pregnant. Now you aren't. That's fact. That's not imagination. Something happened to you. We know that. We just don't know what. But anything I can find at the place where it all started could be a help."

He took a step closer and put a gentle hand on her shoulder. "There's nothing crazy about this. Something really did happen to you. Maybe there's nothing we can do to make it better, but we can find out what happened, and that's a start. If we can't fix it we can at least learn to deal with it. Let me help, Annie. Please?"

Annie took a deep breath, avoiding his eyes, and looked out across the New Mexico landscape. "All right," she said, "let's see what we can find."

From about a half mile away it made a nice tableau: two people talking to a third in the desert. But the two men watching it from the light blue Buick did not appreciate the scene for its artistic merits.

"Eagle, this is Delta," he said. "We have a new player."

"Delta," a voice crackled back on the radio, "this is Eagle Two. We'd like to see it."

"Stand by," the man replied. Turning to his partner, he said, "Let's roll."

The car moved past Frank, Carol and Annie, still clustered at the roadside. As the Buick passed, Annie was pointing up and Frank craned his neck back to look. So he didn't see the small high-speed camera pointed at him from the window of the Buick.

"Gotcha," said the older man; then, into the microphone, he said, "Transmitting now." A wire led from the camera to a control panel under the radio. The man pushed a button on the panel. It was backlit with a red light, and when the man pushed it the button blinked red and there was a whirring sound. "That's it," said the man, putting down the camera and picking up the microphone. "Beta, this is Delta. It's all yours. We're headed for home."

"Frank Cassidy is his name," said Crouch, tossing onto Wesley's desk a glossy picture of Frank craning his neck. "He's an expert on UFOs and the UFO abduction experiences. He's been in *Psychology Today*, and on the 'Donahue' show."

Crouch opened a manila folder and consulted a computer printout inside. "Military service in Germany, nineteen seventy-two through seventy-four, MFA from

Pittsburgh, nineteen seventy-six. Married and divorced, no children. Sir."

Wesley looked up at Crouch and nodded. "Good. It's cleaner when there's no family. I wish he wasn't a veteran, though." He caught Crouch giving the wall behind his head a hard look. "It's time. Get your wet team."

❖

Back in Carol's living room, Annie felt a little less comfortable with her decision to go ahead. "Tell me about this stuff," she said to Frank. "I don't know anything about it and I'd really like you to convince me."

"Well, where to start . . . As far as modern UFOlogy goes, we have to start just down the road from here, in Roswell, New Mexico. In nineteen forty-seven, something crashed out on a ranch near Roswell."

"Come on," said Annie. "I read about that. That was a weather balloon."

"Right. Of course it was. That's what the official government press release said, wasn't it? The second one, anyway."

"Excuse me?"

"That was the second press release, Annie. Quite a while after the fact. The first official military press release clearly said they had recovered some kind of large alien aircraft, saucer-shaped. The crash site took up almost ten acres. But this story was yanked twenty-four hours later and the officer who made it disappeared.

"Several busloads of government experts appeared on the scene within hours, and we have various garbled accounts of what they did. Garbled because, to this day, most of them won't talk. They say it's still classified." And he shook his head. "Forty-five years later and it's still classified. Must have been one *hell* of an interesting weather balloon, huh?

"Anyway," said Frank, "we've kept tabs on most of the people who were in on that. One or two have finally talked and we know that whatever they found out on that farm was not like anything anybody had ever seen before or since. The skin or shell of the thing was light enough that a child could pick it up, and so strong they couldn't scratch it with anything—there's even a rumor they put a hunk of it at ground zero for one of the last aboveground H-bomb tests. And parts were covered with these strange symbols that were not of any written language known in this world.

"Most of the experts who were there are dead or retired or have just vanished. But there is one who's still around and still active. He was a corporal at the time and in on the security of the operation. He stayed with it and rose through the ranks. He's a colonel now and still head of security."

Annie gasped. "Not Colonel Wesley—!"

"Got it on the first try." Frank smiled. "Annie, this is big casino. It goes back five decades, to when Truman set up an organization called MJ-12 to deal with everything resulting from this crash. The panel consisted of the top twelve scientists and intelligence people in the country, with an almost unlimited budget, reporting directly to the President and all presidents thereafter. Their job was to learn as much as they could from the alien technology."

"Wait a minute," she told Frank. "You want me to believe all this? That a, a *flying saucer* crashed forty-some years ago, what, nineteen forty-nine?"

"Nineteen forty-seven."

"Nineteen forty-seven, fine, a flying saucer crashed in nineteen forty-seven and that's why I'm having nightmares today? Why I lost my baby?"

"They didn't just crash. They're still here," Frank said as he took a map out of his battered briefcase and spread it out on the coffee table.

"Look—" He pointed to Roswell, New Mexico. "This was where the Brazel Ranch was, where the crash site was. The wreckage was reported to have been moved here." He moved his index finger an inch to the west to Groom Lake, Nevada.

Annie squinted at the fine print on the map. "Where it says 'Weapons Testing.' "

"It also says DANGER—DO NOT APPROACH when you get within ten miles of it. You want to know why?"

"It's a weapons testing area. They don't want people blown up."

Frank laughed and shook his head. "I was there three years ago, with a MUFON field group. We broke into four teams to hike in. We got closer than anyone before us. Two of the groups did soil sampling, seismic readings, just outside the perimeter fence. Their findings proved there is no weapons testing going on, I can guarantee that.

"The other two groups, one of which I led, were armed with high-speed video cameras. We documented several unusual craft, craft that with further analysis proved able to travel at Mach Six, four thousand miles an hour."

"Maybe they were new military test planes?" Annie shrugged.

"Right, like the Aurora project. You can call it whatever you like, Annie, but what we filmed out there—those aircraft did hard-angle ninety-degree turns, acute-angle turns, without slowing. In other words, at that speed, to bounce like that, the craft had to control gravity. By definition this was a spacecraft, not an aircraft.

"The report we have is that this is an MJ-12 base, that Area Fifty-one is where they keep what's left of the original spacecraft. Some even say there are alien bodies there, in a permanent deep freeze of some kind. Others say aliens are still alive and being held there."

Annie shook her head. "Now you're over the edge."

"Sure. Crazy? Lunatic fringe? Or government disinformation? You can play with the pieces all you like, but you've still got a puzzle. And the pieces are coming together. Not from those sources but from people, like yourself, who come forward with experiences they can't explain, starting with the feeling that they were missing time and ending with the realization that they were abducted. During their abductions they were subjected to strange procedures that range in categories from physical and mental to reproductive examinations by an alien life-form."

Annie blinked. "This is stupid."

"Is it? Annie, what if I told you you're not the first woman I have met who has lost her baby. A viable fetus missing and her OB doctor cannot explain its disappearance."

"I'd say—Carol probably talks too much."

"Annie," Carol interrupted, "we're not the enemy. What happened to you has a psychological classification. It's called Post-Abduction Syndrome. PAS involves a lot of psychological symptoms that are caused by the abduction experience."

"Its greatest effect is on unaware abductees," Frank added. "It's a lot like Post-Traumatic Stress Disorder, but the external forces compel the abductee to repress the memories of traumatic events even though the abductee may want to remember them."

"Excuse me, but you're saying an alien took my baby?" Annie shook her head. "I can't believe that."

"Honey, before you freak, let him finish."

"In six years, I've had sessions with seventy individuals. A psychiatrist worked with me to explore over four hundred abduction experiences. We used hypnotic regressions to help the subjects remember. These people were from different parts of the country, different races, sexes, religions, socioeconomic status, and *all* of them had the same experiences. And yes, many of the women reported sexual procedures, from egg collection and embryo implanting to fetal extraction. Some reported seeing what looked like hybrid babies. These women are not crazy. They didn't suffer from fantasy-prone personalities, hallucinations or Multiple Personality Disorder. These are regular people."

"Well, how, um, would I know? If—"

"If you were one? To start, you're going to have to let go of the screen memory."

"The screen what?"

"Screen memory. An image that is artificially generated to cover the memory of what really happened. With you—I've looked over Carol's notes—I would guess it's the owl. With some people it's deer, or dogs, birds, angels. Whatever seems easiest for the individual to remember and that's *all* they remember."

"So why are parts of my memory coming back? I mean besides owls, I remember doctors now and, and—"

He shook his head. "I don't know, Annie. Your screen memory is coming apart for some reason. I have a feeling if we pry at it just a little, you may be the first to get a peek at the whole picture."

"Uh-huh," said Annie. "Carol—all this flying-saucer talk—"

"Annie, before Frank jumps down your throat you'd better start saying UFO. Flying saucer is for fringe groups who believe the Universal Love Alien Space Brothers are coming to lead us all into a new age of harmony. Frank is dealing with something altogether different, believe me."

"All right, whatever I call it, it sticks in my throat. It just seems so—"

"Unbelievable? Weird?" Carol shrugged.

"Yeah. All that and more."

"That's what got Frank started. In fact, that's what

got everybody started who's serious about this. It seems totally unbelievable, but some very plausible people all say the same things."

"You don't find it hard to believe at all?"

Carol snorted. "Of course I do, doll. But if a couple of million completely unconnected people all said they saw yellow flowers, and they all described the same yellow flower, what would you say about that?"

Annie allowed herself a small smile. "I'd say that somewhere there's a whole lot of yellow flowers. But flowers aren't flying saucers. And come on, Carol—a couple of *million?* Let's be real here."

"That's a conservative estimate, Annie. There have been random surveys indicating that about ten or fifteen percent of the world's population have seen something they can't explain. That's a lot of weather balloons."

Annie opened her mouth "I . . . I didn't know it was so many. . . ."

"If it's even one-tenth of that it's still in the millions, Annie." Carol paused, then said, "So what do you say, doll? You want to find out what really happened? Let's do one more session."

Annie looked between Carol and Frank. "All right. As soon as Stanley gets here."

TWENTY-FIVE

S tan came up the walkway to Carol's house. He glanced back at his car, then down the street. He saw no one. Wesley's very good security, which he had spotted across from his house, had not followed them to Carol's and was not watching now.

Although Stan had been ready to feel irritated at their presence, he now felt vulnerable because of their absence. The Colonel had clearly warned him that he and his wife were in danger, but now—

There wasn't much he could do. He was starting to feel that was true of his whole life—his work, the loss of the baby—and now this idiocy with hypnosis.

He shrugged and knocked. Annie opened the door.

"Come on in," she said. "We're ready to start."

"No," said Stan. "I thought we had settled this."

"We did. This is too important to drop."

"It's also too important for harebrained hocus-pocus."

"Fine," she said. "Then go home and wait for me there." She started to close the door.

Stan stopped her. "Look," he said. "Either hypnosis doesn't work and you're kidding yourself with dangerous delusions. Or it *does* work and you're fooling around with something even more dangerous."

Annie stepped out onto the front doorstep and closed the door behind her. "Carol is an expert, Stan. You can go home if it bothers you. She won't let anything happen to me."

She smiled sweetly and Stan could only throw up his hands and say, "Aw, Annie."

❖

Carol turned to Frank as they stood at the window watching Annie and Stan. "Frank," she asked, "what if they did take Annie's baby?"

Frank shook his head. "I don't know. There's never been a case of anybody getting one back."

Carol glanced out the window again. "Well, it looks like anything is possible," she said. "Stan is coming in." She moved to the front door and opened it.

"Why, Stanley," Carol said as they came in, "how *nice* of you to join us."

Stan turned away for a moment—and the breath

whooshed out of him. Across the street, and maybe half a block away, a blue Buick sedan slid into a parking spot under a tree. So instead of saying something sharp he grumbled, "About time."

"I think so, too," Carol said. "Come on in."

Stan was obviously angry, but there was something very disarming in Frank's demeanor, something that suggested he had taken math courses in college. In Stan's opinion, that was one of the quick tests to see if somebody was human or animal.

So when they were introduced Stan stuck his hand out and said, "Listen, do you really believe all this stuff?"

As Annie and Carol settled on the couch and began some preliminary relaxation exercises, Frank steered Stan into the kitchen to talk about "all this stuff."

"You're an engineer, Stan?" asked Frank as they leaned on facing counters.

"That's right. I work out at Aerocorp."

"Oh, defense stuff. Interesting work?"

"Sure. You know, I can't talk about it or anything, but it keeps me hopping."

"Yeah, I'm not trying to get you to talk about it," said Frank. "But as an engineer, you understand straight-line technological evolution, right?"

Stan shrugged. "Sure. You start with a hand-sized rock and move to a hammer. Step by step, you end up with a pneumatic hammer."

"Now tell me this. How come we've never developed a better vacuum tube?"

Stan blinked. "What do you mean? The transistor

made it obsolete. Why would we want a better vacuum tube?"

"What did the transistor evolve from? Or for that matter, what about today's organically grown silicone chips?"

"Well," said Stan, "those were just, uh, new wrinkles. They didn't really evolve from, uh, what was before."

"It's a quantum jump in technology that came from nowhere," said Frank. "They represent a whole new way of thinking about a technological problem, instead of an upgrade on the old way of dealing with it. Right?"

"Sure. But that doesn't—"

"Of course not," Frank said. "But here's another: Do you know the first time the public heard about laparoscopy? That's the instrument that—"

"That doctors use for examining internal organs, it uses fiber optics."

"It was first reported in early nineteen-sixty."

Stan shook his head. "Impossible. It wasn't invented till the late nineteen-seventies."

"Reinvented. Betty Hill reported it in detail after her abduction on a UFO."

"UFO?"

"At the time, everyone thought she was crazy. That it was impossible. Almost silly."

Stan smiled. "Yeah. So—"

"So where did it come from, Stan? Who was thinking that far ahead, to come up with an advance like that?"

Frank pointed a finger right between Stan's eyes. "I'm not just talking medical advances. I bet even in your own work, you have these kind of jumps?"

Stan shrugged. "That's what guys like me are paid to do."

"And you think somewhere, there's some Air Force engineer who is so good, he's coming up with stuff that's a hundred years ahead of everybody else?"

"No, I mean— But what you're suggesting—it doesn't have to mean that—"

"Not all by itself, no. But there have been a lot of these funny jumps in technology, haven't there? Particularly in the last forty years?"

"Well, you know. Sure, but . . . what are you driving at here?"

Frank pushed himself up off the counter. "Just this. Between World War One and World War Two we improved from the rifle to a slightly better rifle. The machine gun got a little better. Bombs got a little bigger, planes got a little faster. But in the next ten years after World War Two we went from there to the H-bomb, to lasers, to—the modern age. Why?"

Stan played along. "Well, you know. In times of war, technology always goes a little faster, makes these funny jumps."

"Stan, it took three hundred years to go from the musket to the rifle, at a time when the world was constantly at war. No sudden jumps from square-rigged ships to PT boats. What's the difference?"

Stan laughed. "Okay, Frank," he said. "Let's hear it. What's your point?"

"We accept a lot of conventional arguments here that don't really make any sense, that's all. It makes more sense, if we really look at it objectively, to believe that technology is leaking in from some source outside the normal, instead of developing by itself. But we all refuse to think about that because of what 'outside' might mean. In the same way we all just *know* UFOs are impossible."

"But they *are* impossible."

"Are they, Stan?" Frank said softly. "Or do we just want to think so? Because we all keep thinking that, no matter how much evidence piles up. And we swallow the stupidest Goddamned explanations. Mass hypnosis. Earthquake lights. Swamp gas. Demons. If I asked you to believe in mass hypnosis or earthquake lights, you'd laugh me out the door—none of those 'explanations' make any sense at all! But we all believe this totally crazy bullshit in order to avoid believing something that makes perfect sense!"

"Flying saucers don't make sense."

Frank cocked an eyebrow. "Really? What's the most unlikely number in the universe?"

"Sure, the number one is, but—"

"The point is, there are literally *millions* of clues saying that UFOs are at least possible, and there's only an opinion saying they're not—and the opinion isn't even based on science. So why can't people believe the science instead of the opinion?"

"Ah, I don't know," Stan said at last.

Frank relaxed again, leaning back onto the counter. "I don't know either, Stan," he said. "But I don't mind admitting it."

Carol stuck her head in the kitchen door and said softly, "I think we're ready."

TWENTY-SIX

A nnie is in her car and driving along the road from the observatory. She's going a little faster than usual because she is in a hurry to get home, to defuse Stan's crankiness.

But as she drives along the dark road she is not thinking about home, or driving. Her thoughts are concentrated on the tape playing in the dashboard cassette player. The music from space tantalizes her with its elusive familiarity.

And now she's driving through the tunnel—and ahead she sees a light and thinks, that must be a very large truck for the headlights to be so high off the ground.

And now she's out the far end of the tunnel and the lights are above her.

"Go on," said Carol. "What do you see?"

"The light," said Annie. "It's so bright. I've never

seen anything so . . ." Annie trailed off, a small frown on her face. "But I *have* seen it before. . . ."

Frank, sitting slightly behind Carol, leaned forward. "Bingo," he said very softly.

"Tell me about the light, Annie," Carol said.

"It's very bright," she said. "They want me to walk toward it. . . ."

On the far side of the room, sulking in a chair, Stan felt the hair rise up on the back of his neck. Annie's voice had changed. It was higher, less distinct—the voice of a little girl.

Stan stood to look. Frank gave him a warning glare, but Stan looked at his wife.

Her face had relaxed. The worry lines and crow's-feet had dropped away and Stan saw what Annie must have looked like as a child.

Stan sucked in a breath between his teeth and Frank motioned him to sit down.

"I don't want to," said little-girl Annie. "I'll get in trouble."

"It's okay," Carol told her softly, firmly. "They can't hurt you. Go ahead now, Annie. Walk toward the light. What do you see?"

"It's too bright to look. I don't want to—Oh!" Then Annie let out a little girl's giggle. There was no mistaking the sound for anything but a very young girl trying to suppress a laugh.

"What is it, Annie?" Carol asked.

"It's a little man," she said in her five-year-old voice.

"He's very funny. He—" She giggled again. "Okay," she said.

"What just happened, Annie?"

"The little man wants to be my friend," said the girl's voice. "I don't have any friends, so I told him okay. Now he says— Oh! There's something wrong with his hands. Oh. Okay. He says his hands were always like that. They don't hurt."

"Who is the little man, Annie?"

"He says I can call him Mr. Boojum if I'll be his friend. Okay."

"Annie, do you know how old you are now?"

"Course I do. I'm five years old, but I'll be six in, um, July?"

"How did you meet Mr. Boojum?" Carol asked her, and Annie looked confused.

"How . . .?" she said.

"Yes, that's right. Is this the first time you've ever met Mr. Boojum?"

"Yes, the first time." Annie nodded. Frank made a note on his pad and then asked, "Where are you, Annie?"

She is five years old and she's supposed to be asleep because she's already said her prayers and maybe she won't go to Heaven if she doesn't go to sleep after her prayers, or maybe she should say them again just to be sure since she's not under the covers anymore, but has crawled out of bed.

"Mommy?" she says, but there is no answer. "Daddy?" and it's still quiet.

She opens her bedroom door, just a crack, and peeks through into the kitchen. A flake of paint peels off the door and hits her toe soundlessly.

In the kitchen, at the small table, over by the Franklin stove, Daddy reads the Bible, while Mommy washes up the supper dishes, just like they do every night. They never say anything; Daddy just reads while Mommy washes up.

Annie goes back to her bed and reaches under the sheet. At the far side of the bed, against the wall in the safe spot, there's a small lump. It's Gruffy Bear, her only friend. She tries to play with him, but tonight he doesn't have a lot to say and Annie is not satisfied with his bright button eyes.

As she turns to put him back on the bed, frustrated, she sees a very bright light outside her window. It hurts to look at it, but she shades her eyes with one small hand and looks.

What she sees outside makes her drop Gruffy Bear. Her hand goes limp and she gasps in wonder.

She runs to her bedroom door, flinging it wide open and calling, "Mommy! Daddy! Come see! Come quick!"

Mommy is sitting beside Daddy now, and Daddy is still looking down at the Bible in his lap. But they don't move. "Mommy! Daddy!"

They still don't move. Annie looks back over her shoulder at the window. The light is even closer, and now it has a hint of blue to it. "Mommy?" she says. "Daddy?"

And at last her Daddy moves, just a little—and topples sideways out of his chair and hits the floor, still holding the Bible. He lies there motionless.

From the window, Annie can hear music playing softly, and there is light moving across her walls. The light is much

*closer now. She turns back to it slowly. It is not blue/white,
eye-hurting light now. Instead, more colors than she has ever
seen before are playing over her, dancing across the walls, spinning around her room and over her hands and face. "Oh!" she
says, delighted. "Oh, look at the colors!"*

And then a funny little man steps right out of the colors.

*He looks so funny that at first Annie just giggles. He
doesn't have a mouth—but Annie knows he's smiling inside
and he really likes her and then she hears his voice inside her
head, saying he wants to be her friend.*

*And he can move and play and everything, not like Gruffy
Bear. "Okay," she says, thrilled to have a real friend now. And
he wants her to come play with him 'cause they're friends.*

*But Annie's Mommy and Daddy have told her not to go
anywhere, so she tells the little man, "I'm not s'posed to. I'll get
a spanky." His voice comes inside her head and he says she
won't get spanked, Daddy and Mommy are asleep.*

*"They are?" says Annie. And she looks through her bed-
room door again into the kitchen. Mommy and Daddy haven't
moved, but they might wake up. . . .*

*The little man's voice comes inside her head again and he
tells her to come play. "Okay," she says. "But I'll get a spanky.*

*"My name is Annie," she tells him. "What's your
name?"*

*And his voice inside her head says she can call him Mr.
Boojum, and she laughs. "That's a funny name. Are we going
to go play at your house now?"*

Carol took a deep breath and looked at Frank. "Do
you go to his house to play, Annie?" she asked.

Annie frowned a little-girl frown. "Sometimes," she

said. "And sometimes we go for a ride and sometimes he does doctor stuff . . . but it doesn't hurt . . . 'Cause he's my friend. . . . Your friends don't supposed to hurt you, do they?"

"That's right," Carol told her, "nobody wants to hurt you, Annie. Does Mr. Boojum visit you a lot?"

"Oh, yes. I get to see him all the time sometimes."

Frank leaned forward and whispered something in Carol's ear. "Annie, does Mr. Boojum ever tell you *why* he visits you?"

"Oh, yes," said the little Annie voice, "it's 'cause I'm special. And someday I'm gonna do something very special for Mr. Boojum and his friends."

Carol and Frank exchanged a look; Frank nodded and motioned with his hand to go on.

Stan shook his head and whispered urgently to Frank, "Every kid dreams of being somebody special. Reliving a childhood fantasy is not going to help."

"Just give it a minute, Stan," Frank said softly.

Carol turned back to Annie. "Okay, Annie. You're a grown-up woman now."

Annie nodded, and as the others watched, breathless, her face slowly settled, regaining the laugh lines and other marks of age. When she spoke again she used her "normal" mature voice. "Yes," she said.

"Now it's the night you were driving home from the observatory with the space music," Carol prompted her.

"Uh-huh . . ."

"And you see the light. . . . And you stop the car. . . ."

"... Oh ... Yes, it's very bright. ..."

"Annie, is Mr. Boojum there?"

Annie moved her lips slightly but did not answer.

"Annie, some time that night, after you see the light, do you see Mr. Boojum?"

"... at my car ...?" she asked, sounding a little confused.

"That's right," said Carol, but she saw Annie hesitate and added, "And later, when they take you through the tunnel."

"Oh," said Annie, and the sudden change in her voice sent chills through her listeners. "Oh, wait, where are you taking me?"

She is wheeling through the tunnel on her back toward the small circle of light at the far end. She can't move; even though she is not strapped or tied she can't move although she desperately wants to move, to strike out and run.

And now they burst out of the tunnel and into the operating room. She's wheeled up under what she recognizes as some kind of surgical light fixture. She feels her jeans and panties yanked down her legs. The table is cold as her legs are spread.

Small doctor figures move around her. From across the room the taller doctor moves to Annie's side. He takes a thin black rod with a tiny suction cup on the end and slides the instrument between Annie legs.

"Please don't do that," Annie told the doctor, and the heartbreak in her voice brought Stan to his feet again.

"Annie!" said Carol. "It's all right, it can't hurt you!"

But it can. Annie again feels the burning deep inside her. The cold intensifies, builds until there is a sharp cutting sensa-

tion. Finally, the long black instrument is removed. At the end of the instrument is a tiny fetus. Her baby.

"Annie—" Carol started, but she was interrupted by a cry ripped from the very center of Annie's being.

"NO! Oh, my God, NO!"

And as her voice and her emotions peaked and Stan was striding forward to stop it once and for all, she just as suddenly stopped dead and smiled. "Oh," she said, eerily relaxed. "Oh, that's okay then. All right."

"This is—we've got to stop it," whispered Stan urgently. "This is totally out of control."

"I think the worst is over," Frank said, "and we are really on to something here. Just another minute?"

Stan hesitated.

"She's okay, I promise," Frank said, and Stan nodded reluctantly and took a step backward.

"Who's there, Annie? Who do you see?" Carol asked.

"It's Mr. Boojum. It's okay. They're not going to hurt me. He needs my help."

She spoke calmly, but underneath there seemed to be just a hint of something troubling, something the calm couldn't quite submerge, and Carol decided to push for it.

"That's right, they can't hurt you. So what are they doing now?"

Annie, though still sounding calm, began to breathe in small gasps. "They take— They need to— It's . . ."

"Go ahead, honey. What do they do?"

Annie took a deep ragged breath. "They took my baby."

There was a long pause. "Go on," urged Carol quietly.

"It's my baby . . . so small . . . too small . . . It won't live . . . my baby . . . But it's okay . . . They . . . they *need* it . . . they won't . . . hurt it . . . it's okay . . ."

"Who, Annie? Who takes your baby?"

"Mr. Boojum. His friends. . . . There's a doctor there. . . ."

"Who else is there? Anybody else?"

Annie panted slightly, although her face remained calm.

The masked faces bend around her again and then—

"Colonel Wesley," she said.

"Colonel Wesley is there?"

"Yes, he—"

He bends in to speak to the slightly taller one, the one Annie thinks of as the doctor, and Annie can hear his almost uninterested voice, but not the words. But she hears what the doctor says back.

"No," he tells Wesley. "It's still alive. They're keeping it alive."

And as Annie tries to sit up and say something to the doctor, a cool metal rod comes in from her blind side and touches her temple.

There's a tingle, and a blinding burst of light inside her skull, behind her eyes, and Annie sees in complete clarity, every detail precise, an odd diagram. But before she can puz-

zle out what it is a voice is coming at her, demanding to know—

"Where are you, Annie?" asked Carol. "Tell me what you see."

"I see—" and she broke off.

"It's a little later, Annie. Colonel Wesley is gone. What do you see?"

"I see—a wall of . . . blue water . . .? A tank of some kind. There are . . . things in it? Hundreds of them, they're like—"

The thought hit her so hard she felt the hypnotic trance fall away and she sat up, instantly, coldly awake and alert and remembering what she just saw.

"It's an incubator," she said. "They're incubators, Stan—it's alive . . ."

She looked around the room at the three faces staring at her and fought her tears back.

"Don't you understand?" she asked. "It's alive, oh my God, it's alive."

And then she couldn't stop it, couldn't possibly hold it back any longer, and her face fell forward into her hands as the tears poured out of her like summer rain. "It's alive," she sobbed. "My baby is alive."

❄

Down the street from Carol's, in the blue Buick under the tree, the voice of Colonel Wesley crackled over the radio.

"Move in, gentlemen."

TWENTY-SEVEN

It's just a doodle.
—Dr. Annie Katz
Radio astronomer

The quiet in Carol's living room lasted for several minutes. Annie lifted her eyes to the circle of anxious faces surrounding her and tried again. "The machines, the blue tanks," she told them with desperate patience, "the machines Mr. Boojum showed me. They're *incubators*, I'm sure of it. My baby is alive in one of those incubators. We can get it back."

"Annie," Stan said, sweat beading his face, "sweetheart—" And then he stopped, not knowing what to say, and looked over at Carol.

Carol, for once in her life, was speechless, too.

Frank finally spoke. "Don't get your hopes up too high, Annie. We can't prove anything just yet, and even if we prove it—if your baby is alive he's surrounded by fifty miles of desert and the best security in the world."

"It's my baby," said Annie, as if that explained it all.

"I just want you to know what you're up against," he said.

"Wait a minute," Stan said. "This is crazy. I mean, just hold on a second. You're both acting like this was something real that just happened."

Annie turned on him fast and furious. "Stanley, so help me God," she began.

"No, this is— Mr. Boojum, for Christ's sake!? Annie? That's—he's an imaginary friend you had when you were a *kid*, Annie, come on," Stanley pleaded. "Aliens? You can't ask me to take something like this on blind faith. I can't—I just—" Stan put a hand on Annie. "I need some proof. I'm sorry. But—"

"Stanley," said Annie. "Please don't be like this. It's your baby, too."

"*What* is?!" he exploded. "What baby? This is cruel, Annie! Why can't you accept that it's gone and stop this, this—" And he stopped, unable to finish.

Annie let a breath hiss between her teeth. "Stanley— if I am crazy and this is all just a delusion, you owe it to me to go along with it until I see for myself that it's a fantasy."

"Well," said Stan.

"But if it's real—if it has even one small chance of being real—you're blowing your last chance to get the baby back. So you have to either believe, or act like you do, or you're going to regret it for the rest of your life," she said, and sat down on the couch with her arms crossed.

But Stan shook his head. "I need proof."

Proof, Annie thought, exasperated, exhausted, and she closed her eyes—

—*and a cool metal rod comes in from her blind side and touches her temple. There's a tingle and a blinding burst of light inside her skull, behind her eyes, and Annie sees—*

"Proof!" she said, sitting straight up, eyes now wide open. "Mr. Boojum gave me proof! Damn it, how could I be so thickheaded. Where's a pencil? Come over here, Stanley."

Annie meanwhile had grabbed the pad and pencil Frank held out to her and was sketching furiously.

"What," said Stanley. "What are you doing."

"Sit down here, honey bear," she told him. "You're about to get an eyeful of proof."

Stan sat beside her. He looked over at what she was drawing and then looked away. A moment later his head snapped back to the notepad, and in order to see it better he bent over so far he nearly fell off the couch.

Annie finished the last few strokes of the drawing and tilted the pad Stan's way. "There," she said. "You wanted some proof? Put that in your pipe and smoke it."

Stan scanned the sketch from top to bottom. He traced the sketch with his finger and then looked up to see all eyes on him.

Reflexively he snatched up the drawing and held it to his chest so nobody else could see it. He turned to Annie. "Where did you get this?"

"Stanley, I just told you where I got it. Mr. Boojum gave it to me—and I think it's for you."

"That's not possible," he told her.

Annie threw up both hands. "Well, hell," she said. "Then I guess I really am crazy. Totally nuts. I hallucinated the damn thing, is that better?"

"Yeah, but Annie—this thing is *classified*. Except it doesn't exist yet. It *can't* exist, but—"

"Well then, dearie, I guess you're crazy, too."

"But it's not *possible*."

"Tell that to Mr. Boojum."

The doorbell rang.

Frank Cassidy was closest to the door. He looked at Stan and Annie, intent on the drawing, and at Carol, rummaging in her file folder. "I'll get it," Frank said, and stepped into the foyer to open the door.

"Here!" said Carol, turning to Annie with two napkins in her hand from the Astro Coffee Shoppe. "Take a look at these!" She paused and half turned toward the front hallway. "Where's Frank?"

Off to her side, at the now open front door, there was a small sound, as though someone had coughed. Annie looked up and saw Carol frown and step toward the sound.

But half a second later Carol, moving faster than Annie had ever seen her move, leapt back and halfway across the room. Her hand was stretched out in front of her, pointed palm outward at the panic-button switch of her alarm system.

Then several things happened simultaneously:

Frank Cassidy stumbled backward into the room—
and in the half-second glance Annie could see something
wrong with Frank's head. His forehead had a blob of
bright red on it as though a small strange flower had
taken root there and, as he fell and twisted, she saw the
back of his head strangely pushed out.

At the same time, Carol's body, in midair and seemingly frozen in time, jerked once, twice—three jerks as
though some invisible baseball player had hit her with a
bat. But still flying, Carol hit the panic button at a strange,
soft angle, and slid to the floor like a limp doll.

Two men stepped into the room.

Although to Annie's eyes everything seemed like
slow motion, the two men moved so quickly and
smoothly that they alone appeared to be moving at normal speed while everything around them crawled.

One of the men, a young, good-looking black man,
swiveled without strain or haste and yet with incredible
speed. He pointed his very large Desert Eagle .357 magnum exactly between Stan and Annie. To Annie's numb
astonishment, Stan responded by shoving the paper with
the schematic into his mouth, chewing and swallowing it.

"Good boy," said the smiling black gunman.

The other gunman, an older man with dark hair, had
followed Carol's wingless flight and smoothly moved to
stand above her, looking down at the shapeless puddle
she had made in falling.

Annie watched the whole thing happen, the eerie
slow motion making a roaring in her ears and supporting
the unreality of it all. *This can't be*, she thought, *it can't be*

happening. But no matter how hard Annie willed Carol to get up, to stop this graceless joke, to smile and even insult Stanley, Carol remained motionless on the floor, her head bent much too far over to one side, no breath or movement stirring her still body.

The man standing above her bent slightly. One hand still held the gun and with the other he reached down to touch Carol's neck.

"Carol!" Annie called and made an effort to stand. The gun swung toward her.

"Not a sound," said the man. "Not a syllable. Not a whisper." Annie sank back down onto the couch, and the man knelt beside Carol's lifeless body.

"Howdy, neighbors," said the black man with a wide and friendly smile. "Let's be friends. Show me your hands very carefully, okay?"

Numbly, Annie complied, noting out of the corner of her eye that Stan did too.

"Gooood," he drawled, and without looking away said to the other man, "One?"

"All done. Move them."

The black man nodded at Annie and Stan. "Show me the palms of your hands and stand up—slow and careful, neighbor. Slow and careful."

Annie felt as if she were going to throw up and pass out and she was seeing everything through a red haze, but somehow she found her feet and slowly stood, dimly aware that Stan was doing the same right next to her.

"Thank you," he said cheerfully. "One?"

As the other man moved over and quickly patted

down Annie and Stan, the black man continued to smile and, although Annie at first thought she must be imagining it, he began to whistle "Sweet Georgia Brown."

She stared at him, the entire top side of her world still unglued. He winked, and this seemed no more strange to Annie than anything else that had happened in the last two minutes.

The second man straightened. "They're clean. Let's move them," he said, and the black man nodded and gestured with his gun.

"Neighbors?" he said.

TWENTY-EIGHT

Annie still swam in the red fog but thought she might make it all the way to the door until she came to Carol's body. Then she stumbled, felt too weak to go on, and heard herself moan as though from a great distance. But the man behind her nudged her forward with the barrel of his gun, and she somehow faltered toward the door.

Beside her, out of the range of her vision, there were small scuffling noises, and she half turned. Stan had tried to work his way between the guns and his wife. But both gunmen spotted the move almost instantly. They took a half step apart to increase their angle and the black man nudged Stan back beside Annie.

"Sorry, neighbor," he said, sounding like a slightly raspy Mr. Rogers. "Let's just keep moving, okay?"

As Annie moved carefully down the walkway, past Carol's dying rosebushes, her mind whirled in a vague muddle, unable to paste any labels on what had just happened. In place of logical thoughts there were snapshots: *Carol flying through the air; Carol sliding down the wall; Carol lying on the floor without moving* . . .

Try as she would, Annie couldn't make the images mean anything. Like the destruction of her observatory, losing Max, this whole thing seemed to be a random, meaningless chain of violent acts that made no sense at all.

Unless—

She heard a squeal of brakes at the corner of the street and a police car turned the corner and headed toward them. Annie stopped dead in her tracks and was quickly, viciously, poked with a cold steel gun barrel.

"Just keep moving. To that blue Buick, dead ahead," said the cheerful voice. Although a little softer, the voice revealed no tension or uncertainty, even as the police car slowed and stopped in front of Carol's house.

They had reached the blue Buick now and the second, quieter man opened the doors. In the front seat of the police car Annie could see the two policemen who had answered Carol's alarm before, and their names jumped into her mind: Nuñez and Briggs.

Officer Briggs, the younger one, the one with the cute butt whom Carol had flirted with so outrageously, stepped out of the car, adjusting his hat and thrusting his nightstick into his belt. He smiled at Annie and lifted a hand in greeting.

"It's that monkey again, isn't it?" he said to Annie, and took a half step toward them.

So fast Annie couldn't really see how it happened, in perfect unison, the quiet man moved one way and the whistling man pushed her toward the car.

From fifty feet away Annie saw a red dot appear on the cop's forehead and then, accompanied by a small coughing sound from the direction of the quiet man, the top of Briggs's head disappeared. Almost immediately after, the windows of the police car exploded with the next couple of shots.

Seeing Briggs killed suddenly cleared the fog in Annie's head, and for the first time she managed to move into the same time frame as the two men who had hustled her out to their car.

Moving more quickly than she knew she could, Annie yelled a wordless syllable, kicked out at the black man, and dropped to the pavement, rolling away from the car and the two men. As she fell she grabbed at Stan's leg and, in slow motion, he fell after her, a look of surprise on his face.

And as she rolled across the rough pavement she caught a glimpse of Nuñez, the older policeman, aiming across the trunk of his car.

Annie heard several long, deep-pitched blasts, and as her eyes opened again she saw the quiet gunman falling, three red punctures spreading on the front of his shirt. She rolled again and the whistling black man was already diving into the Buick.

With a roar the Buick started. Annie and Stan just

pulled themselves out of the way over the curb as it drove off.

Everything shifted back up the spectrum to normal color and sound and movement. There was a bitter, brackish taste in Annie's mouth and her head ached. She saw the Buick turning the corner at the end of the street and Nuñez crouching, squeezing off two final shots.

"Are you all right?" Stan asked her anxiously. Annie's whole body trembled, the reality of the killings finally setting in. "Annie? Are you all right?"

"I'm fine, Stan," she said. "Just don't ask for any more proof."

Stan stared at her for a very long time.

❈

Nuñez was cold, even hostile, as he collected Stan and Annie from the curb. For several minutes he busied himself with the radio, explaining in thick cop jargon what had happened, and calling for a helicopter to go after the blue Buick.

Moments later the air filled with the sound of sirens as backup arrived, followed immediately by paramedics, detectives, and other cars filled with cops who seemed to come just to make sure Nuñez was okay after losing his partner.

The whole time, through the first ten minutes of arrivals and frenetic activity, Nuñez kept a cold brown eye on Annie and Stan.

A police car containing only one officer pulled up and a large red-faced man, looking almost like a musical-comedy cop, stepped out of the car. He had a hard-looking belly protruding over his belt and the largest hands Annie had ever seen. He leaned his big, jowly face over Nuñez and said something, placing a hand on Nuñez's shoulder. Without looking up at him, Nuñez said something and inclined his head toward Annie.

The large cop looked at them and then stepped quickly over to Annie and Stan. He was surprisingly graceful for such a beefy man.

"Okay, folks," he said with a neutral smile. "Captain wants to see you." He waved a massive hand at his car and helped Stan and Annie in, although in truth they didn't need much help in spite of being shaky.

It was only after the car was on its way, presumably to police headquarters, that Annie noticed there were no handles on the inside of her door and no way to open the door or the window.

Although Annie's head buzzed with the pain of Carol's death and the implications of all that had just happened, it looked a little worse for Stan. He hadn't spoken a word since the gunman got away. His face twitched like a pudding and he shook his head as though a half-dozen improbable ideas were fighting for control. Annie placed her hand on his thigh, and Stan turned to face her.

"Damn Wesley," he blurted out. "They were supposed to be security, not—"

"Stan," she interrupted him gently, and his outpouring broke off just as abruptly as it had started. Annie glanced up at the policeman in the front seat, but his attention was on the road. Still, she lowered her voice.

"I need you to think. Why would Wesley do this? The observatory? Max? Carol—?" Her voice cracked as she mentioned her friend, but she went on, still filled with adrenaline. "It doesn't make sense. What's the connection?"

"I don't know. I thought I knew, but now I just don't know."

She shook her head. "Stan, you've got to know, think."

Stan stared at her for a long moment. Then he looked at the policeman driving the car. He couldn't look long; the sight of the cop reminded him too much of the military, of Wesley. "It's got to be about JOSHUA. Somehow, Annie, I don't know how, but you've got the information to make it work."

She shook her head. "Honest to God, Stanley, that can't be worth killing our friends or kidnapping us."

But she knew it was—to Wesley.

TWENTY-NINE

The Captain's name was J. Riley, according to a bronze metal name strip in a small walnut block on the front of his desk. He was a trim, tough-looking man of about forty-five with a neat mustache and cold brown eyes.

On the corner of the desk to Riley's right sat a police radio. Riley was listening intently to it when Annie and Stan were ushered into the office. He barely glanced at them. "This them?"

"Yes, sir," said the large Sergeant.

Riley nodded briefly. He waved a hand at two metal folding chairs, and they sat. The Sergeant backed out of the office and was gone down the hall.

In the sudden silence, Annie felt very uncertain, even a little guilty—of what, she couldn't say, but she remembered reading somewhere that basic cop procedure was designed to make everyone feel guilty—even other cops, sometimes.

Annie looked at the Captain. But Riley concentrated on the messages coming over the radio and ignored Annie and Stan.

Annie's ears started to get used to the jumble of static and distortion coming from the radio and soon she could make out what the voices on the radio were saying. It was not a terribly hard trick for her. She was used to imposing order on the wild audio jumble of interstellar space, and human voices were much easier.

"—seven-three, roadblock established at grid point one-five-nine-Charlie-Delta. Acknowledge."

The radio crackled and Annie had to strain to hear through the distortion. "Central, this is Delta-Tango-seven-three, we're turning him to one-five-nine-Charlie-Delta." Even over the radio Annie could hear the hysterical whoop of a siren.

"Air One, this is Central. What is your 40?" said the nearly mechanical voice of the dispatcher. It was a woman's voice, completely neutral.

There was a roar of background noise. "Central, this is Air One. I'm holding over one-five-nine-Charlie-Delta. Suspect in sight." The sound clicked off and there was neutral background noise for a moment. Annie glanced up at Riley.

Even this slight movement caused Riley to look at her and focus his chill, dark eyes on hers. Annie felt unnerved, but looked back anyway, and after a moment Riley nodded slightly.

"It looks like you may have him," Annie said, and Riley looked away.

"Central, this is Delta-Tango-seven-three, suspect has halted approximately fifty yards short of roadblock." The radio crackled once. "We're getting out of the car."

Riley continued to ignore Annie. Annoyed in spite of being intimidated, Annie glanced at Stan. She was not sure if she expected to see him looking cowed, or mad or something in between, but she was not expecting what she saw.

Stan had on what Annie called his Lost In Space face, the look he got when he was working a problem through in his head. If they were in some social situation where he couldn't easily start scratching away with pencil and paper, Stan would do the work in his head, and as he did his jaw would drop slightly, the tip of his tongue would rest on his lower lip, and his eyebrows would join together between his eyes.

In his mind Stan had already made the connections that Annie's drawing indicated. It was as if all the work he had been doing was the flip side of the same coin. It pleased him to know that he had gotten that close on his own.

But with the new voltage plate configuration he could take a sound wave, or a partical wave, use harmonic oscillation to reach an instantaneous subnuclear focus. In effect, it was the electronic lens. The result was exactly what he had theorized. JOSHUA could send a wave at molecular level and cause the atoms of the target to vibrate until they simply lost their bond and exploded.

JOSHUA could work.

"Stan," Annie started to say, but she was interrupted by the radio. "Holy Christ," the awed voice said, followed by a frantic, "Eddie! Duck!"

"Please repeat," the voice of Central said, and there was a pause. "Please repeat," the emotionless voice repeated, followed by another pause. "Delta Tan—" the voice started again, but it was cut off. "Central, the bastard blew himself up. He went sky-high here, there's— I've got an injured officer here, uh, Eddie Dobbs got hit by a piece of the bumper—"

Riley frowned slightly and picked up the microphone hooked to the radio. "Billy, this is Captain Riley. Repeat that last."

There was a crackle again, then the voice from the roadblock, sounding a little more formal, came again.

"Uh, Captain. Sir, the, uh, suspect stopped about fifty yards from the roadblock and we ordered him to surrender. Sir, next thing was, the car blew up. Major explosion, sir. No chance he survived it. Officer Dobbs has sustained minor wounds to the head."

"Please remember your radio discipline. Riley out." He placed the microphone back on its hook and turned to Annie and Stan.

"My suspect has apparently blown himself up," he said at last.

The big music-hall cop stepped into the office and placed a manila folder in front of Riley. "Captain," he said very simply.

"Thank you, Smitty," Riley said, opening the folder. The big cop just nodded and walked out.

Riley flipped through the folder for a couple of minutes before closing it and carefully placing it on the desk.

Stan cleared his throat. "What about the other guy?" he asked. Riley, who had been looking at Annie, swiveled his eyes to Stan and looked at him. "Um. You know. The other killer? The one that, uh, they shot?"

Riley let it hang for a moment, just long enough for Stanley to blush at how silly he sounded. Then he nodded slightly.

"We are attempting to identify the other gunman," he said. And watching Stan carefully, he added, "This is a little more difficult than usual as he carried no ID and was wearing clothes that might have been purchased anywhere. Additionally, he seems to lack fingerprints. Just like the other two John Does sitting in the morgue, thanks to your little observatory barbecue."

It took Annie a moment before the last statement sank in. The blush drained from Stan's face. "But everybody has fingerprints," he said.

Riley nodded. "No doubt we just couldn't find them," he said without a trace of irony. Stan opened his mouth but decided not to say anything and closed it again.

"You do government work, don't you, Dr. Katz?"

"Yes. Uh, civilian contractor. At Aerocorp."

Riley nodded. "But you've never heard of a person having no fingerprints?"

Stan's face turned scarlet again, and Annie thought

what an awful spy he would make. "That's, that's—not, uh . . ." Stan trailed off, but it was obvious he knew and was not saying.

"I was in Special Forces, Dr. Katz," Riley said. "In Laos. I worked with a man from Central Intelligence who talked too much."

"I think we should call a lawyer," Stan said. Riley gave him a long look.

"You're not charged with anything," Riley said. "But of course you can call a lawyer if that is your wish." And he pushed the telephone toward them across the desk.

"Okay," Stan said, "then what are we doing here?"

"I have dead bodies stacking up all over town from you two," he said. "One of them is a cop. But I have no killers, no motive, no clues. I don't even have fingerprints. I would say that what you are doing here is voluntarily assisting the police in the course of an investigation. Would you like to check that with your lawyer?"

Nobody said anything.

Riley nodded. "What else am I supposed to do with you people?"

"Let us go," Annie said.

He looked at her with his cold, mildly amused eyes. "Do you really want to go, ma'am? Because I have this funny feeling that maybe this thing hasn't run its course yet. That maybe if there are several guys who can do what you say they did, and one who was willing to blow himself up rather than be captured, there was a real good chance there's a whole organization out there. Now maybe you know who it is. Maybe you don't. But they know who *you* are, and they want you. I think your best chance to stay alive would be to stay here. What do you think?"

And then, with a perfectly straight face, Riley added, "Of course, you are free to go."

Annie let out a long breath. "Captain," she said, and he sat back in his chair and listened politely. "Two of those 'bodies' making your life so untidy are the best friends I've ever had. And I don't know what I'm going to do without them, but I know my life is never going to be what it was. I don't know what's going on, neither one of us does, but I am getting awfully tired of getting tossed around like a beach ball.

"If you want to keep us in protective custody, or hold us for questioning, or whatever you want to call it, then do it. But stop pushing at us. Just—just stop it," she finished, overwhelmingly weary.

Riley watched her for a moment, then moved one finger to a button on his desk. After a few seconds the large cop appeared in the doorway.

"Captain?"

"Smitty," said Riley, "take these people upstairs to an interrogation room. Make sure they're comfortable and secure. We have reason to believe their lives are in danger."

"Folks?" Smitty arched one eyebrow at them. Annie noticed a scar in the eyebrow, directly above the pupil of the eye. Stan offered a hand to Annie. She took it and stood, and turned to look at Riley again. But he was already looking down at his desk, where the file folder lay open.

Annie followed Stan into the hall.

THIRTY

S mitty ushered them past the duty sergeant and toward the back of the building. They followed him through swinging doors and part way down a hall.

A flight of stairs took them to the second floor, where Smitty seated them in a small, institutionally neat room. There was a clean table and six chairs. A mirror stretched along one wall. An ashtray was in the exact center of the table.

"You folks take it easy now. Captain'll take good care of you." And with a twitch of a smile, Smitty sauntered out the door.

Annie saw Stan still wearing the expression of panic that he had taken on in the Captain's office. "Hey," she said, "What was all that with Captain Riley? About the fingerprints?"

Stan shook his head. A little more color drained from his face.

"Stanley," she said sharply. "Whatever it is, it can't be worse than what we've already been through."

"This is top secret stuff, Annie. Look, there's, there's this military security team. With no fingerprints—Colonel Wesley's men. They're a last resort to protect certain very high-priority projects."

"Whoa, slow down, Stan. You work *for* them, why would they want to kill you?"

"I didn't say they wanted to kill me," Stan said. "If they did, I'd be dead already. We'd be dead. They must need you alive, too."

"The drawing," Annie said as it hit her. "That's the only thing that's changed. They want the schematic I got from Mister Boojum. It will finish your project, won't it? It ties your Colonel to this."

"That damned drawing," Stan said. "I should have saved it—it was our bargaining chip." He slapped the table with the palm of his hand.

"It still is." She pulled the pen from his shirt pocket. "Give me your hand," she told him, and he held it out. She turned it over and began to draw on his palm.

"Hey—easy."

Annie shushed him and quickly finished the drawing. It looked exactly like the one Stan had eaten: the wheel-shaped figure with its numbers and symbols.

"There." She put the top on the pen and jammed it back into his pocket. "Now you can't lose it."

Stan was glaring at the drawing with suspicion.

"What's the matter?"

Stan shook his head slowly, stubbornly.

"What?" She felt offended. "It doesn't make sense?"

"No, it *does* make sense. It's perfect. Very elegant. It solves every problem I've been having with this project, and some I hadn't thought of yet. Everything would be so much easier if this didn't work." He let out a frustrated sigh. "Shit."

Annie closed her eyes and put her head down on the table. She let her mind drift, and for the first time in days there was no submerged sense of panic, no fear of her dreams, no terror of what might lie on the far side of the door to her subconscious. There was only soul-restoring sleep, deep and satisfying, the kind that happens when your last thought is simply, *I'm safe—finally safe. . . .*

Annie was jerked awake by the slam of a door. She was not sure how long she had been out.

"Okay, folks," Smitty said. "The Feds are here to talk to you."

Stan looked up quickly. "What Feds?" he asked. "What do you mean?"

"The FBI, Dr. Katz," Smitty said. "We have an attempted kidnapping here, don't we?" And he winked at Stan and held the door open. "They hate to be kept waiting."

"Come on," Annie said. "These are supposed to be the good guys. FBI agents are required to have fingerprints. They might even be able to help."

Stan stood and muttered something. The only word Annie could catch was "naive."

Smitty led them down the short hall to the stairs. At the bottom of the stairs they turned toward the double doors that opened into the main area of the station.

As they approached the doors Smitty stepped ahead of them, making sure to go through the doors first, and Annie wondered at the quiet beyond the door. There was no sound of typing, nor talking, nor telephones ringing—nothing at all.

Smitty pushed the door open carefully and stopped in his tracks.

Annie, right behind him, saw the vein pulse in his neck, and his hand twitch to his side to undo the strap on his holster. She craned her neck for a look, and what she saw made her gasp and step backward. She bumped into Stan.

"What? What is it? Annie?"

She reached to push him back without taking her eyes off the doorway, but he pushed past and stopped dead in the doorway.

"Hey, what—" Stan said softly, before he was brushed back by Smitty's enormous arm.

The police station was quiet for a good reason. Every one of the two dozen cops inside was stretched out, apparently asleep. The duty sergeant had his head down on his desk, telephone cradled in his outstretched hand.

Detective Chambliss had rolled his chair over by the coffee machine and was face down in a box of dough-nuts. The lid of the box was sticking up in the air with the bright illustration of a pudgy, smiling child, and the fat red letters spelling out, HAPPY BOY DOUGHNUTS!

Three uniformed men were just inside the door, scattered on the floor like bowling pins. A detective in a charcoal gray suit was hanging head down off a bench, a cup of coffee spilled out by his hand.

A young woman, her hair pulled into a severe bun at the back of her neck, lay beside him on the floor, and the coffee had seeped into her uniform. Her hand was on her half-drawn weapon.

Captain Riley lay at the mouth of the hallway leading to his office. He alone had managed to draw his gun and he still clutched it in his fingers. Behind him, gray-suited legs were visible—the two FBI men, clearly down and out before Riley.

And then there was a slight thumping sound from the front door. A clatter followed, as though a tin can had hit the wall beside them. Annie looked toward the sound and saw a metallic canister, now lying a few feet from the wall. A thick, oily fog spilled out from the canister and quickly filled the room.

"Get back, folks," Smitty said, his voice sounding oddly muffled. He pushed at them with an arm as large and hard as a dining table, drawing his gun with the other hand.

But before Annie could do more than raise her foot to step back, a movement on the far side of the room froze her.

The figures that moved out of the oily mist were not anything she remembered from her dreams, but there was a haunting, dreamlike quality to the way they looked as they moved slowly, carefully, across the room, and even Smitty paused to stare at them.

There were three, and then five, all identical. They were dressed in black paramilitary fatigues and seemed more or less human, each with two legs and two arms.

But their heads were wrong. Starting with the bulging, glossy eyes, she saw almost nothing human about their faces. Even through the distortion caused by the fog, their heads were out of proportion, elephantine, with a strange, dangling nose hanging down the front of their black tunics.

The lead figure swiveled its impossible head to face them and Smitty raised his old-fashioned revolver into firing stance. He squeezed off two quick shots and the lead figure pivoted and fell, the front of his dark uniform wet with blood.

But before Smitty could squeeze his trigger again, Annie, from her position slightly behind him and to his right, saw a red dot appear on Smitty's forehead. There was the soft coughing sound from the figure closest to them and Smitty's head snapped back as though struck by a hammer.

A hand grabbed Annie from behind, and before she could react on her own, Stan pulled her backward.

"Run, Annie! The back door, at the end of the hall—run!"

Stan pushed her through the double doors and followed backward, keeping his eyes on the methodical advance of the black figures.

The swinging doors whooshed closed, opened, closed, and Annie grabbed for Stan's hand as they ran. But no more than halfway down the hall they heard the soft thumping sound again and another canister flew past them and rattled against the wall just a few feet from the back door.

The oily smoke again poured out, right at them this time, and Annie found that running had suddenly become very difficult. As if in some new nightmare her legs just didn't respond anymore and the smell of slightly metallic cinnamon overwhelmed her. She floated serenely down toward the floor.

The floor was not nearly as hard as she had thought it might be, and she just had time to realize that was because she had landed on top of Stan.

Annie blinked her eyes once and thought she would like a drink of water, but it was far too much trouble to get one, so she simply closed her eyes.

"It's started," Andros said as he looked into the dark eyes of the short gray creature next to him. Blue light from the fetus tank spilled over them both. "Start the signal."

A moment later the room filled with the music of the telemetry sounds.

THIRTY-ONE

I *know that music,* Annie thought as she dozed in a far-away place. *I have heard it some long time ago, some far back time . . . I know what this is. . . .*

But it started to feel like something was wrong with the music, some subtle thing that slipped away when she tried to identify it—and as she came slowly back to the here and now it hit her. The rhythm of the music was wrong; that leaden pounding was not part of it, had never been part of it before.

But maybe the throbbing was a different sound, not part of the music. . . . And then Annie came back a little further from the faraway place where she had been and the pounding was in her head, accompanied by splitting headache pain, made to seem like music by her dream. And the music, of course, was only—

The music was still there.

Startled, Annie opened her eyes. She had no idea where she was and no memory of getting there. Above her curved a strange ceiling and two parallel strips of fluorescent light. None of it looked familiar.

But more important to her now than the fact that she didn't know where she was was that even with her eyes wide open she heard the music. It was faint, but it was definitely there and it was definitely *her* space music.

With a gasp Annie sat bolt upright. That turned out to be a very bad idea, because whatever was causing her head to pound with pain became much worse when she sat up. The blood ran from her head down to her feet with a smashing series of bass drumbeats, and Annie sat and panted for a moment, clutching her head with both trembling hands, willing the pain to go away.

It did not go away, but it did recede slightly, enough for Annie to be aware of a terrible, rasping thirst. Her tongue felt like a block of baked sandstone, thick, heavy and dry.

Struggling against the pain and discomfort, Annie took a deep breath and slowly opened her eyes and dropped her hands from her face. She looked around.

She was in a room with oddly curved walls that arched over her so there was no joint between wall and ceiling, merely a smooth continuation.

In the middle of the floor stood a strange, patchwork piece of machinery, unlike anything Annie had ever seen before. It looked a little like a model of a brontosaurus skeleton built by someone with arrested development and a strong sense of whimsy. But at its center lay a half-open computer with its component-innards spilling out. Beside it lay some very odd-looking sunglasses.

There were four work tables in the room, each about ten feet long and four feet wide. Annie had been lying, and was now sitting, on one of these tables. Two others were covered with electronic test equipment and components. The final table was covered with Stan, still snoring gently with a slight frown on his face.

Annie stood and moved toward him. As she did she saw the room's door. It had a frosted glass panel in it. Through the glass she could see the outline of two figures—guards!—standing one on each side of the door.

Keeping her eyes on the door, she bent over her husband. "Stanley!" she whispered urgently. His eyes fluttered but didn't open.

"Stanley, please wake up!" He made several soft grunting sounds and opened his eyes.

"I was having this terrible dream," he told her.

"I have some very bad news," she said. "It's not a dream."

He blinked at her three times before it registered. "What?" he exploded and sat bolt upright before she could stop him. "Ow," he said very quietly and held his head in his hands.

"Stan, I think we're at that place they took me."

Stan breathed very deliberately for a moment before answering. "What?"

"The place I remembered under hypnosis. Where they took our baby, and I saw Colonel Wesley. I think they've brought us there."

He still didn't look up, still massaged his temples. "What makes you think that, honey?"

"The ceiling," she said. "The way the ceiling curves like that. I remembered, that's how the ceiling looked where they took me."

Now he looked up, carefully and, apparently, with great pain, tilting his head to look at the ceiling. "Quonset hut," he said, and just as carefully looked down again. "War surplus. They use 'em for lots of government places. We could be anywhere."

Annie turned his chin with one finger, until his eyes were aimed at the brontosaurus skeleton. "Is that war surplus, too?" she asked him.

"Oh, shit," he said. "Where in the hell are we?"

"Do you know what that thing is, Stan?" she asked, cued by the scared look on his face.

He turned to her and took a ragged breath. "That's Project JOSHUA."

Annie turned away from him to look again. It didn't really look like much. It certainly didn't look as if it were worth the lives of Carol, Max, Frank Cassidy, Smitty, the young cop—but it was worth it to somebody. And their lives had just been added to the pot.

"Stanley, if you have any ideas, I want to hear them," she said as she nodded toward the door where the two guards were half-visible. "Because pretty soon they're going to come for us, and—I don't really want to die."

A pain throbbed in his forehead and Stan reached to rub his head. But his hand never got to its destination. He froze, and Annie saw once again the Lost In Space look in his eyes.

"Stan?"

"Hold on," he said at last. "Just a second. Wait a minute. Hold on,"

"I'm holding. What is it?"

Instead of answering, Stan stood. His knee didn't lock properly and he staggered half a step, but he recovered and stepped eagerly over to the brontosaurus and ran a hand down its neck, like a wrangler calming a spooked horse. "Okay. Great. Okay," he said, and turned jerkily to the workbench.

"What are you doing?"

He looked at her as if she'd asked him what shoes were for. "This is JOSHUA," he said. "The thing I've been working on."

"You said that already. So?"

He shook his head slowly as he spoke. "Annie," he said, "It's a *weapon*."

It hit her like a hammer. "My God. It works?"

The slightly wicked smile she had fallen in love with spread over his face. He held up his hand and showed her the drawing she had made there.

"Not yet," he said. "But I can *make* it work." And he pried open the back of JOSHUA's computer.

THIRTY-TWO

Today you will finish Project
JOSHUA.
—Colonel John Wesley
Head of MJ-12

F or almost half an hour Stan worked on the circuit
board, frowning, studying the drawing on the palm of
his hand and chewing the nails of the other. He rummaged frantically through heaps of components; he sol-
dered wires and fit in new microchips.

It was too late to change Albright's particle-wave
construction to the less destructive sound waves. But at
least he could finish. Annie's schematic would make
JOSHUA functional.

All Stan had to do now was change the parameters
of the configuration in the wave packets. It was the key
for JOSHUA to be able to destroy the variable molecular
densities of a target's surface.

Annie sat on another table looking from Stan to the
door. She had no idea how long they would be left alone

and so, with nothing else to do while Stan finished the weapon, she watched through the frosted-glass panel in the door for any sign of trouble.

She got off the table and slunk over to the door, as catfooted as she could go, and stood with one ear against the doorframe for a long moment, until she felt too silly to go on.

Then she stepped quietly over to Stan and peered over his shoulder.

"How's this thing work anyway?"

"Think video game. You put on the finger pads, then the glasses. The digitalization system gives the viewer a 3-D heads-up targeting display. A tap of your middle finger to lock on, a tap of your pointing finger to fire."

"Very simple."

"Yeah, if it works." He dropped his head back into his work.

Annie moved nervously back and forth for about twenty more minutes. Then, as she was heading for the table for the hundredth time, she heard a heavy stomp just outside the door.

Annie spun and tried to see through the frosted glass. The two sentries, motionless until now, had jumped to attention and presented arms. As Annie watched, two more shadowy shapes moved to the door, and her heart stopped as one of them reached straight for the doorknob. But the other shape, taller and thinner, said something she couldn't quite hear and the first shape spun to face the thin one.

"Now, God damn it," said the shorter, and Annie's guts twisted as she recognized the voice.

It was Wesley.

Annie spun away from the door, hissing at her husband. "Stan!"

"Almost. I just have to—" he said absently.

"No, now! Not almost—now! They're here!"

Stan's hands shook as he slid the completed circuit board back into the computer. "Who is it?"

"Colonel Wesley! Get away from that thing."

He blinked at her. "Why?"

"Stan!" she hissed again with all her might, and he dropped a Phillips head screwdriver and backed away from JOSHUA as the door swung open. Annie spun to face the door, her hands out behind her as she backed up against the table.

Colonel Wesley stepped in, paused, and locked eyes with Annie.

Annie knew that five other men in the crisp black uniforms had come in with him, but she also knew that only Wesley mattered and she glared at him as two of the soldiers took up guard on either side of the door.

For a long moment she simply stared at him, and he stared back with reptilian amusement.

"Well," said Colonel Wesley at last. "Dr. Katz. And," he bowed to Stan, "Dr. Katz. How are you feeling?

Thirsty? A little headachey? Sorry about that, unavoidable side effects."

"What do you want?" Annie demanded.

"Just what the hell is going on here?" Stan said.

"Why, it's simple, Dr. Katz," Wesley said, and now Stan could hear the dry rattle of evil in his voice, as loudly as Annie had heard it all along. "It's just another day at the office." And he gave Stan a smile that shot a mountainous row of goose bumps from Stan's neck all the way down his spine.

"Today you will finish Project JOSHUA." He looked at Stanley, calm, mild and matter-of-fact.

"That's impossible," said Stan, closing his fist. "There's no final stage schematic."

Wesley's smile widened. "Oh, stop it. You know as well as I do exactly where it is," he said, and nodded to Annie. "And I'm going to get it now."

He motioned to three Black Berets. One of them handed Wesley a black medical bag. "Bring her here," Wesley told the other two. He opened the bag and pulled out a syringe and a small glass vial filled with amber liquid.

Annie felt no fear as the soldiers stepped toward her. There was nothing about them that suggested humanity, but Annie was no longer afraid. She was filled with the purest hatred she had ever felt. She took a step forward to meet them.

"Wait," she heard Stan say, stepping in between Annie and the two soldiers.

The two soldiers did not hesitate. They pushed Stan

aside without even the appearance of effort and he half stumbled, catching himself on the bench.

They took Annie by the arms and she stepped forward with them, toward Colonel Wesley. As she locked eyes with Wesley again, a thought flitted into the back of her head.

It was not a plan. It was more of an impulse, but even so she held it tight. She knew it was the only chance for her, and Stan, and for their baby, which she knew was alive somewhere nearby.

Wesley pulled back the plunger on the syringe, filling it with the deadly amber fluid. "Just a minute, Colonel," she said.

Wesley held the syringe at eye level and squeezed the air out. A drop rolled down from the needle's tip. "Yes, Dr. Katz?"

"I just, I'll do whatever you want. If you—"

Wesley blinked, something red smoldering in the back of his eyes. "Dr. Katz, you're in no position to bargain."

"What are you going to do to her?" Stan gargled.

Wesley looked at him for a half moment, then turned back to Annie. "Think of it as downloading a computer. That's what our brains are, just organic computers, in which, chemically speaking, we can download, place a virus, or even crash the hard drive."

He held up the syringe. "Of course, there are a few severe side effects, but—" Wesley shrugged.

Stan jumped for Wesley, already swinging a schoolyard roundhouse of a punch. "You bastard!" he shouted. One of the Black Berets easily stepped between Stan and Wesley and grabbed his swinging fist. He used the momentum to pivot Stan into a headlock with smooth, practiced economy. Stan struggled briefly and yelled out, "Don't touch her!"

Wesley watched his hopeless struggle for a moment. "Don't hurt him too much," he said to the soldier holding Stan in the headlock. "We're going to need him in a few minutes."

Then Wesley turned back to Annie. "Ready, Dr. Katz?" Wesley thumbed the plunger to remove the last bit of air from the needle. A tiny geyser of liquid spritzed upward.

"All right," said Annie, "just a minute. I—I already know the schematic. I can draw it right now. I'll do it if—I can just see my baby." She didn't dare to look up, but there was a long pause and she prayed that Wesley would go for it.

"All right," Wesley said finally, after a long and terrible silence while he took into account that he still needed Stanley to cooperate. "After all, we're not monsters here." Wesley motioned to the soldiers, who pushed Annie and Stan over to the workbench beside JOSHUA.

"Give me some paper and a pencil, Stan," Annie said. "I'll draw the schematic."

She saw him blink and prayed he would understand what she was trying to do.

Stan took a deep breath and reached for a legal pad on the bench. "Here you go, honey," he said. "What do we do first?"

Annie stepped to JOSHUA and put her hand on the power switch. She looked at Stan, who nodded almost imperceptibly.

Annie took a deep breath and turned to Wesley. "The problem is all in the, uh, this last circuit here," she ad-libbed. "You see, when you power up, um—"

Annie flipped the switch to the On position. A row of four lights winked on and the room was filled with a low humming sound that rose up through the scale, one octave at a time, until the sound had gone over the top threshold of human hearing.

Annie was startled, but luckily, Wesley didn't notice. He watched her with interest, waiting for her to make the next move. "Go on, Dr. Katz," he told her. "What happens next?"

"The, uh, the virtual-reality interlock relay system has to be brought on-line," she said. Stan helped her into the acrylic glasses and the targeting glove. She gasped as the computer-generated image surrounded her. The room was clear in 3-D, only the colors were wrong.

Twenty feet away, in brilliant orange and yellow, she saw Wesley.

"Dr. Katz. Cut to the chase," said the orange and yellow man, his mouth a slash of red.

"Tap the middle finger," Stan whispered.

Annie tapped against the boron carbide armor of JOSHUA's body. The targeting grid formed. In the col-

umn on the left the readout gave: FIVE TARGETS,
LOCATED: 2 METERS AHEAD, HALF A METER
APART. MOVEMENT: NONE. WEAPONS:
IDENTIFIED, M-16, GLOCK-45.

There was no mistaking the heat-sensitive image of
the Berets and Wesley in red and orange. The weapons
they held were a cool dark blue.

"Oh," said Annie, trying desperately to learn to see
with the grid.

"All right, Dr. Katz," said Wesley, and stepped forward. The movement caused the orange and yellow to
stand out like tiger's stripes. The readout flickered with
his new range. "I think we've wasted enough time with
this."

Now or never, Annie thought, and swung her hand
toward Wesley. She heard the servomotors on JOSHUA
whine in response as the neck turned to follow her aim.

But instead of locking on to a living target, JOSHUA
swirled straight up as a startled Annie glanced at the ceiling and tapped her pointing finger.

A long slow arc of the room's ceiling rippled outward in a silent fury of red and then vanished.

Annie gasped. A second chunk of the ceiling, its
beams half gone and now unsupported, teetered for a
moment, creaked and dropped to the floor in a shower of
dust.

"Well, I'll be damned." Wesley nodded to the soldiers. "Take it."

THIRTY-THREE

Stop," Annie ordered. The soldiers hesitated, and Annie fired at the table in front of them. It disappeared. "I *mean* it!" Annie barked. "Freeze!"

They did freeze, and, backing up a half step, they looked to Wesley for new orders.

"My God, Stan," Annie whispered through the tension. "What happens if this thing hits a person?"

Stan gulped. "Remember that old story about the poodle in the microwave?"

"Oh, Lord." Annie hoped she wouldn't have to see what that would be like. She looked at Colonel Wesley. "Don't make me use this thing," she told him, almost pleading. "Give us our baby. You have what you want—let us go."

"I'm sorry, Dr. Katz, but you're not going anywhere.

National security," he said, and pointed. "Take her." The soldiers stepped toward Annie.

"For God's sake, Wesley!" Annie shouted.

"Shoot! Shoot!" Stanley yelled, ducking behind JOSHUA's boron carbide armor.

Annie could see the advancing Berets in her grid. She locked on. The Kevlar turret took aim. She tapped her finger, holding her breath. Everything seemed to go in slow motion.

At the last half second she saw the faces of the two men she was about to turn into loose molecules and she spasmodically jerked her head downward. JOSHUA, cybernetically linked to her movements, jerked down, too.

One of the men screamed briefly as the lower half of his leg disappeared and blood spurted across the floor, bright yellow in her display. But then the floor was gone, too; a slanting crater opened up beneath the charging soldiers and they slid, off balance, deep into the new hole and vanished into the darkness.

Annie gulped hard to keep down a rising nausea and turned the targeting grid to Wesley. The servomotors spun the Kevlar turret directly at the Colonel. For a moment they simply looked at each other, Annie pale and shaking but more determined than ever, and Wesley still cool, aloof, slightly amused in his devilish tiger glow.

"All right, Colonel," Annie began, but there was a clatter of feet in the hallway and a file of Black Berets, led by Crouch, ran into position.

"Hold your fire, Crouch," Wesley commanded.

"Sir!" he gave a hand signal to his troopers to fan out into covered positions around the equipment and tables, their weapons ready. Annie could see the orange-and-red figures moving through the cool blue of the room.

"I'm sorry, Dr. Katz," Wesley told her. "You no longer have anything to bargain with. It's over."

Annie stared at his mocking half smile, dark red in her visor, and she felt the hatred rising in her again.

"You bastard, come and get me!"

"Take her, Captain," he said, and the thin Captain signaled his men with one hand.

The soldiers began shooting as they leapfrogged forward. The first careful shots came from the hall and spanged off JOSHUA's armor.

"Annie!" Stan called in panic. He turned over the lab table in front of JOSHUA, hoping for cover, and leaped to grab the weapon from her.

"Get down, honey." Stan tried to force her down to semisafety behind the overturned table.

Off to the side, Wesley, pistol in hand, yelled encouragement to the soldiers. Annie half raised herself to a crouch in time to see him level the pistol and fire. The shot hit Stan in the arm and the force of it turned him halfway around. Stan fell to the floor.

My God, thought Annie, *they're really going to kill us.*

And something clicked in Annie's head. Her eyes and fingers worked with the speed of a twelve-year-old pro in a video arcade. Grabbing the controls back from her fallen husband, she turned her tracking grid on the red glow of Wesley. The adrenaline raced through her and she almost laughed at how Wesley looked. His mouth was a dark O in a red and yellow face.

The Kevlar turret pointed right at him. She locked on at the same moment he raised his pistol at her.

In the blink of an eye, they both tried to fire. The tap of a finger won.

Wesley's surprised look vanished as the heat of the particle wave hit him. From the inside out, a chain reaction started. All the cooler colors she saw in him vanished, replaced by white hot swirls across a background steadily rising from red to yellow to white. The internuclear separation began, the thermal heat built from the separated atoms, and Annie was nearly blinded by the blast of pure light in the goggles. She blinked and flipped them off.

Only a red mist remained where he had been standing.

Colonel Wesley was gone.

Annie had a moment to catch her ragged breath as the soldiers dove for cover, and she looked down to her wounded husband.

"Stan!" she yelled. The blood had soaked his shirt around the bicep and dripped down as far as his wrist, but he still struggled to get back up.

"I'm okay. I'm okay," he said.

She wanted to tell him Wesley was dead, but didn't have time. Three new bullet holes ripped the steel table just above Stan's head. "Jesus!" he yelled. "Shoot!"

Annie again grabbed the glasses and risked a quick peek over the top of her meager cover. Half a dozen more shots rang out and she ducked back.

I'm going to have to kill them all, Annie thought in terrified panic as she locked on and fired JOSHUA at anything moving. And although the thought made her insides churn, it was up to her to save her family, which included a small life somewhere in a hidden room of this terrible place, and she would do anything in the world, absolutely anything, to find that baby and make it safe.

She crouched again, getting as much cover as she could from the boron-carbide frame of JOSHUA. More gunfire came from a half section of wall. She fired. Almost instantly the shooting stopped, and Annie risked a quick peek.

The wall where the soldiers had been hiding was gone. Half a rifle lay on the floor. There was no other trace of the soldiers.

Another cluster of Black Berets began firing from a new position. Annie ducked again. Terrified for Stan and herself, she found it that much easier to keep firing, watching the soldiers vanish.

She did it so well that she stopped the rush of troopers momentarily. She had also caused most of the cover in the room to vanish, leaving them no place to hide.

The thin officer shouted something Annie couldn't quite hear, and the remaining troopers scrambled back to the shattered hallway for cover. In the long, tense silence that followed, Annie bent down to Stan, who was muttering and trying to bandage his bleeding arm with pieces torn from his shirt.

Annie slipped the glasses up onto her forehead.

"Stanley, are you okay?"

He looked at her and she felt a great burst of relief at how clear his eyes appeared. He was pale, but in control.

"I'm okay," he told her, and bit his lip. "But Jesus Christ this hurts. How do those guys on TV sound so tough when they say it's just a flesh wound? This really hurts." She helped him tie a quick knot in the rag. "What's going on?"

"They went back into the hall," she said. "I think they're waiting for reinforcements or something." She hesitated and then said, "Stan—"

He gave her a spasmodic smile that seemed to say his arm was hurting more than he let on. "I know it," he told her. "But we can't stop now." He reached his good arm over to squeeze her hand. "Would it help any if I said, 'Now I believe you'?"

She smiled briefly. "No, I know what that would cost you," she said. "Save your strength. We still have to find our baby."

She gave Stan's hand a squeeze and then, slowly and carefully, somewhat nervous about how quiet it had become, she peeked up and over the frame of JOSHUA.

The room looked quiet; there seemed no new movement from the Black Berets, and there was no sign of them or of their thin officer.

And then, out of the corner of her eye, she saw a red light wink.

She gasped and turned to see the thin officer in person, his laser-sited Desert Eagle pistol pointed directly at her and the red dot of its aim unwaveringly on her heart.

Behind him a squad of five more Black Berets fanned out to cover her, weapons at the ready.

She could not slip the glasses back on without drawing fire. It was over.

The red dot did not waver and Annie could feel the tension and helpless rage boiling up like some furious stew and she wanted to scream, "Shoot! Get it over with, damn you!" But at the very moment when she had to do something or burst, the red dot wavered . . .

And then slid off her chest, down her arm onto the floor, and winked out.

※

Annie looked at the officer. There was no expression on his face. He slumped to the floor and remained motionless.

Behind him, like bowling pins, every trooper in the squad simply toppled over.

For a long moment she couldn't do anything. Then she felt Stan tapping at her leg from the floor. "Anne? Annie? What is it? What's going on?"

She ducked down beside her husband. "I—don't know," she told him.

And then there came a soft, lizard-like scurrying sound, as though some small night creatures were scuttering across the floor, and Annie carefully hauled herself up for a look. Slowly, with all the caution her shattered nerves could muster, she raised her head up high enough to see over the framework of JOSHUA, and . . .

"Oh—!" she said.

Someone was looking back at her from no more than six inches away.

He was less than four and a half feet high and not quite human. His skin was leathery, a strange off color that fell somewhere between gray and beige. He had no hair and no chin and the dome of his forehead would seem too big if it had not served as a setting for those eyes. Annie looked into the eyes and—

His eyes were dark, lustrous and bottomless pools that led her further and further into herself, into peace and the promise that everything was all right. And the hand he reached up— that, too, did not look quite right, not quite human, but Annie did not care about that at all. She barely noticed.

What was important was that it was the hand of comfort that had soothed her dreams. Its light touch had stroked her face many times, as it did now. Annie swam in the promise of the eyes and remembered. . . .

"Mr. Boojum!" she gasped, and she found that tears were running down her face as, for the first time, she really started to believe it was going to be all right.

The small, leathery hand with its four long fingers dropped from her cheek to her hand, and they stood there for a moment, just holding hands.

THIRTY-FOUR

S tan finally got Annie's attention by tapping her leg repeatedly and demanding to know what the hell was going on.

With a tremendous effort of will, Annie broke eye contact with Mr. Boojum, holding onto his hand as she looked down at Stan with an enormous smile. "It's Mr. Boojum, Stan," she said. "It looks like my imaginary friend just saved our lives."

There was a long silence from Stan. "Oh, uh-huh," he finally said.

Annie had to laugh, and the sound startled her. It was a lighthearted sound, a laugh with no more pain and worry to it, a laugh that said the heartache of the past few weeks was over.

She looked at Mr. Boojum, and although that face had not been made to show emotion of any kind, she could feel the laughter that sparkled inside him.

Annie reached down and helped Stan to his feet. He did not look happy, but when he saw Mr. Boojum he gave a gasp that once again pulled the giggle out of Annie.

"I—I—It—" said Stan. "That's not— You weren't kidding."

But before they could say more there was a rapid patter-scurry from where the door used to be and a gang of five or six gray aliens scuttered in the door.

Physically they were just like Mr. Boojum, but as much as a foot shorter and, to Annie's eye at least, not nearly as attractive. There was something mechanical or reptilian, and vaguely repellent, about the way they moved with no apparent joints and quickly swarmed over Stan's brontosaurus skeleton of JOSHUA. Their movements seemed to be without haste and yet very rapid, and before the humans could register what was happening they had the circuit box unbolted.

"Hey—" Stan started to protest, but there was a tug at his arm. Mr. Boojum looked at Stanley with his giant dark eyes. He placed a careful hand on Stan's cheek and looked back at him.

After a long moment in which Annie could hardly hear Stan breathe, he spoke.

"Oh. Well, okay then," Stan said. He looked up and caught Annie's eye and gave her a strange, shy smile.

"He says they needed JOSHUA. That's why they had me build it." And he looked back at Mr. Boojum with an intimacy that Annie found unsettling.

"What do you mean he *needs* JOSHUA?" Annie asked Stan. And then it occurred to her that the real question was, "What do you mean, he had you build it?"

"Mr. Boojum's people designed it," said a voice from the doorway.

Annie whirled to see a tall blond man in an Army uniform with a Major's insignia on the collar. As she realized she had seen him before, the man continued. "Then they gave the final design to you, Annie," Major Andros said.

To Annie, it was like being hit in the stomach when she realized why she recognized him, and where she had seen him before.

He bends over her, part of a circle of strange faces, and Colonel Wesley stands beside him, asking him something. "No," the tall Major says, "it's alive. They're keeping it alive—"

"You!" Annie snarled at him, reflexively reaching for the JOSHUA cannon. But there was no effect when she tapped the trigger.

The Major shook his head. "Annie," he said, looking embarrassed. "I mean, Dr. Katz, Mrs. Dr. Katz—I'm sorry," he said, "but we haven't—uh, I'm Major Andros, ma'am."

"We've met," Annie hissed, her skin crawling at the memory. "You're one of Wesley's flunkies. You—you took my baby!"

"Actually, ma'am, I'm more like Mr. Boojum's flunky—and *he* took your baby."

But Annie felt outraged at this horrible *thing* who had done something to her with the owl doctors—

And as another realization overcame her Annie turned to Mr. Boojum.

". . . the owls . . .?" she said, dazed.

Major Andros nodded. "As you know now, it was, uh—a screen memory. To keep you from thinking about it. We can't make you completely forget something without doing real damage to your, well—Mr. Boojum doesn't believe in that. So we cover up the real event with some memory that makes you, um . . . not want to think about it?"

Annie turned accusingly to the small figure beside her. Mr. Boojum focused his wet black eyes upon her.

"But why?" she asked. "Why my baby? What were you covering up—what . . ."

Without saying or doing anything, Mr. Boojum stopped her cascading questions. Their eyes locked and she was mesmerized. He reached a slow finger up to her temple, and another to Stan's, never breaking eye contact, and as his dry leathery finger brushed her face a series of pictures formed inside Annie's head. Without transition the room she stood in was gone and she was . . .

. . . *out in the desert and a warm wind blows the tumbleweeds along. A farmhouse stands in the distance with a 1940s military truck next to it. She can see large silver-gray pieces being loaded onto a truck.*

The truck arrives at a remote air base. There are tall

mountain ranges surrounding the hangar. The door to the hangar is huge, one hundred feet tall by four hundred feet wide. The entire complex is surrounded by armed guards dressed in black—and Annie feels her stomach churn as she recognizes a much younger Colonel Wesley among the uniforms, looking too young for the Corporal's stripes he wears in these early years.

More pictures: Annie is aware that the years are moving past with only a little progress, but that does not seem as important as the fact that some progress is being made. The base grows larger. The help grows more sophisticated and increasingly able to understand the more complicated things they are shown. The humans build wonderful new devices based on what they are shown. Some of the devices are a great surprise to Mr. Boojum's people, using their ideas in new and different ways.

Increasingly, these new devices are twisted and violent, and often seem aimed at the very beings that showed how such things were possible. And also increasingly—in fact, on a directly parallel track—a young soldier rises in rank and gains more and more power over the ship and its crew and the repairs made on it.

Captain Wesley demands greater and greater access to the ship's secrets, and returns less and less for the access.

And the ship is slowly reassembled, the blue tanks replaced. The scout crafts make short trips for suitable donors. A new stock, perhaps even better than the first, is bred for the tanks and once again there is hope for the home planet.

But security precautions surrounding the base get tighter. A huge perimeter goes up, patrolled by an elite security corps.

Mr. Boojum accepts this as a gift from his hosts, but in fact, it is his first mistake and he learns a great deal from it.

Later, in a scout ship, there is a bright, loving picture of Annie, a little girl of five. She doesn't know whether to weep or shout aloud as she sees her small self in her first magical encounter with Mr. Boojum. And she sees the medical work she had long forgotten, though she remembered something small, like a BB, being put inside her ear and how it had made her cry.

But Mr. Boojum always makes the pain go away. And Annie again lives through the first steps in this long, strange friendship, from Mr. Boojum's perspective this time. She is dimly aware that there is some purpose beyond mere friendship in Mr. Boojum's visits, and that the purpose is connected to the work Boojum means to do—and that, somehow, the visits are part of Boojum's plan to get home; but how this might be true is not clear. Mr. Boojum is not showing her everything in these images.

Throughout her life he has been there, although she now realizes that she has forgotten most of his visits—has been made to forget, by Mr. Boojum himself. But he had been there when she met Stan, and she could sense his . . . Approval? Satisfaction? It was more than a friend's positive reaction to a good match. It was as if it somehow affected Mr. Boojum, in some way that he— But the image is gone, lost in a whirl of new pictures before she can get more than a hint of purpose.

As the partly repaired mother ship begins testing its functions on a limited scale, the helpers from the government begin to worry about losing this wonderful bounty from the stars. One man plays on that worry, using it to drive himself to the top of the pile.

Wesley is middle-aged now and wearing a Colonel's uniform when he is finally elected chairman of the top-secret panel that deals with Mr. Boojum's people and their gifts of technology. He wants more than Boojum can give.

Boojum's people are highly specialized, a hive society where every member has a different area of knowledge. None of the surviving members of the crew can give Wesley the kind of details he wants. Boojum knows that Wesley, suspicious by nature, believes the aliens are holding back on purpose.

Boojum, however, also realizes Wesley is not angry at the aliens but instead sees himself in a no-lose situation. Either he forces Boojum to give up major technology, or he consolidates his power in the Pentagon by proving that his suspicions about the aliens' withholding information are correct. He believes he has pushed Boojum into a corner.

Mr. Boojum knows that Colonel Wesley is wrong.

There has finally been communication with the home planet—not in words, of course, since Boojum's people do not use sound for speech. But they do use sound, and they use it to send help. A new ship is not possible. But when human technology has been pushed along far enough for the aliens' purposes, instructions for final repairs for the drive unit are sent, encoded in a stream of musical pulses.

"My space music!" Annie was startled out of the rapport with Mr. Boojum. She turned to Andros to demand more explanation.

"This is more than music, more than encoded information," Andros said. "It seems to be some form of energy for them. I don't know how it works, but I have heard it from their scout ships."

He shrugged and broke off, exchanging a look with Mr. Boojum. "But there's a lot more here, Annie—Dr. Katz," the Major said. "It's kind of—" And he broke off, glancing at Mr. Boojum.

"He better tell you," said Major Andros.

THIRTY-FIVE

Annie allowed herself to be drawn back into the deep liquid eyes of Mr. Boojum. In an instant she could feel his images move into her mind. If she had wanted to, she couldn't have stopped them. But there was no hesitation on her part. She let her mind fill with the images.

She sees Mr. Boojum's people working in unison, almost insectlike in their physical movement, bound into their hive-society mentality.

None of the survivors of the crash could have used the instructions to build the needed parts. It is not that they don't know how; they don't know how to be capable of knowing how. Each one of them is genetically programmed from pre-birth for a certain specific function.

Mr. Boojum's specialty is alien psychology. He has been studying humans for almost fifty years. Most of that time, he has also been studying one specific human named Wesley. Mr. Boojum has not revealed all his secrets, not by any means, and although in its present state of repair his ship cannot yet travel, his crew can defend it from sabotage by Colonel Wesley.

Mr. Boojum's crew release a jelly-like barricade to keep out Wesley and his men. He sends a peace offering consisting of an idea, a new way of thinking about sound waves.

The bait is savagely snapped up. Annie feels a sense of triumph/satisfaction run through the crew. Mr. Boojum's plan is working. Wesley is confident that he has at last forced the opening he needs to create Project JOSHUA, the ultimate weapon of destruction.

What Wesley doesn't know is that Boojum has created his own perversion this time. Taking the heart of his damaged ship's drive system and twisting it into a Wesleyan mold, he gambles that Wesley will do just what he has done: rush to finish the weapon, without knowing that in reality, he is rushing to finish the repairs on the ship.

It has taken almost fifty years for Mr. Boojum to slowly, carefully, create an Earth technology capable of building this one device so the ship can once again travel in space, swimming home in the dark interstellar sea on currents of sound.

Annie returned to the present with a gasp as Mr. Boojum's hand gently dropped away from her face.

Major Andros nodded at her. "It's quite a story, isn't it?" he said.

"It's impossible," said Annie. "Even Mr. Boojum couldn't have done all that."

There was liquid amusement in Mr. Boojum's eyes and he looked at her for a moment. Annie felt a hand on her shoulder and looked up to see Stan standing beside her.

"You believe him, don't you?" And Stan blushed.

"Yeah," he said. "Yeah, I do."

Annie looked from her husband back to Major Andros, who radiated a calm confidence.

"All right. That isn't important right now," she said, letting her breath hiss out between her teeth. "What about our baby?"

Major Andros smiled. "If you'll come with me," he said.

Annie shook her head, her jaw tightening. "Come with you where?"

"Your baby is all right, Annie," Andros said. "It's in a kind of special facility."

"What does that mean, special facility?" Annie snarled. "What have you done to my baby?"

Major Andros became very serious. "It, it, ah—your baby was very sick. It was not a viable fetus, in fact, not at all. You would have lost it, Annie. That's why—Mr. Boojum suggested we take it and, um, fix it. You know, correct the problems with a little genetic engineering. Which I have to say, they know a lot more about than we do. So . . ."

Annie just stared, so he repeated it. "It's okay, Annie, ah, Dr. Katz. Really it is."

Annie couldn't breathe, and the room seemed darker. "My baby is all right?" she heard herself asking from a great distance.

Major Andros's mouth twitched in a half-suppressed smile. "Oh, yes," he told her. "Maybe even better than all right."

Stan stayed behind as the Major led Annie away with Mr. Boojum. They walked along a hall where whole rooms were gone, rooms that had stood in the path of JOSHUA's beam. Walls, ceiling and furniture had been vaporized.

Annie felt nervous, not sure what was going to happen and not sure how to deal with scenes like the Black Beret squad room, where five soldiers were slumped over, in various stages of arming themselves.

One soldier, obviously pulling on a boot, was toppled over in half a chair. The back half had stood right in the path of the beam from JOSHUA and the soldier, leaning forward to lace up his boot, had narrowly missed vanishing along with the chair's back. He was now sound asleep, bent double over his boot.

"Are they dead?" Annie asked.

Andros followed her stare. "Oh, no," he said. "No. They're just switched off—" He wiggled his hand in a circle to indicate something he didn't have a word for. "You know. It's like asleep, pretty much. Mr. Boojum's people do it."

"How do they do it?"

"Well. There is an awful lot I don't know about their physiology and mental capabilities, but if I had to guess,

I'd say they access a part of our brain that controls motor functions, and—there's like a switch they can turn off or on, so they don't have to hurt anybody."

He put a surprisingly soft hand on her arm.

"Come on." He turned down another ruined hall. Annie was increasingly surprised at the damage the JOSHUA cannon had caused. There seemed to be no limit to its range, at least within her field of vision.

Andros led her to a room at the end of the building. It was off to the far side and largely undamaged, except for one panel of the wall in the hallway, which was neatly sliced away.

Annie stopped dead in the doorway. She had been in this room before, although it took her a moment to remember when she had previously seen the wall with the tank of blue liquid and gleaming machines that worked as—

"The incubators!"

Andros nodded.

Still dazed, she found herself turning and following the tank of liquid. Hundreds of fetuses were growing in the tank, each with a small wire attached to it.

Which one is mine? She slowed her pace, to really look at them, but then— No, there was something wrong, disturbing, about these fetuses, they looked—different. Their eyes were more like Mr. Boojum's. Annie turned away and hurried down the row of incubators to the far end, where a second door opened into a hallway that led down into darkness.

Annie stepped down into the dark hallway. She felt

pulled along by what she half remembered and soon she had gone down to a point where the hall became a tunnel. She stooped to negotiate the low, packed-dirt ceiling. Then she was going back upward again and moments later she came out of the tunnel.

She was standing in the operating room, the room where they had taken her baby from her—there stood the table with its OB-GYN stirrups in the middle of the room. Next to it, on a small table, a small blue liquid-filled tank with a large fetus. It looked almost human.

My baby.

She whirled to Andros. "What did you mean—better than okay?" she demanded. "What have you done—?"

But before she could speak again, there was a small four-fingered hand touching her arm. She looked down into Mr. Boojum's dark eyes, the warmth and depth and strangeness, and he reached his hand up to touch her face again.

Almost against her will she relaxed. As she did, a picture formed in her mind and she knew why she had been brought again to the operating room.

"Ooohhhh," she breathed, "yes. Okay."

Once she was on the operating table again Annie's daze deepened. Mr. Boojum stood directly beside her, his eyes only inches from her. She never saw what Andros was doing. Instead she relaxed, smiling, drifting, thinking about a sunlit field. In the field a Labrador Retriever played with a small child while she and Stan watched fondly.

Her daydream was briefly interrupted by the feel of something cold between her legs, and she gasped involuntarily as something pushed hard up into her—

But never mind. Mr. Boojum stared into her eyes, pressing his soft hand on her forehead. The feel of his hand was almost like a warm, pliable plastic, and Annie allowed the pressure to push her back into the sunny field again until, some time later, she heard Andros say, "All right. Good."

Mr. Boojum took his hand away and Annie got up to go tell Stan the wonderful news.

EPILOGUE

It's a shame that ninety-
eight percent of man's greatest
technological achievements
started as weapons.
—Major Michael Andros
Head of Genetics, MJ-12

Annie had watched carefully all day and, whether because she was watching or for other reasons, nothing had been broken. The large and solemn black man with the clipboard and his three helpers were gone. Only a half-hour ago the big orange moving truck had pulled out.

Annie stood now just inside the front door, looking out for the last time into her flower garden. She had left it intact, hoping the next person who lived here would appreciate it and care for it.

The house had not sold yet. The real-estate agent, a middle-aged woman named Marge who wore too much makeup, said the market was soft now and if they could wait a few months they should. Stan and Annie had agreed to try.

Annie sighed, very tired now, and leaned her new bulk against the wall. She was still not used to being six months pregnant. The missing weeks before she got her baby back had taken her mind off the mental preparation necessary for so drastic a physical change and over the weeks following the return of her baby she had been constantly bumping into things and clutching at chair backs as she swayed through the house packing everything they owned.

But it was done. Even the three large cartons of model train pieces and tracks had gone onto the truck. All that remained of their years in this house was packed in four large suitcases stacked there in the front hall, right where the telephone table used to stand.

In a few minutes, Stan would return with the Volvo wagon. Always fussy about machinery, he has taken it to have a full safety check, get the tires rotated and the oil changed. And even as Annie thought of him, she heard the car pull up in the driveway.

Annie stepped back from the door to let her husband enter. Stan seemed breathless, and as excited as a kid with a new bike. He pecked at her cheek and pushed past to stand in the hallway and survey the empty house.

"Well," he said, "car's ready. Are you all set?"

"Of course I'm all set, Stan. I've been packed for three days."

He nodded without really hearing her. "Uh-huh. Okay, well—" And he broke off. Annie knew he was reluctant to leave this house. It was the first either had ever owned and so it would always be special to them as the

first place that was ever *theirs*. But their life had moved
beyond this place now.

Stan moved beside her and put an arm across her
shoulders. For a long moment they just stood together
and let memories of the place wash over them.

Stan was the first to break the mood. "Well," he said,
giving her a delicate squeeze, "I'd better give the place a
final once-over."

Annie smiled. "Again?" she asked. "That's fourteen
final once-overs since you got up today."

"It'll just take a minute," he said, and strode off to
look in closets and corners.

Annie sighed and leaned again against the wall, her
hands cupped protectively under her belly.

Moving to Syracuse was a major change. The money
would be less. Stan's teaching salary was good, the benefits were excellent, but it was only one salary instead
of two, and not as much as he had been making at
Aerocorp.

Still, Major Andros—Colonel Andros now—had
promised that there would be something coming to them
from time to time, small chunks of found money. "Con-
sulting fees," Andros had called them with that annoy-
ingly enigmatic smile of his. It was understood that
keeping them on the payroll bought their silence; Annie
doubted that either of them would talk anyway. It would
seem like a betrayal of Mr. Boojum, no matter what the
money.

But money was not the issue. It was important for
them both to get away from this place where too much

had happened. Too, Stan no longer wanted anything to do with weapons research.

Besides, Syracuse was a good place to raise their child, and that was all that really mattered. Good schools, surprisingly pretty countryside—and winters, real winters with snow piled high on the ground and cold wind whistling down the chimney. Annie hadn't really experienced severe winter before, except in the canyons of Manhattan, which did not really seem the same at all as a house with a wood-burning fireplace set in rolling, snow-covered hills.

They were both looking forward to sledding with the baby, lounging in front of a roaring fire, and Stan even swore he was going to go ice-fishing. Annie considered that very unlikely—but then, after what had happened to them, what did "unlikely" really mean anymore?

In just a few minutes Stan was back. "Okay," he said. "All clear."

She stroked his cheek fondly as he bent to pick up a suitcase. "You sound disappointed," she teased.

Stan dropped the half-lifted suitcase and gave Annie a full-body hug. "Not me," he said. "I'm off on a great adventure with the world's most wonderful wife."

Annie hugged him back, hard. "And baby makes three," she said in a husky voice, and felt a tear roll down her face and onto Stan's shirt. For a moment they stood like that, lost in each other and what was to come. Then Annie looked at her wristwatch. "Hey," she said, "we'd better hurry."

Stan stepped back, looking at his own watch. "Yikes," he said. "We can't be late for this."

Stan stooped again and picked up two suitcases. He staggered out to the car and back again for the other two bags as Annie stepped down the walkway and stood one last time in her garden. She reached out and with the back of her hand brushed the petals on a blossom of her favorite rosebush.

In the dying sunshine the yellow-orange flower seemed filled with light from inside itself. Annie felt just about like that herself. She was achingly aware of saying good-bye to too many things, and the bright color of her emotions seemed to have a sharpness that filled her and still spilled out.

She missed Carol and Max so much—nothing would ever take the pain away. In three months the baby would be born, and how she wished they could have been there. But maybe she could talk Stan into changing his idea of the baby's name. So if it was a girl, her name would be Carol, and if it was a boy, Max.

A foot scraped the path behind her and she released her grip on the rose. "Time, honey," Stan said, and Annie turned to him.

"I'm ready." She took his hand. They walked together to the Volvo. Annie hesitated as Stan held the passenger door open. She took one last look at the house, then ducked her head and climbed in.

They drove out into the desert. It was a long drive and by the time they reached a good spot at the fence it was dark. "Made it," Stan told Annie. "Best seat in the house." He pocketed the keys and hurried around to the other side of the car to help her walk the twenty-five feet over to the fence. Reaching it, they both stood silently and watched a spot to the west.

The Dreamland base. The place where so much had happened, and now, one last thing was—

"There!" said Stan suddenly.

Three pulsing fingers of light slowly climbed into the sky. They shimmered and moved slightly, like the aurora borealis. "Oh," Annie said as she watched the glowing colors.

There was a burst of white light from within the color. It speared upward, gaining momentum at an exponential rate, and was quickly gone. It left behind a trail of cooler colors, running down the spectrum from white at the head to red, orange, purple and finally a cool blue indistinguishable from the night sky.

"Bye, Mr. Boojum," Annie said softly, and Stan took her hand. They watched for a long time, even after the colors had faded and the bright stars had come out in the clear depth of the sky.

When there was nothing left to see, they still watched for a moment, thinking back over all that had happened.

Only one small worry still nagged at Annie. "Stanley—"

"Hmm . . .?" her husband said, neck still craned up at the spot where Mr. Boojum's ship had vanished.

"Major Andros said the baby was 'better than all right'—what did he mean by that?"

"He meant not to worry," Stan told her, taking her hand. "So don't."

Then, as the chill of the desert night started to settle on them, Stan put an arm around Annie's shoulders and they got in their car.

But as they began the long drive to Syracuse, Annie could not help wondering—*Better than all right? What does that mean?*